Worse Than Myself

Worse Than Myself © 2008 by Adam Golaski
All rights reserved

Published by Raw Dog Screaming Press
Hyattsville, MD

Second Edition

Book design: Jennifer Barnes

Printed in the United States of America

ISBN 978-1-933293-67-7

Library of Congress Control Number: 2008925625

www.rawdogscreaming.com

Worse Than Myself

by Adam Golaski

RAW DOG SCREAMING PRESS

for David Longhorn

One: New England & New York

| The Animator's House   9

| In the Cellar   29

| The Animal Aspect of Her Movement   43

| The Demon   59

| Back Home   73

| A String of Lights   89

Two: Montana

| What Water Reveals   105

| They Look Like Little Girls   129

| The Man from the Peak   145

| The Dead Gather on the Bridge to Seattle   161

| Weird Furka   183

New England & New York

The Animator's House

Nothing could be weirder than discovering you are related to a priest, as Molly discovered when her parents told her they were going to visit Father Mike, who was, in fact and also, Cousin Mike. A cousin twice removed, so calculated Mom. Not, obviously, a cousin Molly's age, a being Molly longed for when lonely, which was often. The reasons Molly didn't know she had a cousin Mike were several: his entry into Holy Orders was sudden and alarming to his family, all only feebly Christian, and even fewer actually Catholic (Molly's family, the May family, were among the few, though the Church was for them very much a Christmas spectacular only); Mike was located by the Church in the Southwest, far from his East Coast relations; and, finally, Mike was a terrible correspondent. However, when the Church relocated Father Mike to a parish among the Finger Lakes of New York, Cousin Mike sent a card to the May family, with a short but entertaining note, and a holiday photo of himself, standing with a group of overweight, old ladies, and another priest, in front of St. Joseph's Church.

Mom asked, "Where's his collar?" To which Molly said, "Here," and pointed to the collar of Cousin Mike's purple shirt. Mom and Dad laughed. "Not all priests have to wear collars," Dad explained, and to Molly her father explained what her mother meant. "The Church is lightening up," Dad said.

"Whatever," said Mom.

A month passed, but the May family's resolve to visit Cousin Mike remained strong enough for a call to be placed and for plans to be made.

That the May family car was not outfitted with a DVD player or a game console was a cruelty Molly was forced to endure because her parents thought it was better for the family to play travel games and to listen to Dad's music (some of which Molly very much liked) and to talk and to sing. Mom's beautiful voice effortlessly eased Molly into sleep or at least into Molly's sleepy daydream house, but when Dad joined in and Molly was expected to, the magic disappeared. "Dad, can just Mom sing?" Dad seemed to understand and would be quiet for a while, or absent-mindedly whistle which was okay. And Molly really enjoyed travel games because she was very good at them, often beating Dad (Mom was more of a challenge). All this was to say that mostly May family drives were pretty fun, but a DVD player would have been nice. Even Mom and Dad had to admit that by the fifth hour of the drive to Cousin Mike's they themselves were ready to call it quits. The sky was gray the entire time, and for a little while there was snow, and then rain. Mom asked Dad a hundred times if he needed a break from driving; he was a little afraid to let anyone else drive; at last he acquiesced, and snoozed for a half hour before Mom woke him to navigate the minor right and lefts that would lead to St. Joseph's Church.

"I don't know how to act," Mom said, as they drove into the empty parking lot between the church and the rectory.

"He's just family."

"Your family."

Cousin Mike must have been watching from a window, because he appeared at the driver's side door with a huge umbrella and opened the door for Mom. She stepped out, under the umbrella, and Cousin Mike leaned into the car, "Just hang on a minute, and I'll come back for you." Dad opened his door anyway, and opened a little Tote umbrella over his own head. "Wait for Cousin Mike," he told Molly, and walked round to the trunk. There wasn't a lot of luggage. The plan was to spend the night with Cousin Mike, then visit Aunt Amy on the way back. Molly sat up on her knees in the backseat and watched her father through the small gap created by the open trunk lid.

"Molly?"

Cousin Mike's voice startled her, and she jumped.

"Didn't mean to scare you. Come on, I'm sure you're tired of the backseat."

Cousin Mike was right about that. Molly got out under his big umbrella, and felt safe under the big umbrella, next to the priest who wore khakis and a Polo, button-down shirt. He had a big stomach, though not in a gross way, and a moustache, which Molly found very interesting.

Once inside the rectory, Cousin Mike led everyone to a sitting room. Set out on a side-table was cheese, a bottle of wine, a slim pitcher of grape juice, and a box of crackers. Everything in the room was dark. Above a fireplace was a clock, a circular slab cut from a tree with Roman numerals and brass hands. There was a couch with a high back, nothing too comfortable, and brass lamps on either side. Two wing chairs were set side-by-side, with a small table between them. Most of the pictures on the walls were photographs of churches or clergymen; above the couch was a brass bas relief portrait of The Last Supper; one of the pictures, a contrast to everything else in the room, was a drawing of the evil fairy from Disney's "Sleeping Beauty"—Molly recognized it immediately and said, "That's Maleficent!" Cousin Mike rewarded her with a great smile.

"Absolutely correct," he said.

Dad strolled over to the picture and looked at it closely.

Cousin Mike put a hand on Mom's shoulder and said, "Would you like some wine?"

Mom visibly relaxed. "Oh, yes."

"After a long drive in bad weather," Cousin Mike said, without bothering to finish his sentiment.

"Yes," Mom said.

"And Molly, would you like some juice?"

She nodded, still very pleased with herself for correctly identifying the picture.

Much to Molly's pleasure, her juice was poured into a crystal wine glass.

"Is this real?" Dad asked.

"It is," Cousin Mike said. "It's the only thing in this room—aside from the cheese—that I bought. The wine is courtesy of Father Dale, by the way, who isn't here but wanted to wish you all a pleasant stay. And, frankly, to show off his excellent taste in wine. He has a bottle or two set aside to go with dinner."

Mom helped herself to a few slices of cheese, then sat down on the couch.

"Wow," Dad said. "Molly, take a look at this."

Cousin Mike said, "Take it off the wall so she can see better."

Which Dad did, gingerly. Molly approached the picture hesitantly, keen to the fact that it was somehow valuable, though she wasn't sure how that could be. "This," Dad said, "is an animation cell." He looked at Cousin Mike. "Is that right?"

"Yes." Cousin Mike put together a big selection of cheese—he looked at Mom and said, "Triple cream—be sure you get some." He put his plate and wineglass on the little table between the wing chairs, and set to making a fire.

Dad explained to Molly about how animation was done before computers, "One frame at a time, all hand-drawn." Molly hadn't considered this before; she'd seen plenty of the old animated films, but was more familiar with, and preferred, digitally animated movies. They looked more realistic.

"That sounds so boring," she said.

Cousin Mike said, "It is." A few flames ate the paper beneath the logs and kindling; the kindling caught. "But it has its satisfactions. Working like that, drawing a film frame-by-frame, reminds me of hand-copying the Bible." He sat down on the wing chair closest to the fire. "Is that predictable of me?"

Dad made up a plate for Molly, who sat next to her mother. She tasted the triple cream brie; put the rest on Mom's plate. "Careful with your grape juice," Mom said.

"I will."

Cousin Mike said, "Don't worry too much. That couch is supposed to be stain sealed, or something like that. You could test it out. It's an ugly couch besides."

Molly liked Cousin Mike, and so did Mom and Dad. He put them all at ease.

"I bought that cell as a souvenir, of sorts. Before I went to seminary I thought my calling was to work as an animator. Got all the way out to California and even got myself hired to work on a cartoon." He addressed Molly, "Did you ever watch *Spider and the Undiscovered Bug*?"

Molly shook her head.

"Well that's good, it was terrible. I guess you're not like every other child who'll watch anything so long as it's on T.V."

Mom said, "No, she'll watch anything."

Molly poked Mom, "That's *not* true. I just never heard of that show."

"Maybe it was a little before your time. You're ten, right?"

"Yes!"

"Very good. I try not to ask children their age." He popped a cracker, smothered in brie, into his mouth. "Too much computer work, too little drawing. I did that for about a month. I was miserable."

Mom said, "And that's when you decided to become a priest?"

"Well," Cousin Mike smiled. "Soon after."

"Why did you decide to become a priest?" Dad asked.

"Why did I decide… you know, I tell most people that I was moved by the Holy Spirit, who blew into my life as the Spirit does, and that I felt empty doing what I thought I wanted to do, and that the Lord spoke to me in His way and that's true but… that's not the whole story." Cousin Mike got up and brought the pitcher of grape juice to Molly. "You look like you could use some more." Molly smiled and held out her glass. "And who wants more wine?" Cousin Mike poured more for everyone. "Father Dale does know good wine. Always finds it cheap, too. This bottle—" Cousin Mike poured the last of it into his glass— "just ten dollars." Cousin Mike sat down, picked up the poker and adjusted one of the logs in the fireplace; the flames grew brighter.

"I don't usually tell the whole story because it's personal. And because I don't want to be known as Crazy Father Mike. But this is what happened.

"After I quit my job I sold what little I had and bought a tent, a sleeping bag, some basic camping supplies, and headed for Glacier National Park. I planned to stay for as long as I could. Turned out, that was just one night.

"Once I pitched my tent, I spent the day hiking. I saw all kinds of animals, I even saw a bear. I was on a high trail, which curved around a mountain. I took a turn and the bear was just a few feet in front of me, tugging at a huckleberry bush. Instead of being frightened, as any rational person would be, I felt calm, and in fact I thought to myself that this was the first time in months—maybe years—that I'd really felt calm. I stood perfectly still. The bear ate for a while longer, then walked off. A beautiful moment. A moment full of grace, really, and truly."

"And that's why you became a priest?" Mom asked.

Molly said, "Mom, that can't be it." She looked at Cousin Mike. "That's not it, right?"

Cousin Mike laughed and said, "Oh no. If that had been the most extraordinary occurrence in Glacier, I might've gone back to school for biology. Or headed for the hills and built myself a cabin. No.

"I returned to my campsite around seven o'clock. The folk at the neighboring site had a little motor home with a striped awning, and they were grilling, and when they saw me, all alone and munching on granola, they invited me over for dogs and beer. By the time I finally went to bed—these were very friendly, talkative people—I'd had more beer than I was used to, and was a little drunk.

"I fell asleep right away, but I didn't stay asleep." Cousin Mike looked at Molly. "One of the downsides of beer drinking, besides turning some folk into fools, is that it goes right through you, if you know what I mean."

"You had to pee," Molly said, her delight, obvious.

"I had to pee. Real bad.

"You might think, being out in the woods, that I could just go behind a tree."

"Gross."

"Park rangers feel the same way, Molly. In fact, Glacier's pretty civilized.

A short walk from the campsite is a public bathroom. It's a cabin, one half for boys, one for girls.

"There are no streetlights, no porch lights, no nothing, except the moon, which was just a sliver that night, and not much good for light. I climbed out of my tent into the first real darkness I'd ever been in, I think. Before I clicked on my flashlight, I looked up, and folks, the sky is full of stars. And satellites, I'm told, but they all looked like stars to me, on the blackest background the universe has to offer. That was another nice little moment. Maybe I would have become an astronomer. Or an astronaut.

"But as lovely as the night sky was, I had to pee, and besides, the stars would be there when I got back. I switched on my light—a pitiful, cheap little flashlight—and started up the slope to the bathroom. I couldn't find the trail I'd used earlier, so I just made my own trail, shining my light back onto my tent to keep myself oriented. Pretty soon I could see the light from the bathroom.

"The park bathroom was unheated, and lit only by a few, bare, incandescent bulbs. Screened openings, just beneath the ceiling, provide the only ventilation. Because of the bulbs, there were insects everywhere; anytime the door is opened, more come in. While I stood at the toilet, I watched moths and long, spindly bugs creep along the wall in front of me, and I tried not to think about all the bugs that were probably just above my head, and I tried not to look at all the bugs swimming in the toilet bowl. Even though I was slathered in insect repellent, bugs still flew into me.

"As I relieved myself, that was when I heard the noise, a clicking sound, like this." Cousin Mike made a noise with his mouth. Molly lifted her legs up from the floor, curled up against Mom. "The sound came from behind me.

"You all know how vulnerable you feel when you're in a public bathroom, especially when you're using the toilet. I got pretty scared. I figured an animal had gotten in, and I didn't like the idea of being caught by a bobcat or a wolverine with my pants down. I zipped up quick, wet myself a little—Molly, I'm sorry, I'm being gross."

Molly didn't say a word. Mom was starting to wonder if she should cut Cousin Mike off, if he was going to scare Molly.

"So I go back out, a little shaken up, trying to laugh at myself, but feeling very exposed and ill-equipped. My cheap flashlight flickered a bit—I turned back toward the bathroom—to keep my bearings—I certainly didn't want to get lost—the idea terrified me—and I saw a figure step out of the men's room, and I could have sworn it was a woman.

"Oddly enough, that was kind of comforting. I could laugh at that. A female camper went into the wrong bathroom and when I came in she was embarrassed, so she hid in a stall. That made sense, it explained everything, and so I moved toward my tent with a slightly renewed sense of confidence.

"When I shone my light back toward the bathroom again, I caught a glimpse of that figure again, and the way it moved—I couldn't tell anymore if it was a man or a woman—the way it moved horrified me. Instead of walking like a man, it moved rapidly side to side, its legs wide apart, making an upside-down 'V.' Its legs didn't bend—I couldn't see how it moved, exactly, but it did move, and was moving toward me, crossing back and forth over the path I'd made.

"I ran.

"A tent is a funny thing, because it's no protection from anything, really, except bugs and small animals and the elements. But once you're in it, you feel safer. So I got into my tent and zipped it shut and turned off my flashlight and sat as still as I could. I was out of breath; I fought to breathe as slowly and quietly as possible.

"I knew it was outside my tent because I heard the sound I'd heard in the bathroom." Cousin Mike made the noise again, and now Molly was frightened, but also needed to hear the end of the story, and Mom was worried for Molly but engrossed and Dad was too.

"My heart hurt inside my chest, and it surely skipped a beat when something scratched the outside of my tent. Ran its nails or claws all over the tent, to taunt me, because surely it could tear the tent apart if it wished to.

"I knew it was not an animal when it pulled at the tent zipper.

"I had no weapon and so I prayed. I spoke the Lord's Prayer as loud and clear as I could: 'Our Father who art in Heaven, hallowed be Thy name'—the zipper, inched upward—'Thy Kingdom come, Thy will be done, on Earth as it is in Heaven'—I grew more confident and raised my voice—'give us this day our daily bread, and forgive us our trespasses, as we forgive those who trespass against us'—the zipper stopped, and I finished out the prayer—'and lead us not, into temptation, but deliver us from evil.' When I said 'amen,' I had the strength to open the tent and step out into the night. I turned on my flashlight and walked around my tent. There was nothing."

No one said a word. Cousin Mike broke the spell by tossing another log onto the fire. The room brightened. Cousin Mike said, "There are demons in this world. And God has provided us with a way to protect ourselves."

Cousin Mike stood and said, "You can see why I don't often tell this story. And I hardly intended to tell it tonight! Now—" and Cousin Mike slapped his stomach— "I didn't mention this when you came in, but I've a roast cooking for dinner tonight and—" he sniffed the air— "judging by the smell, dinner will soon be ready. Why don't you folks go upstairs and freshen up? I'd take you up—I should have—but I think I'd better boil the potatoes. Follow me."

And the May family stood and followed their cousin. No one spoke, except Dad, who muttered that a roast would really hit the spot. Cousin Mike pointed up the stairs and gave them directions to the guest room. "There's only one guest room, I hope you don't mind. I put a cot in for Molly."

The guest room was very spare, and so the painted statue, set beneath a lamp, really stood out.

"What is that?" Mom asked.

The statue was of a woman, dressed in blue robes; she was unexceptional but for what she held: a silver dish with a pair of eyes on it.

"That is awful," Mom said.

Molly found it very curious, but not awful. The woman had a very placid expression on her face, and her own eyes were where they were supposed to be. "Maybe she was a doctor, Mom." Molly read the plaque on the base: "St.

Lucy of Syracuse—that's where we are!—'Lucy-light, the shortest day and the longest night.' That's solstice."

For a moment Mom's disgust with the statue dissipated. "That's right, Molly." Her disgust quickly returned and she directed it at Dad: "I am not happy. That story was completely inappropriate. Imagine." She turned to Molly. "You're not going to have nightmares, are you?"

"I don't know."

Dad said, "He's a priest."

"Is that how you explain his lack of common sense? You don't tell a story like that to a ten year old girl."

"I thought it was really interesting, Mom."

"I'm sure you did. Crazy Father Mike sounds right to me."

"He's not going to kill us in our sleep," Dad said. "Unless, of course, he thinks you're a demon." Dad winked at Molly. "So maybe you should tone it down."

"I'm not laughing."

"Okay. I agree. He's eccentric. Let's try to have a nice dinner."

"Fine. But I want to leave first thing tomorrow."

"We're going to leave first thing tomorrow. That's the plan."

"Fine."

The May family went downstairs, and in spite of Mom's sour mood, the conversation was convivial, being about family and school and favorite movies, and the food was excellent, as was Father Dale's wine. "Just ten dollars a bottle. It's a miracle."

That night, Molly did have a nightmare, and worse, she did not wake up; her nightmare went on and on until the morning, when her mother woke her from her whimpering sleep. Molly could not remember much about the nightmare except that she waited and waited and while she waited she could not move.

Cousin Mike was sorry the May family had to leave so early. "I spent too much time away from family," he said. And Molly was sorry too—she thought he was sad.

Dinner had gone a long way toward calming Mom down, and though she planned to leave as soon as the car was packed—and said so to Dad—she gave in when Cousin Mike insisted they have some kind of breakfast, which was eggs, bagels and bacon. During breakfast, Cousin Mike excused himself. When he returned to the table he brought a wrapped gift—"I had some tissue paper lying around, that's all"—which he gave to Molly.

Molly unwrapped it and Dad said, "That's not the one from the living room."

"She can't accept that," Mom said.

"Sure she can. No, it's not the one from the living room. I bought the cells as a pair—this is a frame or two further along. You see Molly, how little Maleficent has moved? I had this one in my office. Will it look good in your room?"

"Yes! Thank you!"

Mom said, "That was very nice of you."

"And it was nice of you all to come. I'm sorry I didn't write sooner. Molly, here's something else for you," Cousin Mike handed her a laminated card. "I'm sure this doesn't seem very exciting, but I want you to have it." One side of the card depicted a long-haired, doe-eyed Jesus standing on top of a hill, arms raised. On the other side of the card was The Lord's Prayer. "It's a dreadful picture, I know, but the prayer's still good," and Cousin Mike winked at Molly's parents. Mom didn't like this gift at all. Dad promised himself he'd take Molly to church more often. Molly thanked her cousin, and tucked the card into her pocket.

"One last thing. I looked over some maps last night and I think I found a good route for you to take to Aunt Amy's. I think I shaved a half hour off your trip." Cousin Mike handed Dad a piece of paper with new directions. "Thanks," Dad said. And the May family went on their way.

Three hours into their drive, the May family followed directions from a roadside sign to a restaurant called Diner at the Animator's House. The signs indicated that the diner was a few miles further than Mom and Dad really cared to stray from the road—they were ever-calculating miles and time-to-go—but the signs were brightly painted and it was time for lunch. Dad guessed it was no coincidence that Cousin Mike's directions led them past an "animator's house," and smiled; he was pretty sure he liked his cousin. Mom was hungry and started to imagine a hamburger, and Molly was excited, she thought she might see people drawing cartoons, "Like Cousin Mike," she said.

Ultimately, a dirt parking lot and just one other car, a red Pontiac circa 1985, coated in a yellow layer of pollen. Not very appealing, but behind a row of empty parking spaces, each indicated with a stone marker, was the restaurant, all shiny chrome, looking every bit like an Airstream trailer, and—seamlessly attached—a little red house, presumably belonging to "The Animator." All this was bright and very welcoming and so Mom and Dad's worry about being away from the highway melted a little, and Dad said, "This looks pretty nice," and Molly couldn't wait to see if the inside was as toy-like as the exterior.

And, indeed, it was. Bright yellow and blue stools in a short row before a tall, chrome and Formica counter; a glass cake-dish with pink-frosted donuts under the lid; a couple of booths, all vibrant green vinyl ("Everything looks brand new," Mom said); and a jukebox, a "Wurlitzer of wisdom." Three walls of the restaurant were tile, white and pale blue checked, but one wall was shingled and featured a plain brown door—the door to the Animator's House, the May family presumed, though there was no sign, nor any evidence that the house was open to the public. Perhaps, Molly thought, the animator lives there still, and was even then quietly making cartoons.

Mom would have preferred a booth, but Molly begged for the counter, and Dad didn't mind and neither did Mom, not really, and when Mom thought of the milkshake she was about to order she found that she really didn't mind. Molly saw, between a pink espresso machine and a small soda fountain, a black wire rack which displayed little books, books no bigger than cell phones, each with black covers but bound with gold tape. "Mom," she said. "What are those?"

Before Mom could figure out what Molly wanted to know about, Mathilda—so said her name tag—emerged from the kitchen. "Hello y'all,"

Mathilda said, with absolutely no southern accent. "Y'all hungry for a late lunch?" Dad nodded, a little wide-eyed and why not, Mathilda was splendidly endowed and wore her blouse open a button lower than Mom thought respectable, revealing the decorative edges of a lacy blue brassiere. Mathilda's hair was black, really, really black, and this startled Molly—why she was startled was not clear, but she leaned against Mom and Mom put an arm around her, glad that someone else was a little off-put. Dad, being neither foolish nor crude, turned from Mathilda and said, "This is my wife and my daughter. We're driving to her aunt's house and we needed a break." Mathilda smiled and that smile put everyone at ease; Dad no longer worried he would look too much and upset the waitress or his wife, Mom saw that Mathilda was a little older than she initially appeared (crow's feet, just like her own), and Molly saw a sense of humor and—in Mathilda's eyes—a sweet beckoning.

"What are those little books?" Molly asked.

Mathilda tilted her head a little and said, "What little books, darling?"

"Those," Molly insisted with an outstretched arm.

Mathilda turned, and all three watched her take several steps toward the rack, all watched her body move beneath a stiff, blue and white striped uniform, all watched as she slipped a single finger through a loop at the top of the rack, lifted the rack from the counter, bent a little and blew, "It's a little dusty, honey," and carried the rack to the counter. "Why don't you take a look, sweetie, while your parents tell me just what they want."

Molly was delighted to have the mysterious books all to herself, but she was also a little worried—what if she damaged one? Were they expensive? If you break it, so many store keepers said, you've bought it. What a cruel world we live in. Mathilda, without turning her attention from Molly's mother, who was ordering a milkshake and a hamburger, said, "You go ahead, doll, don't fuss over those, they're meant to be bent and broken in."

And when Molly took one from the rack, she saw exactly what Mathilda meant: they were flip-books. She took one, bent it back and let the pages go. Molly didn't like what she saw.

Mathilda placed a hamburger in front of Mom and a hamburger in front of Dad. She winked at Molly and set down a plate of breaded chicken fingers. "You want some barbeque sauce to go on that, or some honey?" Molly wondered if she had ordered and forgotten doing so—chicken fingers was exactly the food she'd thought of when she'd walked into the diner—but then maybe her parents ordered for her.

Dad reached in front of Molly and took a flipbook "I always loved these things." He quickly flipped through the book and he laughed.

Molly asked for honey. She couldn't help but watch Mathilda as she walked toward the kitchen. Mathilda's waist was so narrow, her hips so wide.

Mathilda retuned with Molly's honey and Mom asked, "Who is the Animator?"

"He drew those little books," Mathilda said.

"Does he live next door?"

"Oh, no. He's been dead for a while. The house is an homage to his memory, a museum."

Molly looked at her plate and found she'd eaten all her food, even the lettuce garnish, and the honey-saucer was clean too (her finger was sticky she put it in her mouth), and this disturbed her, because she did not remember eating the chicken.

Dad asked, "Was he famous?"

"To a small, inner circle." Mathilda angled her head. "Excuse me one minute, that's the cook," she said. Molly heard no one, and in fact, she'd not once heard a sound from the kitchen, not a pot or a dish or the chop of a knife.

Mom said, "My you were hungry. Have some of my fries." Mom bit into her pickle. She'd not started her burger.

Molly didn't want a French fry but she ate one and then another.

Dad said, "This is an excellent burger."

The door to the museum opened, just a hair.

"Would you like to play something on the jukebox?" Dad held up a quarter.

Molly brightened, the little confusions fled, and she leapt from her stool.

As she flipped through the song titles, she was reminded of the flip book: a black scribble moved from left to right, flickering and twisting as it moved. Half way across, the scribble froze—pages kept flipping—too many, the book wasn't that thick, but the scribble was caught. The scribble changed, a smudge, a fingerprint, dust, several blank pages, and finally the pages were bright red.

The quarter Dad gave Molly was gone from her hand and she heard the machine work: an arm on a 45, the record dropped onto the turntable, the needle—shush, shush—and then the tune, a familiar song, one Molly might have chosen, but not exactly, not even the version of the song she was used to. The lights on the jukebox bounced to and fro.

"That's a funny choice," Dad said.

The record caught; the song jumped back on itself; a lyric repeated more times than was right. "It's skipping," Mom said. Then the record corrected itself and the song proceeded to its end.

Mathilda, back behind the counter, topped off Dad's coffee and, with her fingernail, tapped the metal cup that contained Mom's milkshake: "Need a little more?" Mom said yes, her mouth full. Mom swallowed and before Molly could climb onto her stool said, "The museum is open. Mathilda says you can go right on in. Your father and I will be a little bit longer with our meals."

The May family watched Mathilda as she walked to the museum door, already ajar, and pushed it open. Film canisters were stacked on the floor alongside thick pads of paper. "Go ahead on in," Mom said. Molly, hesitant but curious, crossed the threshold. As soon as Mathilda took her hand from the door the door drifted back, stopped just ajar of its frame.

And Molly was in the museum. Dust-color, the dull, sticky color of pollen, gray shadowy black. Her parents' voices—clear for a moment: Dad, "What kind of films did he make?" Mathilda, "He had a knack for children." Mom: "A knack?" Her parents' voices: gone.

Some museum, Molly thought. The room was quite bare. Against the far wall was a drafting table, with a lamp clamped to its side, and a metal stool.

There were no bookshelves (which would have comforted Molly). Where Molly had walked were footprints, the image of the cartoon character on the bottom of her shoes—a smiling rectangle with arms and legs—stamped into the dust that covered the floor. She laughed when she saw the imprint, but her laughter soured; the friendly rectangle's smile did not seem kind, reproduced as it was in dust. Two filthy windows offered a view of the parking lot; the light outside was low, the sky a deep and dark blue, the trees black. The May family car looked as forlorn as the Pontiac parked just beyond.

Molly lifted the cover of a drawing pad on the floor. In pencil, the words, "Emily stands still." Molly didn't like the image: a beetle, back split, withered wings up. Did they buzz?

"Mom?"

Her mother did not answer.

Molly went to the door, and peeked out into the diner. Her parents were sitting at the counter, eating their hamburgers. At the far end of the diner, the jukebox boiled with colored light.

"Molly."

"Mom?"

But Mom was eating, pushing food into her mouth with her index finger.

"Molly."

Mathilda was on the ceiling, tucked into the peak, partially obscured by ceiling beams and shadow. She clung upside down, her head thrown back, her black hair long, her pale throat exposed. Molly did not scream, but put her hand into her mouth and bit down—honey and dust. Mathilda scuttled across the ceiling without taking her eyes from Molly. Briefly, Mathilda was directly above Molly, head at an impossible angle, and Molly spat out her hand and said, "No." She was sure Mathilda would drop down on top of her, press her face into Molly's own. And Mathilda's face was no longer beautiful, but distorted, muscles taut, teeth bared to the gums. Mathilda did not drop from the ceiling, but crawled to the place where the wall and ceiling met—just above the door to the diner.

Molly shouted, "Mom!"

Mathilda said, "Mom."

Molly shouted, "Mom! Dad! I'm in here!"

Mathilda said, "Mom. Dad. I'm in here."

The door to the Animator's House opened wide, and Molly's parents walked in. "You didn't let me finish my burger," Mom complained. Molly thought her mother meant that she had interrupted her mother, but Dad said, "You're a slow poke." Molly shouted, "Look behind you," and she pointed up at Mathilda, who jiggered on the wall. A noise like dishes stacked. Dad turned around, and looked out into the diner. "No, up, Dad, on the ceiling." But he only peered out and said, "Mathilda? Don't clear away my wife's dish." He turned to Mom. "Huh. I thought I heard Mathilda out there." Mathilda's eyes shifted left to right.

Mom and Dad walked past Molly. Dad asked, "Is she out at the car?" Mom went to a window, "I can't really tell. These windows are filthy." "Nice museum," Dad said. Molly couldn't tell if her father was being sarcastic or not, but what upset her most was his disinterest in her, and that her parents had not noticed Mathilda, clinging to the wall. Molly screamed, as loud as she possibly could.

"Well, I don't want her walking around in a parking lot when it's so dark outside."

Dad said, "It has gotten dark, hasn't it?" Then, "Okay, yeah, I'll go out. Why don't you have your burger wrapped up."

Dad left the museum, passed right under Mathilda, and Mom did too; Molly—afraid to get close to Mathilda—hung back but watched her mother through the half-open door. Mom sat at the counter and said, "Mathilda?"

Mathilda on the ceiling said, "Mathilda."

Molly watched her mother take a bite from her hamburger and saw that it was not a hamburger but a clod of dirt. Mathilda stepped out of the kitchen, wiping her wet hands on her apron. "Just washing up," she said. Mathilda was also on the ceiling in the museum.

Mom asked, "Can I get this wrapped up?"

Mathilda on the ceiling said, "Can I get this wrapped up."

Mathilda behind the counter said, "Why of course. I'm glad you enjoyed our humble fare."

Mom offered a weak smile.

Dad came in from the parking lot. "Honey, I don't see Molly out there." He addressed Mathilda, who stood with Mom's plate of dirt: "Have you seen Molly?"

"No. No I haven't. Didn't she go into the Animator's House?"

Mathilda, on the ceiling said, "Didn't she go into the Animator's House."

Dad said, "I thought so, but she wasn't in there when we looked."

Molly made a dash for the door, but Mathilda, quick as a millipede, banged the door shut. Molly cried out and stumbled back—the windows, she thought—and then she saw that the stool at the drafting table was occupied.

An ordinary looking man, a little thin, perhaps, bald, in fact, sat on the stool with his back to the drafting table. "Hi," he said, as if nothing at all terrible were happening.

Molly glanced at the window and saw her parents, looking around the parking lot, hands cupped to their mouths, presumably calling out her name, but there was no sound in the museum, except Molly's breathing and an occasional click, click from Mathilda, her long fingernail on the shut door.

"I suppose I ought to get to work, right?" The man turned to the drafting table, adjusted the angle of the lamp but did not turn the lamp on—the room was dark. And dark. The man picked up a pencil and a little brass pencil sharpener—Molly heard the sound of the pencil as it turned against the sharpener's blade. "I guess the best place to start is where you stand now," he said.

Outside, Molly's parents were hysterical. Mom shouted Molly's name in the darkening parking lot. Dad used a phone in the diner as Mathilda stood by, a worried expression on her face.

Mathilda in the museum clicked at the door.

Molly said, as calmly as she could, "I want to go."

The man said, "Oh, but look, you can't." He gestured for Molly to come join him at the drafting table, to see what it was he drew. Molly read the title: "Molly stands still." And while she didn't look anything like what the Animator had drawn on the page, she would not be able to move until he was finished. The laminated card with the Lord's Prayer was in her pocket. She had never learned the prayer, not by heart, and her cousin's recitation of it in his story was the first time she'd heard it since Christmas. She could not remember any of it; at least, she could not seem to bring any of it to mind. And so the prayer, her salvation, cruelly mocked her ignorance. If only she could read the words, if only Cousin Mike were here.

The Animator drew, and Molly hoped he would draw her hand to her pocket. Though she could not imagine why he would.

In the Cellar

Ironing naked, Joseph's wife Marguerite asked Joseph to tell her a story. He was dozing, and he was watching her breasts shift as she rearranged a blouse on the board, watching her mouth purse as she got the tip of the iron into a corner of fabric, but mostly, he was dozing. His legs and arms were spread across the bed, his penis relaxed, spent, his breathing drifting into snoring. Joseph acknowledged that he would tell Marguerite a story, and then he snored a little. It was late, he was tired, but she had decided after making love that she was going to iron her blouses, to be ready for the week, and while she was at it she would iron his shirts, so: "Joseph. Tell me a story." He moved again, jerked awake, then closed his eyes again. "Come on, Joseph. Tell me a story while I iron." "Okay," he said with his eyes closed. "Okay," he said to the white ceiling. "Okay," he said, as he looked at his wife.

Because he was not fully awake, he told a story he didn't expect to tell. He said, "I remember the stairs that go down and I remember the little girl who led me." Marguerite stopped ironing for a moment, to take in what Joseph had said. She frowned. He woke up a little more and started again:

"When I was living alone, in the apartment, I woke one night from a nightmare. I tried to go back to sleep but every time I closed my eyes the images that had terrified me came back. I turned on my bedside lamp which cast my bedroom a dirty yellow. I wrote the nightmare out, hoping to exorcize the images into my notebook; no good, they were still firm. So, exhausted, I got out of bed and walked into the kitchen, flipping light switches the whole way. I poured myself a glass of milk and sat at the small card table where I used to eat my meals. As I sat there, a memory came back, in toto, all at once."

Joseph appeared to be in contemplation, but his snore gave him away. "Joseph," Marguerite said. Joseph said, "The off-season cottage. The yard. Lilacs. Abigail and the steps." Marguerite set her iron down and started to come around the ironing board, because it looked to her as if Joseph had slipped into a nightmare. But he opened his eyes and said, "I'm sorry. I'm not making any sense, am I? Let me make some tea."

He returned to their bedroom with two cups of tea, set one on the night table and another on the end of the ironing board. Marguerite moved her cup from the ironing board to the night table and Joseph told this story:

When Joseph was eight, his family moved, for an off-season, to a small cottage in the seaside town Marion. The air smelled of lilac and ocean. The trees were still green but for patches of color: an oak in the back with an iris of red. The drive was a gravel roundabout, with a great pine in the center which cast a shadow over the house. To the left of the house was a small shed, slightly dilapidated, painted white with green trim to match the house. The shed's window was thick with dust; through it, only vague shapes could be seen. The backyard was the cottage's most impressive feature. An enormous field of carefully trimmed green grass, marked at its halfway point by a row of apple trees. At the far end of the yard was a flat granite boulder and a split rail fence, which right-angled and ran along the right, street-side of the yard. The left side of the yard was delineated by tall, thick, lilac bushes.

Joseph's bedroom was bright during the day. One large window opened out over the backyard, and another faced the shed. For the first week he and his parents spent in the cottage, there were no curtains up over those windows: during the day Joseph didn't care, but at night he felt vulnerable. He liked least his view of the shed, which, even on dark nights, was bright white.

Toward the end of the first week, he woke in the middle of the night, opened his eyes and saw a little girl at the shed window, screaming. He whimpered. Her hands were pressed to the glass, her mouth was wide open. Behind her, something moved. He screamed, "Mom!" And, "Dad!" His father flipped the light switch, flooding the room, and erasing the image of the screaming girl: his bedroom window went dark. Joseph's mother pushed into the room, alert, awake. She touched his face, his arms, pulled back his covers to examine his body. "What's wrong Joe, what's wrong?" His father crouched in front of him. Joseph said, "There's a little girl in the shed and she's screaming. I saw her in the window." His father walked around the bed to the window, put his hands to the glass and looked out. Joseph's mother looked at his father, who turned and said, "I don't see anything, Joe. But I'll go out and check." Joseph's mother kept caressing him and reassured him that his father would make sure everything was all right. When his father got to the bedroom door, his mother asked, "Should I be calling the police?" His father replied, "Just keep an eye on me."

 Joseph's mother turned on the small light by Joseph's bed, then stood— "I'm not going anywhere," she reassured—and turned off the overhead light. Now they could see out the window into the side yard. Soon they saw Joseph's dad, leather jacket on over his pajamas, work shoes without socks and a heavy flashlight. He walked to the shed. He checked the door. Apparently it was locked. He walked to the shed window and shone the light inside. For a moment, Joseph and his mother could see the cluttered interior. Joseph's dad pointed the light into the backyard and walked a little ways into it, out of sight. When he came back into view, he gave Joseph and Joseph's mother a thumb's up, then headed back toward the front of the cottage. In a moment, he was standing in the door frame of Joseph's bedroom. "I didn't see anything, Joseph. And you saw me look around. But it sounds like you had a bad nightmare, so feel free to join us tonight if you want." Joseph's mother smiled, and Joseph, getting sleepy amid the comfort of his parents, mumbled that he wanted to sleep with them. Joseph's father picked him up, and the three of them left Joseph's room. Once Joseph was tucked into his parents' bed, Joseph's father signaled for his mother to step out into the hall. He said, "I didn't see anything, Mary, but I heard something in the backyard. Toward the left, by the bushes."

"Was it an animal?" she asked. "Probably. But I'm going to make sure all the windows and doors are locked before I join you two for bed."

When not at school or in his room playing, Joseph took long, exploratory walks. These walks never took him far but there was a wealth of detail to be found close to home. Along the left perimeter of the backyard, among the short trunks of the lilac bushes, were gaps large enough for him to crawl into, which gave him glimpses of the yard beyond—his only glimpses: the house was otherwise surrounded by a high, unpainted picket fence. There wasn't much to be revealed by his spying—another backyard, another flat plane of bright green grass. The only mystery a cellar entrance, a slanted cement bunker with metal doors. Joseph could lie for hours watching those doors and fantasizing about the people who might exit from them.

On a bright, cool afternoon, as he squirmed under one of the bushes, turning up the pale, dry dirt—tendrils of dust rising to his nose—he unearthed something metal. With his fingers he began to dig around it, to assess its size, his goal to remove it from the earth. He cut several inches into the dirt on either side of the object, and then it dawned on Joseph what it was he'd discovered; a rail. To confirm this, he began to dig a few feet to the left of the single rail he'd uncovered, and then a few feet to the right. Eventually he located the parallel rail, and, with a little more effort, a rotting wooden tie. He slid out from under the bushes, astonished by the thought of a buried train line—from where, he wondered, from the ocean? He began to walk a straight line from the rail he'd discovered across his backyard, mumbling to himself as he did. His mother, who was in the kitchen, noticed him doing this when she glanced out the window to see what he was up to. She dried her hands on a dish towel as she walked toward him. She called out his name. He stopped, looked up and eagerly waved her over. When she was close enough to speak to him without shouting she said, "It looks like you're marching."

"I'm following train tracks."

"Train tracks?"

Too excited to explain, he said, "Let me show you." He took her hand and led her to the bush he'd been under. As they walked she noticed how dirty he was; she refrained from commenting. "Look at what I found," he said, pointing under the bush. His mother had to get on her knees—for a moment he saw just how small he was and how his world was full of extraordinary minutia—then excitement rushed over him and the thought was gone, never fully formed.

Before his mother understood what it was Joseph had found she saw the glint of metal and wondered if he'd unearthed something electrical. Her heart sped up, and she began to back away and admonish her son. Then she saw what actually he had unearthed, and linked it with what he had been saying, and her concern vanished, and she was taken by curiosity. "These are train tracks."

"Yeah. I was following where they went."

She stood up, brushed off her slacks and looked across the yard in the direction Joseph had been walking. "That would take the train right into the ocean," she said. She regained her sense of concern and said, "You shouldn't dig in the yard like that. You might hit a wire and electrocute yourself." Then she said, "But this is interesting. I'll have to stop by the library, see if a line ran through here."

"Why would a train go into the ocean?"

Joseph's mother looked in the direction of the beach that lay across the street, just behind a great yellow house with a widow's peak she found romantic. "Maybe there was a loading dock at one time." She doubted this; to have all signs of commerce cleared away for what was now a residential area seemed unlikely. "Or maybe the tracks curved that way into town." She turned and faced the road to town. She imagined a train roaring through the house, tearing up the earth as it rode on its sunken rail. "Come on," she said, back from her reverie. "Let me make you some lunch. We'll figure it out later."

Late October, walking home from school, kicking through fallen leaves, Joseph spotted a cat. Instead of running away, the cat stood still, tail raised and curling like smoke from a chimney. Joseph crouched in front of it, letting his backpack drop to the ground behind him, and opened his hand to the animal. It approached him and licked the tips of his fingers—the roughness of its tongue pleased Joseph. He saw that the cat had no collar, so he named the cat: Marla—after one of the girls in his class (who was always nice to Joseph).

When Marla began to walk away, he followed. She walked past the cottage toward the house next door. She slipped under the picket fence. He tried to see between the fence slats, but the pickets were tight together. He backed up, considered running to the lilac bushes and crawling underneath, but opted instead to climb the tree which stood in the center of the roundabout in front of the cottage, so he could see over the fence and see where the cat had gone (maybe it would go into the cellar?). Once in the tree, he spotted Marla immediately, bright white and black against a backdrop of dried leaves.

Adjusting his position on the branch he'd climbed to, Joseph glimpsed something white in the uppermost window of the house next door. He focused his attention on the small pane of glass and saw that at the window was a little girl in a white dress. He was startled, and for a moment lost his balance—she reminded him of the girl he'd seen in the shed (and mostly forgotten about, except when he couldn't sleep at night). Once he regained his balance, he looked again at the window, and realized she was watching him. Hesitantly, he waved. She waved back. He stared at her for a long while, and when she backed away, into the darkness of that upstairs room, he continued to stare, until the muscles in his arms and legs began to tremble from the strain of keeping him balanced in the tree.

Joseph spent the following afternoons prowling around the perimeter of his neighbor's house in hopes that the little girl would come outside. He thought about knocking on the door and once stood at the front gate—considering the possibility—but got no further. Sometimes, as he crawled along the lilac bushes Marla would join him, slinking in and out between the trunks. When he lay still long enough, she would climb onto his back. When she did, Joseph tried not to move, because he liked the company and the weight of her warm body. Eventually she would grow restless and walk out into the yard Joseph couldn't bring himself to explore. He'd often end his outings—as the sun set—by climbing the tree in the front yard and staring at the window where he'd seen the girl.

One evening, after dinner, when his folks had finished washing up and were chatting over cups of coffee, they mentioned the house next door. They were discussing the neighborhood and Joseph's father asked, "Have you ever seen anyone come in or out of that big house next door?" Joseph stopped playing (he was under the dining room table, steering his cars along the pattern on the carpet). His mother said, "No. I noticed that too. I was chatting with Mrs. Garnett—she lives at the top of our street—and I asked if the house was vacant. She said as far as she knew, it wasn't, that a family of three lived there. She said they were very private people—they were the ones who put up the high fence. One of the ladies at the school told her that she thought the family was very religious and home taught their child." Joseph's father said, "A fundamentalist family in this town? Maybe there's an invalid next door, and everything's delivered." His parents' speculation ended soon after, and as far as Joseph knew, his parents' promises to investigate further never materialized, much the same way his mother never followed up on the buried tracks.

The first snow of the season left only a dust of powder on the ground. The second snowfall buried Marion in a foot of snow. Having not seen the girl in nearly a month and with the cold growing bitter, Joseph had become less vigilant about his watch. Occasionally he sought out Marla, but she, too, had become of dim interest. Now he tended to spend his afternoons in his bedroom, playing on the floor with his toy men or cars or blocks.

One such afternoon he happened to glance out his window and saw, behind the now bare lilac bushes (a fence of black, pointed sticks), the little girl. She wasn't wearing a coat, just a little white dress and white stockings pulled to her knees. Her feet were hidden by the snow. Joseph took his jacket and was outside, was in the backyard, was facing the little girl through the grate of bare branches.

"Hello," he said.

"Hi," she said. "Is that your yard?"

He looked over his shoulder at the enormous white plain around him. "Yes. Do you live in that house?"

"Yes. What's your name?"

"Joseph."

"That's a handsome name." Which sounded very adult to Joseph, and made him feel he was dealing with someone not only mysterious, but more mature and probably smarter. "I'm Abigail. I hate my name. How old are you?"

"Eight," he said, careful to answer her questions directly.

"I'm nine."

"Is that your room?" He pointed to the small upper window. "Up there?"

"Yes."

"It must be great, living so high up. Can you see the ocean?"

"No."

He was unsure if she was telling him she couldn't see the ocean or that it wasn't so great to live so high up. Her answer was so abrupt, though, he was afraid to ask for any clarification.

"Why haven't I seen you out?" he asked.

"My parents won't let me. They're away. I'm cold. Will you come in?"

Joseph knew he shouldn't without telling his parents, but she wasn't wearing a jacket and it was terribly cold. "Okay," he said.

He expected they would go around to the front door, or that there was a side door he'd never seen, but instead, as he crawled under the branches (they made zipper sounds across the back of his jacket), she opened the cellar doors. When he stood up and could see down the yellow-lit steps, his chest filled with terror. Before he could back down, turn and go home, to his room, to the kitchen where his mother was cooking, Abigail stepped over the bunker lip and down the first few cement steps. She turned and said, "Come on."

What, from the top of the stairs, had looked like a square of the cellar floor, was in fact only a landing. At the second landing, which Joseph had also hoped was the cellar floor, he stopped and said, "Where are we going?" Above his head was a bare incandescent bulb, screwed into a socket which was set into the wall.

"I want to see if I can get to the trains. You can protect me."

Though he was now very interested, he was also frightened. "From what?"

"The dark. I get scared in the dark. But with a boy… you can hold my hand."

"It gets dark?"

"Darker. But you're a boy."

Misguided pride took him landing to landing, which, thankfully, were each lit by a single bulb.

The pair arrived on a landing that was wet. The lip of the landing was crumbled, exposing iron rods and a wooden framework. The next set of steps were wood. Abigail took Joseph's hand. "You're so brave," she whispered. She did not look at him. She led them down the wooden steps to the next landing, which was also wood, weathered, unpainted, warped up at the edges.

"How much further do we have to go?" he asked.

"I don't know."

They walked down another set of wooden steps, which creaked, and halfway down, canted slightly. They froze, then went forward, down.

There was no light bulb in the wall at the next landing. Joseph said, "It's dark."

Abigail squeezed his hand; his was clammy (beneath his fear, he was embarrassed by this); her hand was warm and dry.

At the next landing, which was lit by a greasy yellow bulb, the stairs became spiral. Black iron, narrow, a corkscrew into the ground. From where they stood it seemed as if there was light below, but from no identifiable source. The pair continued to descend. Joseph's mind whirred. He thought of his parents and how worried they might be (what time was it was it close to dinner time?). He wondered about this girl, who was older and quiet. She scared him. He kept one hand on the banister, one in Abigail's. And then—

"The banister," he said.

His hand slipped off the end of the banister. He stopped. Abigail tugged at him and he nearly lost his balance, but he pulled back and stopped her. He felt for more banister—perhaps only a link in the rough iron rail had fallen out. He gently pushed Abigail forward, cautiously looking for firm footing. "The banister is gone."

"We can be careful."

The light was only enough to cast a glow over Abigail's white dress and white skin. Where her hair fell, black. The narrow spiral staircase was black. Joseph looked up, and saw that the light behind him was feeble. He would not have gone further, but Abigail slipped her hand from his, and continued down: his fear of being left alone in the dark overcame his reason: he saw white faces before his eyes.

He learned the shape of each step. Though there was nothing to catch him from falling over the edge (and what was below and where?), the outermost end of the step was widest. There were no risers, so his ankle hit the hard lip of each step as he sought to establish its contours. The metal rung with each step. Abigail moved too fast and was vanishing. "Abigail, wait." She would slow, then move on, and he would have to call to her to wait again.

She stopped. "Abigail?" Joseph, slow, caught up with her. "Abigail?" He whispered her name into her ear.

"Shh. Listen." Joseph stood still. The air smelled like mildew and—he smelled his own sweat.

And he heard a sound coming from below. "What…"

"Shh."

The sound was like the rumble of an empty dump truck. The scrape and grind of the shovel-end of a front lifter dragged across pavement. The scrabbling of crab legs?

"What is it?"

"We have to go back." There was the lilt of panic in her voice. "It's coming up."

Hopeful, he asked, "Your dad?" To Joseph, the thought of her father—any parent—was reassuring. But she was so scared and upset—it couldn't be her father. The dull thump of a heavy book dropped on thick carpet, the sound of a boot sucked at by mud. Joseph had the impression, too, that the sounds were moving up and gaining.

She pushed at him. "We have to go fast."

Just turning around on the spiral staircase with no banister made Joseph panic. She put her hands on his waist to turn him—he didn't like that—he got over his fear and moved—still slow, though, careful to firmly find his footing. He focused on nothing else and that helped and it was easier to move up than down, so he did move quicker, but not fast enough for Abigail, who slapped and punched at his back and butt.

When he found the railing, he was able to go much quicker. Her blows landed less often.

Behind them, the noises boomed, clicked and scratched, faster. They gained on the pair.

When he came to the first landing—below the greasy bulb—he could run. He could see and the stairs were straight and wide. They rocked beneath him, his legs burned, he was soaked in sweat, but he could run and he ran.

The sound like a squall like a piano lifted and let go.

His shoulders grazed the cement walls as he hit each landing and turned to run up the next flight of stairs. He tried to glance back, to look for Abigail and to see if the monster (he thought of it as a monster now) was behind them was so close its face could be seen. But he couldn't slow down to twist his body around.

He saw the night sky framed by the cellar doors. He felt sharp air blow down and around him. He couldn't tell if the whine—a tinny screech—was a noise the wind made or a cry from behind—Abigail or their pursuer.

The deep snow made Joseph stagger, but he did not fall, and he built up enough momentum to crash through the lilac bushes into his own yard. He stopped to look behind him and saw that Abigail was not with him. He crouched forward, wheezing. He kneeled on the snow, peering through the bush-screen of sticks, listened for sounds from the open cellar. He heard his own labored breathing. He tried to hold his breath, to silence it so he could listen for footsteps, for the grinding, drumming noise, but he couldn't, he couldn't even draw enough breath to hold.

Still, Joseph was able to hear the train, which must have run underground, below Abigail's house. Announcing its arrival, the train's whistle blew, and the sound filled the air like wind.

Joseph fell onto his side in the snow. He couldn't breathe. He blacked out. That was when the memory of the stairs going down and of Abigail buried itself, to emerge only years later, prompted by a nightmare.

"After I remembered the stairs that went down and the little girl who led me, I became driven to deal with what my mind at eight would not let me deal with. Without turning on the light in my bedroom I found clothes I'd let fall on the floor, dressed, grabbed my keys and left my apartment, determined to go to Marion, to see the cottage my parents had rented for the off-season, the shed, and Abigail's house.

"Of course, I had no way to get to Marion. I didn't have a car. I was a student then and had no money—I couldn't take a cab or a bus. I ran to a pay phone and called a friend who had a car—this was at four, five in the morning. This friend got out of bed and met me in front of her apartment building with the keys to her car and a cup of coffee in a go cup. She wanted me to better explain what I was doing with her car and why I needed it so suddenly, and I think I tried, but I'd run to her place, was out of breath and too focused on my need to get to the cottage.

"With a map I purchased at a gas station spread out across the passenger seat, and the coffee cup between my legs, I drove to Marion. Once in the town—though I'd only lived there a few months—I was able to find the cottage without thinking. By then the sky was growing light—the sun would come into view in an hour. I parked the car on the street.

"The cottage itself looked the same. The tree in front had been cleared away. I walked to the side yard and the shed was still there. Behind it I could see the yard. Someone had removed the lilac bushes. Abigail's yard and mine now merged seamlessly. I walked past the shed about half way across the yard—the trees which once marked this halfway point were gone too, cleared away for the hoops and wickets used for croquet. But I knew where I was because of the bunker. I looked on the ground for the railroad tracks but of course the grass had grown over the hole I'd dug when I was eight. I walked to the cellar doors and saw that they were padlocked.

"I decided that I wasn't going to let that stop me, so I went out into the yard looking for something I might smash the padlock with. Walking toward the shed, where I thought I might find a hammer or a sledge, I stumbled over a brightly colored, wooden mallet. With this mallet in hand, I walked over to the cellar doors, took careful aim and swung at the lock.

"The sound was outrageously loud and I accomplished little. Still, filled with a feeling akin to rage, I swung again and again. The lights in the house I was attacking came on, as did the lights in the cottage behind me. I kept swinging. As a man appeared—holding a flashlight and with a jacket on over his pajamas—the mallet head shattered. 'Goddamn it,' I shouted.

"The figure turned and ran back toward the cottage, and it dawned on me what I was doing and that I was going to be arrested if I didn't get away. I dropped the wasted mallet, ran to the car and drove.

"Just before I reached the highway, I pulled the car over. I was exhausted and shaking. I took my seat belt off and opened the car door. I swung my legs out, put my feet down in the grass. I leaned over my knees, and vomited. Bile came up without effort, in a single great gush, and splattered onto the ground. I swung my legs into the car, leaned back in the driver's seat and began to cry."

Joseph was done telling his story. Marguerite was on the bed next to Joseph. She was uncovered, still naked, her back to him. The ironing board had been left set up, a shirt out for ironing but the iron up and cold—Joseph had unplugged it when Marguerite had stood staring at him, her face full of concern and, gradually, distress. Now, at the end of his story, he regretted telling it. Had he been fully awake, he would not have. It was not the kind of story he told to Marguerite. In his full consciousness, he felt the brunt of the wicked guilt he had felt while hammering at that padlocked bunker.

Marguerite was off in another place. Marguerite knew what the story meant, of course, because her father had raped her night after night while her mother lay awake in her father's room.

The Animal Aspect of Her Movement

Brian

Sun caught the chrome bumper of the little red car that cut in front of me, my eyes drawn, then dazzled, and for miles that little red car seemed to settle in, locked into my line of sight. I only kind of noticed, my mind stuck on the failed sales call I'd made an hour earlier. I guess I really started to pay attention to the little red car when it signaled for an exit, seconds before I signaled, and I thought, that little red car has been ahead of me for a while.

Better than worry over my customer's dismissal ("I've never heard anything about your company"), I played a game with the little red car. I sped up to pass; the little red car blocked my advance in the passing lane. I slowed, to let another car in between us; the little red car slowed till we were nearly bumper to bumper. I changed lanes without signaling; so did the little red car. Odd, but not outrageous. Nonetheless, and backwards, surely, I felt followed.

A sign for a scenic turnout (three miles) presented a course of action. From the leftmost lane and at full speed I'd exit without warning, let the little red car get far ahead, get gone so I didn't have to think about it anymore. Determined not to give myself away, I moved only my eyes, from odometer to the little red car to the dirt and pine along the right side of the road. A quick scan of my mirrors—

and the little red car crossed the highway traffic and exited. So. Simple enough. All I needed to do was not exit. But I did exit, unable not to, unable to change my plan.

And there was the little red car, parked, stopped for a while so its driver could enjoy the scene, valley, river, mountain. Whatever. The sky. I parked alongside the little red car, afraid, adrenaline-jittery, eyes forward, a bird, some raptor, its path, down. I was in that little red car, years ago. The nose of my car touched the wood guardrail set a few yards from the lip of the cliff that fell to the valley bottom. I remembered, I knew the little red car. A few folks had spread a picnic across a shaded wooden table. They paid us no mind. I'd been a passenger in the little red car many times. I became aroused.

The driver-side door of the little red car opened. A girl, seventeen years old, emerged from the little red car. She stood at the guardrail like anyone would who stopped at a scenic view on the way to… on the way to wherever. I didn't get out of my car. I was too afraid. But I didn't turn the engine over and escape, either. The girl stepped over the guardrail—her skirt, very tight, very short, rose and stretched. Near the cliff-edge, she kicked at the dirt. Dust rose up around her feet. In heels, her action was horse-like, only, she was far too delicate to be a horse, she was more like a fawn. Finally, my hands fists pushed hard against my thighs, the girl turned her back on the valley and I saw who I knew she must be, Marianne Ferris, and—impossible. Marianne Ferris was in my high school graduating class and so should be thirty-four, or thirty-three, or thereabouts. My age. Instead:

seventeen year-old Marianne Ferris returned to her car, shut the door, turned on the ignition, drove through the wood guardrail, and over the edge of the cliff.

I followed. With deliberation, I backed up and drove my car through the gap she'd made in the guardrail, across a few yards of crumbling dirt, over, down. I caught a glimpse of the picnickers, a delightfully absurd sight, as my stomach laughed its way up my throat to my brain. My car hit the dirt, nose-first. The river loud, a short distance from my shattered windshield.

The little red car lay on its back, to the left of my car. Marianne drove the little red car to school every day. I rode with her many times.

I was unharmed, awake, alert. The engine and other under-the-hood-inner-workings of my car were shoved into the passenger seat beside me, stinking hot oil. My legs were free, the driver's side foot-well untroubled by the impact. I unbuckled my seat belt and clumsily tumbled out of my car. Marianne's dusty high heeled shoes; she stood over me. Marianne smiled and tilted her head—just a hair, as she'd often done, a gesture she may once have cultivated but by the time I met her was her own, a gesture I loved. I got up on my knees and she sprinted, her skirt (I recognized that skirt) rose and stretched as it had before, rose high and tightened around her buttocks as she ran, accentuated the animal aspect of her movement. She ran through the grass that grew tall along the river's edge, followed a secret path.

I raised my right leg, angled forward, my instinct to run after her—I resisted, planted my feet, dug into the soft of the muddy river's edge. A while—Marianne gone, the tires of her dead car still—sirens and people shouting down at me. I couldn't understand the words.

I was later coming home than expected.

And I expected Janie to be worried, to have called and left escalating messages on my phone (lost in and with the car), but when I parked the rental in our driveway, the house was dark. The car clattered as it cooled. Janie must be asleep, I was relieved she was asleep, I hated when she worried, her worry made me feel guilty, and I wasn't sure how to explain why I was late or why I didn't call because I didn't know what had happened that morning. Marianne, Marianne Ferris, I'd thought of her often, grown erect and sleepy with nostalgia on long drives, remembering her as she was, as somehow she was still.

Janie was in the backyard, I caught her movement at the corner of my eye.

Janie was my wife. Her name was Jane and no one, not even her mother, called her Janie. Except me. It's a babyish thing to call a woman, I suppose, but I did once and it stuck, for us, she gave me permission to call her Janie, and from that permission came a pleasure hard to quantify or explain.

Janie stood in the yard, at the far end where the grass met a small stretch of trees. My mouth opened to call to her, but something about the way she moved—slightly, with her hands up in front of her face—caused me to shut my mouth.

As quietly as I tried to approach, Janie spotted me before I was halfway across the yard. Beyond her, something large and hidden among the trees, quickly moved away. Janie's body relaxed; her head dropped, her stance made it look as if she were sleepwalking, but she called my name, so I knew she wasn't. She wore jeans and a sweatshirt. I asked, "What are you doing out here?" She didn't reply right away, but walked to close the gap between us. She put her arms around me and pressed her face into my chest (except for her breasts, she was very small). Her hair was wet and it glistened. She'd just showered, the perfume of her shampoo. "Are you okay?" I asked. She nodded. I put my arm over her shoulder and we walked toward the house.

"Whose car is that?" she asked.

"It's a rental."

"Where's our car?"

"Our car is totaled."

She stopped and looked up at me, eyes wide.

"Janie, I'm fine. Look at me. I'm fine."

We resumed our walk to the house. The grass shushed as we moved over it. A branch snapped—Janie tensed, relaxed. She asked, "How did our car get totaled?"

"It fell off a cliff."

Janie laughed, then stopped mid-stride. "You're serious."

"I am." I told her the official story, which while more reasonable than the true story, didn't add up, didn't explain why next to my car was an abandoned little red car, or why I was unharmed after driving my car off a cliff, but the police didn't seem to want to know, didn't ask a lot of question and, when I think back, they supplied more answers than I did. Ultimately, the official story became: "I stopped at a scenic turnout to enjoy the view. Something in the car malfunctioned. The car accelerated on its own and drove through a gap in the guardrail." Janie interrupted and stumbled out an, "Oh my God."

I squeezed her shoulders and urged her to keep on toward the house. We walked up a slope to the driveway. She touched the rental car as we passed. I continued: "The police think that the car was angled just so, and so while the front of the car was crushed, the driver's side was largely undamaged and me, I mean, I was undamaged."

In the kitchen, Janie squeezed me around my middle, squeezed tight enough to expel breath from my lungs and that felt good. She released me, a little, arms still around me, and we went upstairs to our bedroom where I took off her clothes (she'd worn no underwear) and we made love, quick, not great sex but good, and I thought of Marianne Ferris as I'd seen her today, exactly as I remembered her. Janie and I lay side by side, eyes open in our dark bedroom, eyes to the humming white ceiling, and I asked, "What were you doing in the yard?"

To which she replied:

"There was a deer in the yard."

She said, "I was undressed, about to put on pajamas, when I spotted a deer in the yard."

"A deer."

"Hmm," she said. "I almost went out naked."

I didn't understand why she almost went out naked, I almost asked but instead at that moment it occurred to me what I should have told my customer when he said he wasn't going to let my company manage his money. I should have said, "All you don't know is how good we are." To that, I smiled, woozy with exhaustion.

Janie said, "I went out into the yard. The deer didn't run away. It stood, with its head turned so it could look at me over its shoulder. I got really close. The deer moved away from me. I got close again. It led me, slowly, across the yard. And then you came home."

"Huh," was all I managed before I vanished into sleep. I felt sleep rise up around me and with it, memory.

Marianne Ferris was great looking and wore short skirts and I steered clear of her for the longest time. I thought, she's way more sophisticated than I am, and I'll never know her in any way at all. Next year she and I were in a class together and I found myself in brief, exhilarating, class-related contact. Senior year she often approached me during the free minutes before class to say hello and maybe to ask a question. History class, for instance:

"Hey, Brian."

"Hi."

"I can't remember the name of Otto von Bismarck's dog."

She leaned over my desk and her hair fell against my face as I flipped through our history text. I pointed to a caption: "Tyras," I read. "But, didn't he have lots of dogs?"

My thick-headed belief that Marianne Ferris could not possibly be romantically interested in me died one afternoon when she and I ran into each other in the city. Dressed in her street clothes, I didn't recognize her at first. The jeans she wore were not tight like her skirts, and instead of a blouse she wore a man's plaid shirt. Her hair was down, just straight. She said my name and I stopped. "Marianne Ferris," I said. With only a few months left of high school, we were still declared class couple, and girls said things to me like, "I can't even remember what it was like when you weren't together," and asked, "What are you buying her for your one-month anniversary?" I bought Marianne nothing. We laughed at our breathy classmates. Guys asked other questions, which, had I not actually cared about Marianne, I would have gladly answered. But I did care about her. And in that way we were mysterious. We were glad when school was over, both of us going to local colleges, me with a summer job at a movie theater. She worked at an ice cream stand. She was seventeen.

That day that we ran into each other in the city she bought the skirt that she would wear fifteen-plus years later, on the day she drove her little red car off a cliff and I followed. I was with her when she bought it; she stepped out of the dressing room, plaid shirt bunched up in her hand to better show the skirt and revealing a slim line of her belly—she turned—a slim line of her back. Of course I liked it, and said so, I was still amazed she'd said my name and further amazed she'd asked me to wait for her while she tried on some skirts. "That'll make Mrs. Kirk flinch," she said. "It is short," I said. Marianne twirled for me.

While with Marianne, my confidence emerged, but was unwieldy, and thus the screw up, at a summer party, the last house party Marianne's cohorts at the ice cream stand threw (they had the best parties, they knew everyone). I went to the party late, the last show over after midnight, sweeping popcorn well after the ice cream stand was shuttered. I walked over in my theater uniform, bow tie unhooked (a clip-on). The girl who answered the door was Susan, she answered with a drink in hand and said, "I made this just for you," though it was half gone, obviously her own, and she touched my nose with her pinkie before she gave me the glass, rum and diet Coca-Cola. Susan led me to Marianne, who was sweetly drunk and happy to see me, in the middle of an extra-soft couch with two co-workers, girls like Susan. Marianne tried to get up, failed, she took my hand and I pulled her up and we kissed and danced, and her co-workers teased us and all was good for a while, until Marianne and I were separated, somehow, and I wound up in the backyard on a hammock, very drunk, and Susan climbed into the hammock with me, and Susan and I kissed, my eyes half closed, my hands on Susan's breasts and down the back of her pants as far as my reach allowed. I blacked out some of the time, distant party noise, glass beer bottles, a television. Marianne found us like that. I was too drunk to apologize or to show remorse or even to take my hand out of Susan's pants. A week later Marianne and I met for coffee, not a cup drunk. A couple weeks after that we went to college, both broken-hearted (I think she was; I was, and I felt stupid, too. I felt stupid and bad for a long time).

The night of the party, after Marianne found me with Susan, after Susan crept away, I hung in the hammock, struggled with my drunk, and heard an animal knocking trash cans.

When I woke up, next to my wife, the morning after the accident, I felt guilty. I put a tie around my collar, looked at Janie as she slept a little extra, and I went down to the kitchen for a bowl of cereal. I felt guilty. Not for the car, but because Marianne Ferris was on my mind all the time, I couldn't remember when she wasn't on my mind, maybe, maybe for a while when I first met Janie, when Janie and I were first married, but ever since, Marianne Ferris. I didn't want breakfast. I said to myself, I did nothing wrong. That wasn't quite true, but I knew what I meant. I hadn't hurt Janie.

Before I left, Janie joined me in the kitchen, bathrobe, hair up, sloppy. She asked, "You totaled the car? Are you sure you're okay? Shouldn't you take the day off? Are you okay to drive today? Our car malfunctioned?" I said, "Everything's fine."

Janie

From the bedroom window I saw a girl as she walked along the far end of the backyard. She moved along the tree line, in and out of shadow. I knew some of the high school girls in the neighborhood, sometimes they came to me for advice, I wasn't too old, and I was always around. The girls would walk into my yard when they saw me out on the back steps drinking vodka/pomegranate/soda. There was Kathy, Carrie, and Maureen, and there was Jenny and Darla. They all lived in nearby houses. Once or twice a girl showed up late in the day, shadowing our house, looking in windows to see if I was around. I turned off the lights to better see the yard. Brian was very late coming home from work. The bedroom clock: 9:37. I was undressed, still damp from a bath. I stood at the window, put my forehead to the cool glass and watched. The girl moved slow, her steps herky-jerky, as if her feet were asleep/not her own. She wore a blouse and a short skirt. Heels would explain that walk.

I was downstairs and at the kitchen door before I noticed I was naked. I put on the jeans and sweatshirt that I'd draped over the back of a chair to dry after an afternoon sun shower and went out into the yard. Barefoot, I enjoyed the shock of cold grass. I said, "Kathy," though I was sure it wasn't Kathy, and I said, "Jenny," though sure the girl was not her, either; the names were a comfort to me, real girls I knew and cared for, silly girls.

I stood halfway between the house and the tree line, in a pool of shadow where the yard dipped, and saw no girl at all, and felt lost. The air smelled of gasoline and of something else. Popcorn. A cool breeze caused the trees to shiver, their leaves turning, dark green/black, dark green/black. A deer moved along the tree line. Had I mistaken a deer for a girl?

The deer took a step away from me, stopped, looked to where I stood, and I very nearly pointed to myself, as if to ask, *me?* I approached the animal. My first feelings were this deer is a beautiful creature, how special this moment is, etc., but all those sentimental, automatic feelings were gradually replaced by lust. Not desire: bloodlust. I wanted to kill the deer, but I did not know how.

Brian touched my shoulder, I started, the deer disappeared among trees. My bloodlust transferred briefly onto Brian, then dissipated, almost wholly, but not completely, and so I was glad Brian wanted sex, quick and simple.

The next day, Brian at the office, doing the horrible job that sustained us ("I sell asset management plans"), I slept on the couch till noon, ate lunch, felt gross and forced myself to take a walk around the block. I considered walking into the woods behind our house, a little nothing patch of trees that kept the main road from sight, but the overgrown ferns and vines and probably poison ivy put me off. I stood at the end of a deer path and looked but did nothing. The sun filtered through green, lots of green and was pretty, and the green nearly put me to sleep where I stood. Around three I sat on the back steps with a glass of vodka/pomegranate/soda staring out at the yard, which I needed to mow and would later or the next day if I could muster the energy. Darla, sans her gal pal Jenny, stood at the edge of my backyard, with her hand up to shade her eyes and she waved when she saw me.

"Hey Jane," she said, as if she'd bumped into me. She lit a cigarette, a recently developed habit, some stupid boy's fault, so I gathered from Jenny, who would surely be carrying her own cigarettes soon enough. Darla didn't ask if it was okay to smoke, nor did she offer me a cigarette; she was low on etiquette. I vaguely wanted one, but mostly didn't.

"Darla," I said. "Where's Jenny?"

"David, *I think.*" Darla touched her lip and asked, "What're you drinking?"

I held my glass up to my eyes: "This has a stupid name I won't say. It's vodka, pomegranate, and soda." I tipped the glass to my lips.

She wanted some; I would give her none. She'd never ask but she added:

"I like vodka." She paused for my reaction. I sipped. She sat down beside me.

"So," she said.

She pulled and puffed at her cigarette, then bent over and rubbed out her cigarette on the last of the steps where I sat. She didn't know what to do with the butt or with the black smudge she'd left on my step. She rubbed at the smudge with her foot and slipped the butt into a little coin pocket on the front of her jeans. There was hope.

"Don't worry about it, Darla."

She folded her arms.

"What's on your mind?"

Her lips moved, a little. I looked out across the backyard and decided I wouldn't have the energy to mow the lawn. I squeezed my eyes a little and the trees bent together. Or: did an animal move behind the trees?

"Darla, did you see something?"

"Where?"

I pointed with my glass.

Darla leaned forward, squinted, put her hand up to her forehead as she'd done from the street: was it really so sunny? Darla's lipstick was too orange. I asked, "What's on your mind?"

"David."

She touched her pack of cigarettes but I guess she decided not to smoke. I was a little sorry because I would've had a puff, but I didn't want to ask for a cigarette because that seemed too much like encouraging her, and I felt some vague urge, as an adult, I guess, to promote not smoking, or something to that effect. Perhaps, I thought for an instant, I didn't care at all, and I should pour Darla some vodka, and the two of us should get really drunk together, and watch television until her parents sent the police out looking for her, if her parents cared, and if they didn't then I don't know what.

She said, "David and Jenny are going out. They've been going out for two weeks. Last night the three of us went out to see a movie. Before the movie started Jenny went out to the lobby to talk to Sarah, who had some news she wanted to tell Jenny, and while she was gone I put my hand on David's leg."

"You did?"

"Yeah. I put my hand on his leg and, you know, I felt it get hard."

I finished my drink and said, "On his leg?"

"You know."

"Sure."

"So?"

"Um?"

"What should I do?"

I took Darla's cigarettes and put one in my mouth. Lighting my bummed cigarette did not occur to her, so I put it to my mouth and tapped the filter with the tip of my tongue, waited a second, took the cigarette from my mouth and said, "Maybe, don't touch David's penis?" I tucked the cigarette behind my ear.

"I know that."

"Why did you?"

"I like David."

"Trust me. You don't like David more than you like Jenny. She's your friend. Come on. I need to get a refill." In the kitchen, Darla watched me make another vodka/pomegranate/soda. Not offering her a drink, of any kind, was my revenge for her not offering a light. I lit my cigarette off a stove burner, smoked for the first time in… I couldn't remember, I wondered if I'd smoked with Darla before, felt woozy, then calm, then guilty: in Brian's kitchen, I thought. From the back step I saw movement in the woods. "Darla, do you see something?" I pointed.

"Yeah, a deer," she said. "How sweet," she added.

"Yeah."

Then Darla said, "I know Jenny's my friend, but I don't think you realize."

"Maybe not, Darla." I saw the next few months of Darla's life play out: summer would come, she'd be at a party with Jenny, and David, no doubt Jenny's ex by then, would be there, and late at night, in the backyard of whomever was throwing the party, Darla would make out with David. And Jenny would be pissed off and Jenny and Darla wouldn't return to school as friends, and David, stupid, stupid David, well what could it possibly matter?

Darla stayed longer than she usually did. Eventually, we shared things: Darla, my drink, me, her cigarettes and her lighter. When Brian came home Darla said, "Hi," and then wandered off, coin pocket full of cigarette butts, hers and mine. She wandered across our backyard, to a spot where the trees were parted, a little doorway in the woods.

"What's wrong with her?" Brian asked.

"A boy," I said. And I said, "Let's order Chinese, shall we? I was too tired to go to the grocery store today and besides I don't feel like cooking."

Oh, Brian, the way you sighed. If only you knew how I exhausted I was all of the time. Pour me another! But I didn't ask for another. I nibbled at the steamed vegetables. Later, I thought, I'd eat all the fried rice. I would sit on the back steps with a tablespoon and shovel rice into my mouth. Soon after dinner, Brian went to bed. I sat in the living room, television on but the sound down—occasionally a glimmer of laughter. The book on my knee was spent, damp, pages dropped out onto the floor. When the television screen went dark between programs, I saw reflected the living room. And beside the television, the window, blinds up, it also reflected the living room, and me, but in that reflection was the dark grassy backyard. A deer put its face to the window and I screamed.

The deer's oval-shaped face emerged, like something floating up from the bottom of a murky pool. A white, ragged stripe from the deer's nose to its forehead. No horns, a female, the same, I knew, as I'd seen the night before. And possibly that afternoon.

Brian did not come down the stairs. My scream had not been enough to rouse him after an exhausting, dreadful day calling potential investors, most smart enough to know that the firm Brian worked for was worthless.

The deer's face disappeared from the window. I carried my drink, less pomegranate, less soda, and went out into the backyard. The grass, black. Faint light only exaggerated the darkness of the woods where I was sure I saw movement, the deer or the girl. I rushed across the lawn, my drink sloshed onto my hand, cold; it dried and that felt good. I stumbled, that dip in the yard, and very nearly dropped my glass. A sip. I walked on, into the woods, I crashed into branches, and my drink slipped from my hand and the glass shattered. Brian, you idiot, I thought, you wrecked our car. I stepped into a stream. The water was cold and polluted, and soon my bare feet were sticky. Again, I'd rushed from the house without shoes. At least I was dressed, I thought, and I laughed, a kind of a snort. I walked without caution and soon my feet stopped hurting, didn't hurt when I stepped on sharp rocks or sticks, when my foot went sideways into a hole, some animal's burrow. The trees were luminescent with a mossy light. I waked through a shallow pond, felt slime coated stones and living things, they swam up the cuffs of my pants, attached themselves to my legs. My heart beat hard and steady. Ahead of me the trees fell away

a backyard.

Jenny's.

Jenny and Darla and I had walked in Jenny's backyard once before, on a calm afternoon. A cool afternoon. Even night, now, was warm. My body was hot and prickled.

The yard was a dark plane, the house ahead was white. A single window on the ground floor was lit, the blinds up, a hot square. Jenny's bedroom. From the dark yard my view was perfect, Jenny on her bed, sitting up on her knees, and a boy—surely, David—in Jenny's bedroom. Her parents out or asleep. From where I stood, beneath her window, they moved without sound, but I put two fingers to the window and felt the glass vibrate and so I knew, they talked, there was sound. The yard was endlessly silent, no clicking crickets and frogs, only black grass growing up around my bare feet.

David wasn't naked—why was that?—her shirt, off, her bra, unclasped (it unhooked in the front), her belt undone and he pulled at her jeans, tugged while she sat up and wriggled her little hips, helped him to undress her. She reached for the buttons of his shirt. He dipped forward and kissed her clavicle, her breasts. Jenny's head back, she sighed; her excitement breathy and sick, my terror for her huge:

I slapped the glass and shouted,

I shouted, "Jenny! Don't!"

Jenny and David turned to the window, frightened, blind. With the light so brilliant in Jenny's room, they surely couldn't see me, or saw only a shape, an animal tapping its head on the glass. I slapped the glass again, with both hands, "Jenny! Don't ruin everything!"

She didn't cover herself, as I would've. Nor did David panic. He dashed for the light switch and I ran, a flash burning across the yard. I burned through the little forest, through the muck and wet, stopped for a breath only when I at last stood in my kitchen. And though the kitchen was cool I could not get cool, I sweated and my abdomen turned, I felt my intestines working feverishly to expel some rotten thing I'd consumed. At the kitchen table, I put my hands palm-down, tried to push the table into the linoleum. I could imagine pouring a vodka, but I could not get up from where I sat until

I heard a noise from the bedroom upstairs; a noise like an animal crashing through a forest.

As complex as the sound was, it did not last. But it had been real and real enough to move me from my seat, bare feet sticking to the floor, wet pant-cuffs stiffly shifting with each step I took, up, upstairs to the bedroom. I opened the door.

My husband, Brian, lay asleep, naked and uncovered, his penis semi-erect and wet—it glistened as it had the night before. Beside him, on my side of the bed, was a deer. (All our bedclothes on the floor in a heap at the foot of the bed.) I squinted in the dim-lit room. A doe, that's what they're called, lay on her side, peacefully, I supposed, sleeping. Eyes shut, belly (flank) rising up and down as she breathed, a doe, and from between her hind legs a slick trail to Brian that would dry white and stain.

I clapped my hands together once. The doe started, her head rose quick from my pillow, her legs, too. Brian stirred, but did not wake. She was awake, though. The doe scrambled upright, stood ridiculously on my bed, caused the mattress to sink deep where I usually slept so lightly. Brian woke when she trotted off the bed onto the hardwood floor. The noise her hooves made—

Brian shouted, then he shouted my name, "Janie!" and yelled, "Look out!" as if I might not have noticed the deer, as if he was surprised we were all there.

I ran at her. She dodged my attack with ease, her reflexes fast and natural. My wet pants tripped me up, they were loose on me and heavy, so I stepped out of them, free now half-naked.

I ran out of the bedroom, after the doe. She stumbled in the hallway, her big body crashed into the wall (the plaster cracked), and I caught up enough to give her a big push: I put my hands on her rump and shoved and she stumbled forward, toward the stairs, and at the top step she lost her balance, crashed down the stairs and collapsed, a disaster in our living room, broken legs, more than that, probably. She writhed, turned her head up—I glared down from the top step. She mewled, pitifully, and I felt sorry for her, a dumb animal.

And yet, she had tricked me, lured me into the woods she knew so well, saw me lost and double-backed. So, perhaps not so dumb, not so dumb as Brian, wrecker-of-cars, foolish enough to keep a dreadful job and to fall asleep with his girl-animal, when he must have known I wouldn't be lost forever.

Brian stood in the doorway of our bedroom. He wore only his slippers. His thick, dark hair was matted, pushed flat. He held out his arms and said, "That was terrible, how horrifying, are you okay? I just can't believe, I just don't know how she got in. Oh, Janie."

"Don't call me that!" I shouted.

And then I said, "Brian."

And I said, "You will drag her carcass out. You will put her carcass in the car you've rented. You will leave, and you will never come back."

Worse Than Myself

Brian wanted to explain but instead told me about a girl he dated when he was in high school. I said nothing. He told me he needed clothes. I said, "You're perfect the way you are." His pitiful, pale, naked butt exposed, he followed his girlfriend down the stairs.

[*for* Jaime Corbacho]

The Demon

A pair a pair of lips. A set full, soft-peaked. When kissed a hard tongue emerges. A set high-peaked, bright red; perpetually chapped and waxy with Carmex.

"I'm out."

"—."

"What are they?"

"Export A."

"Now you have to smoke like Sartre?"

"Fuck you."

"Matches?"

"Here."

—

"Did you hear about the Solar Temple cult?"

"Like, 'The Saint'?"

"?"

"Simon Templar."

"I'm not—is that a joke?"

"No, I haven't."

"Mass suicide. Only everyone didn't go willingly. People were shot with plastic bags on their heads. They used garbage bags filled with gasoline to blow up these chalets in Switzerland where cult members were meeting. Look. I'm shaking all over."

"You are—"

"I need another."

"Take it."

"So they— So they were forced to die. Kids too."

"Damn."

"They were led by this guy, Luc Jouret. He had pictures of Jesus Christ with his face painted in. Nailed to the front door of one of the chalets was a sack with a tape in it, with him raving about the sky and the way the planets were coming together."

"Crazy."

"Yeah, I mean, well— You know. Like all religions, it was just a scam for money. These people turned over their accounts and he didn't kill himself. He has property all over."

"Oh."

"You look— You look disappointed."

"Kind of takes away from the—I don't know—from the weird religion."

"There was a room full of corpses. What else do you need?"

"I don't know."

"Shit. Look at me. I gotta go."

"What? No. Chad, you said you'd stay. You said you wouldn't, tonight."

"I can't stay still. I gotta go."

"Have another whiskey with me. That'll settle you."

"It won't. But I will. Another smoke? And one for the road?"

"I'll buy more tonight."

"No. Just the two. These're expensive."

"I know what—chalices of blood. Candles made from human fat. Demons. Despair. Depravity."

"What the fuck are you talking about?"

"Weird religion. The cult. It should have been really weird."

"They had a pentagram."

"My boyfriend in high school had a pentagram tattooed on his arm."

"You're fucked up."

"Tell me about something mysterious."

"Like, my drink is gone and I'm going."

"Come on."

"No. I need to go."

"Will you come back tonight?"

"Maybe," Chad says.

"Okay," I say. "Kiss me."

A fleck of tobacco on a pair of soft lips. Fine, transparent hairs, like a mist. A pair of lips a raspberry popsicle. A fleck of skin.

October 28th, 1994, late. Our invitation—an elegant invitation—a thick, folded rectangle of paper, the invite and directions drawn in careful calligraphy. Glued to the front of the invitation a dry oak leaf, now cracked, missing points, as the invite has been read and is being reread by James. James says, "Our right should be soon."

I'm driving my father's car. Chad is in the back—he prefers the backseat, where he can recline. He's unbuckled, head at an uncomfortable angle against a leather arm rest. "I can't believe you won't let me smoke," he says. James and I say, "Shut up," and I add: "Make sure you don't get make-up in the leather."

"Right, right."

"Turn here," James says.

I turn the car off the two-lane onto a narrow road—even darker, I think, than the two-lane. "I can't believe there aren't any streetlights," I say.

Chad says, "Change the tape. Change the tape. We've heard this."

James yanks the cassette and puts on another.

"What's this shit?" Chad says. "Put on Jane's."

I say, "That, we've heard a thousand times."

"Come on."

James looks at me, switches tapes. A languid bass rolls through the stereo.

Chad and James are the official invitees—Chad knows one of the girls who lives in the house—Suzan—James another. They're both pretty sure there's a third housemate—a man, they think. Chad had something going on with Suzan before we started going out. He's always cagey about just what was going on when I ask. I don't want to be clingy, so I don't push.

Now, way out in western Massachusetts, the car's high beams illuminate only a small stretch ahead of the car. I'm awed by the darkness—nervous, too—just a couple of hours out of Boston, I think.

James shouts my name—I hit the breaks—a deer—its eyes—in front of the car. My heart beats hard. Chad—thrown against the front seat, bitches.

James says, "Drop the highs."

I do. Our pocket of light shrinks. Three deer staring at me— "They're beautiful," I say. "I haven't seen deer in—"

"Turn the headlights off," James says.

I do. The dark is complete. I feel a hand on my breast—a quick touch that frightens me—"Chad, fuck off," I say—he must have reached up from behind—an awkward reach. I turn on the headlights. The deer are gone. For a long moment, it seems, their shapes linger.

Chad sings. Even with the tape, he screws up the lyrics: "Me and my girlfriend, don't have no shoes, her nose is painted bright sunlight—"

I laugh. He sings it this way all the time.

Chad continues to sing his lyrics, slightly off, but right, "She loves me, I mean it's oh, so serious, it's serious candy.'"

I laugh.

James says, "Turn here."

"There's no sign," I say.

"I've been counting. And isn't that a red mailbox?"

We drive another mile along an uneven dirt road. Chad sits up between the two front seats. "It is goddamn dark," he says. "Goddamn dark. Turn off the music." I'm glad for Chad and James. In the car, with them, I feel protected. There's light ahead.

Hanging from the trees are long, filmy, white shreds of cloth. On a small mound are gravestones—perfectly round at the top and carefully illuminated by flood lights set in the ground. A shovel stands in the dirt. The drive bends, and the house is directly in front of us. The house looks like two boxes stacked one atop the other, the upper box askew, creating a triangular upper deck. There are great square windows on the upper story, and tall, narrow windows all around the first floor, warmly lit. I can see people moving inside—they appear and vanish and appear, as if pictures in a zoetrope.

James puts on his mask, a translucent face that distorts his own face just enough to be off-putting; he's otherwise wearing a mismatched brown suit bought at a second hand store and a brilliant green shirt—"candy pumpkin green," James told me when I picked him up earlier that evening. Chad gets out of the car—slugs out of the backseat. He's wearing what he wears all the time—unstylish, tight, faded black jeans and a worn tan and black flannel shirt—but he surprised me by showing up at my apartment with a drug store make-up kit, and by asking me to, "Paint me like a skull-face." He is so skinny, his face so gaunt, the make-up seems only to accentuate an already skeletal physicality. He walks loose. I lock the car and catch up with him. James walks a few steps ahead.

The walk is decorated with carved pumpkins. Simple carvings, jagged cuts for mouths, eyes.

"Who spent their fucking lifetime decorating the front yard?" Chad asks.

"I'm guessing," James says, "that'd be Heather. She's passionately domestic." James' voice is muffled, as if he's talking through crumpled tissue paper.

A flight of wide, wooden steps, every other with another jack-o'-lantern. Their eyes flick like tongues. One has no mouth. The deck railing is decorated with cotton cobwebs, plastic spiders the size of a little girl's hand and dismembered, skeletal hands. The yard slopes into a dark basin, lined with loose teeth stones—a farmer's wall.

James rings the bell and with no delay the front door is swung wide open—a woman dressed as an angel: a bell-shaped, thigh high negligee over a silky slip, white hose, a gold crown with a halo attached—bobbing above the woman's head—hand-made gold wings visible just over the woman's slight shoulders.

Chad whispers to me, "This must be Heather." I laugh.

Heather hugs James and kisses him on the jaw. Kisses him again just above the mouth. "I'm so pleased you came—and so amazed. We live so far away I didn't think any of my friends would come. Are you Chad and Rachel? Suzan's told me all about you, Chad. All of you come in. Are you hungry? There's soup and hors d'oeuvres. Oh, come in." She steps aside and the three of us pass her into a single, great room. We've come into the kitchen area, separated from the rest of the first floor by a low wall. There's a long table covered with food and wine, and a smaller table, where a group of men and women, all in their thirties, sit talking. Everything is decorated with gourds and dried wheat and corn. The living area is occupied by a small group of costumed people, chatting, holding wine glasses and black or orange paper plates. I see a little girl in a pink princess dress dash across the floor through a doorway to a dark back room.

Chad fills a glass with liquor, and asks where he can smoke.

Heather says, "On the deck or upstairs, on the balcony—don't you want to say hello to Suzan?"

Chad grins, "For Suzan I need to be fortified." Heather smiles. "Besides, she smokes. I don't see her here. She must be out smoking."

"Well then, you really should go, it's lovely up there."

"Lovely," Chad repeats, and nods. "You are as Suzan said. I'll go upstairs then. You comin', Rach?"

"I'm hungry," I say. I'm not ready for the fray.

"Whatever," and Chad moves swiftly across the living area to a staircase that disappears through a rectangle in the ceiling.

James says, "I can't believe this house, it's amazing."

Heather points, timidly, to a man dressed as a murderous doctor, seated at the kitchen table. "He designed it, built it. He's renting rooms to me and Suzan."

A woman, dressed as a devil—a red miniskirt and a red turtleneck sweater, red stockings, red high heel shoes and with horns protruding from her black hair—steps out of a room on the far side of the living area.

"There's Suzan," Heather says.

Suzan says, "I'm Sue, welcome." She angles her hip just so when she says "welcome."

"I'm Rachel."

"Oh?" Suzan looks around. "So where's our lothario Chad?"

James looks at Suzan's legs, her breasts, goes for a glass of wine and some soup.

Heather follows James. I can't decide for a moment; I finger the pack of smokes in my bag, follow James instead. On my way I'm stopped by the house-designer—"And who are you?" he asks. The rest of the table goes on talking. I hear a man—not costumed at all—say the words, "…to capture Saddam." A woman, dressed in a vinyl French maid outfit, answers, "It's just Clinton trying to distract us from Whitewater." I say, to the house-designer, "I'm Rachel. I'm with Chad and James. They know Sue and Heather."

"Well, delighted to have you. Did you come far?"

"Boston."

"That's not too bad. Though everything seems far away when you live out here. Especially at night. Sometimes I feel as if I've been dropped into the middle of nowhere. So glad to have roomies." He winks. "Oh. I'm Stephen. Hey guys, can we stop boring each other with politics for a second?"

I'm certain Stephen is gay, which makes his choice of roommates seem less odd to me. He's at least ten years older than Heather and Suzan. He introduces me to three others at the table, all of whom eye me up and down.

"But I shouldn't stop you from getting some libations," he says. "Heather spent so much time preparing everything—or ordering it with my credit card." Again, he winks. I wonder if it's actually a twitch.

I ask, "Who's little girl is here?"

"Little girl?" Stephen raises an eyebrow. "Did someone bring a child to our little bacchanal?" He looks around the table. The man who isn't wearing a costume laughs. "Maybe one of Heather's friends?" Stephen points in the general direction of the people grouped in the living area. I see Chad and Suzan come down the stairs—I'm relieved. Surprised by how relieved.

"This house is beautiful," I say.

He gestures the compliment away with his hand. The woman in the fetish French maid costume says, "He's a genius." The man without a costume says to her, "Don't be such a fag." The man who hasn't said anything, wearing the lower half of a gorilla suit, snorts out a laugh.

Chad, Suzan, Heather, James and I stand around the long table with the food. James has a bowl of soup in his hand. Heather watches him eat; she's got doe eyes, I think. I try to catch James' attention, to see if he knows that Heather obviously wants him, would tear off her slutty angel outfit in an instant for him. He sees nothing but soup, apparently. Chad says, "Rach, you gotta come upstairs and have a smoke out on the porch with me and Sue—this house is fuckin' amazing." I look at Suzan and think, Do those legs go all the way up, and laugh out loud. "What?" Chad asks. "Nothing," I say. I stand next to Chad, and take his hand. He leans over to me and says, "Upstairs. They told me they have some," he puts his lips to my ear—his dry, waxy lips brush against my earlobe—and he tells me what exactly they have upstairs. I jerk my hand away, "You said you would never." He grins at me—at first I think he's mocking me but he says, "I'm only messing with you." He smiles until I do and he goes to the living area, grinning at the people gathered there. He sits on the piano bench and begins to play, a little too fast but with great ability, the Rondo from Beethoven's, "Pathétique." The group in the living area and even Stephen's friends stop what they're doing to watch. Heather gives a cute little clap. I smile; the jolt from what he said slips away, tingles out through my fingers and my feet.

I know I'd better go down and sit on the bench with him before anyone else—before Suzan—does. Chad's done this at parties before and there's always some girl who goes for it. I grab what looks like a shrunken quiche, slosh wine into a glass and go sit with Chad.

Suzan steps into the living area and watches for a moment. James finishes his soup and fills a plate with little food. Heather explains what each item is that he's picked up. He nods and looks out at one of the women on the floor; she's dressed as some kind of forest pixie, in a long, green dress with green eye make-up and lipstick and leaves in her hair. Standing next to her is a thin guy, wearing a t-shirt and jeans. He looks dirty, his hair is matted and disheveled. I can't tell if he's in costume or not.

I see, out of the corner of my eye, the little girl dressed as a princess. The little girl waves to me. I hesitate a moment, but Suzan heads toward the stairs, so I slide off the piano bench and go to where the little girl was, a small ante-room preceded by a screened-in porch. I hear movement, push open the feather-light door and step out onto the porch.

"Hello?"

On the floor of the porch is a metal tub. The tub is filled with water and things floating in the water—hard to determine what in the darkness—apples. In the far corner of the porch is a figure; as my eyes adjust I see it's a straw man. He shivers—the little girl brushes against him.

"You startled me," I say. I feel nervous and I feel silly for feeling nervous. I hear the piano from the living area, and laughter. I calm down, a little. "That's a nice costume. What are you? A princess?"

The little girl steps a little closer.

"Why aren't you in the room with us? We're all having fun. My boyfriend is—" The music from the piano stops. I strain to hear what's going on, wait for the music to start again.

The little girl dashes out a door that leads to a set of steps down into the backyard.

I run after her, fly down the stairs. At the bottom I hit a patch of wet grass and fall—hard—onto my butt. I slide down the hill a bit, coming to rest flat on my back. Stars through the bare branches of oak trees. I sit up and see that my feet are just inches from a black pool of water. "Holy—" I say aloud. I hear talking, turn and see windows open in the second story.

I walk carefully around the pool, half looking for the girl, who I'm pretty sure must have been playing a prank—a nasty one at that, I think—and half looking up at the windows, to see what might be going on. Instead of warm, yellow-orange, the windows are flat panels of purple light. I see shapes, the talkers, but they are only black, wavy lines from where I stand.

"Well this was stupid," I say. I light a cigarette, which I suddenly realize I sorely need.

The living area is empty; the party has moved upstairs. I smoke my cigarette and ash on the floor. What a strange house, I think. It occurs to me then that Suzan and Chad are upstairs. I go to the kitchen and fill a water glass with wine and eat a piece of salmon. I throw my cigarette butt down the disposal.

The first door I pass is closed and I don't hear any sounds. The next door is slightly ajar and I catch a flash of green—James' shirt. I stop at the door, hand on the knob, when I hear Heather, who sounds as if she's in tears.

"Everything was so nice," Heather says. "Now he's so—he looks at me, there's a way he puts his hands on me. There's nowhere I can go. I don't have a car. I rely on him. I don't even have any money."

I don't want to get involved with Heather histrionics. I move on and into a large, empty master bedroom. There are coats on the bed. Outside of the bedroom is the balcony and a group are out, smoking. I hear Chad's voice, and smile.

Chad is not on the balcony. The woman in the fetish French maid costume waves me over.

"Do you have a cigarette? I don't feel at all like going in."

"Sure." I squeeze past the forest pixie and a man in a silver space suit. I hand the woman a cigarette and ask, "Have you seen Chad?"

"Chad?"

"He played the piano."

"Your boyfriend? He's cute. Very cute. Tiny butt."

I grin. Maybe this woman's okay. I have half a glass of wine left. I didn't even notice I'd been drinking.

"There's a door—" The woman points into the bedroom. "That leads to another hall. At the end of that—"

I didn't notice the door when I first walked through the bedroom because it's blended with the wall. I push on one side, and it gives, a spring mechanism, and then opens inward a little. I pull the door open with my fingertips and step through.

There's no decoration in the hall on the other side of the door—no pictures, no carpet, no little tables with flowers. Even the lights seem bare, harsh. At the end of the hall is a room with its door ajar. A triangle of purple light falls like a welcome mat in front of it.

The room is packed and thick with smoke. There's a large stereo with a turntable. The crackling record is of some endless guitar and keyboard wash. Something Chad would listen to while stoned—and not all the smoke in the room is cigarette smoke, and the idea of smoking with Chad sounds just about right. The man without a costume from the kitchen table smiles at me, looks me up and down without trying to be subtle about it. Some of the other party-goers are sitting on the floor. The room seems crowded, but there are just a lot of people gathered close to the door and I can't see past. Then the man without a costume steps aside, to talk with someone else, and I see that the room is quite large, and largely empty.

I see Chad first, lying on a twin bed. His sneakers look massive compared to the rest of his body. Seated on the floor in front of Chad, leaning with his back against the bed, is the dirty looking guy I saw in the living area. His head is lolling side to side. Something red draws my attention. Suzan in the far right corner of the room. She's kneeling with her back to me.

Then I see him—Stephen, the house-designer—standing in that shadowy corner, arms up, hands on the walls. Suzan's head bobs at his crotch. Instead of an expression of pleasure, he stares at me, a smile, like a pen-knife slit on a pumpkin face. I let out a gasp, a, "Chad," and turn back to where Chad lies. And now I see the silver tray on the floor next to the dirty guy, and understand what it is. Half on, half off the tray is a compressed syringe. I drop my empty glass. Chad's been talking about "taking the next step" for weeks now, and I've been getting him to promise he wouldn't.

"You fuck," I say aloud, to Chad. I'm furious.

The dirty guy's head lolls up to look at me, drifts back down to his chest.

"You fuck," I repeat. I'm amazed at how furious I am.

I see Stephen's smile grow wide. He tilts his head back as if he's cumming, and says to Suzan—but to me, too, I think, "No, you're not done, make it hard again."

I shout at Chad "You said you wouldn't." He doesn't move at all.

A few people in the room stop talking and glance over to see what's going on; most people ignore me. The French maid slips in.

"Okay," I continue. "Ignore me. Fuck you. You're on your own." And I mean it. I turn and rush for the door, bumping the guy without a costume. His boney shoulder hurts my arm. The French maid says, "Aw, baby—" and I'm in the hall, trying to find the hidden door, pushing open the hidden door, through the bedroom, back into the first hall. I burst into the room where I saw James and Heather. Heather is in the process of showing James a glass statuette she has on her shelf. James looks up. His mask is hung around his neck.

"I'm going now," I say.

James nods. He says, "I have to go."

Heather looks as if she's going to cry: "You'll come back soon?"

James promises that he will. Heather kisses him, holds him and kisses him firmly on the mouth. Everything about Heather pisses me off. I say, "Now." James breaks off the kiss, touches Heather, just above her left breast, looks her in the eye, and then James and I are jogging down the stairs. "What about Chad?" James asks. I say nothing; we're out the front door and at the car.

"You drive," I say. I'm too angry, probably drunk.

"What about Chad?"

"He's staying."

"Did you fight?"

"Not now."

"Not with Suzan?"

I glare at James. "Not now."

James turns on the car. The music we were listening to blares for a second before I shut off the stereo. James slowly rolls the car down the drive, past the gravestones, past the ghosts in the tree. "Look. Are we just going to be turning around to get him in a minute—"

"James," is all I say.

"Okay then."

James drives a little faster than I did, but I want him to. I know he'll know how to get out of these forests, back home to the city. I know he'll suggest we go to one of the other parties he was invited to and I'll go. I know he'll offer to go up with me to my dorm room, and that I'll probably accept.

We turn at the end of the long driveway, high beams swing across trees to the narrow road in front of them—

and James hits the brakes.

"Holy fucking shit," he says.

Steaming on the road is an enormous red pile of meat and bone. The mess stretches back, out of the circle of light cast by the headlights. My mouth opens wide, goes dry.

"Someone must of hit it going really fucking fast," James says.

I start to gasp, to cry. I whimper, "Get it away. Get it out of my sight. I can't stand it."

"I think there were more than one—"

I scream, "James!" I pound the leather car door.

James backs the car up a little, and takes as wide a circle around the carcasses as he can. I can't help but stare at the heap of wet innards. I recognize a hoof. And I turn to see the carcass made even redder in the light of the car's taillights. I see in it Chad, lying on that narrow bed, unmoving, arms crossed like a corpse.

Two days later.

A pair of lips. A set full, soft-peaked. Fine, transparent hairs, like a mist.

"Is there enough wine?

"I mean, for the night? For the both of us?

"I just bought a new pack so go ahead and—

"I don't know.

"You're sure you don't have to go?

"You're so good to me, James. You've been so good.

"What do you think about Iraq?

"No. Me neither.

"I don't know.

"I just heard someone talking about it. Now it's all over the papers.

"I don't know why.

"Yes. Please.

"How about the Knights of the Solar Temple?

"I hadn't heard of them either. It was one of the last things Chad talked about. Hang on. So. So, I've been thinking about them. Anyway—

"I don't mean to cry. I just haven't been able to stop crying. I need another.

"Okay. I've stopped. So. They're a cult. Or—they were.

"Something about Jesus Christ, the stars— You know, some cosmic event and the second coming all mashed together.

"I don't know I have no idea.

"You don't have enough.

"No. No. Have more. You're staying, right?

"So drink, then.

"Shit, I'm crying again. I just can't believe—

"I can't believe he's gone.

"You're religious, aren't you?

"You know. I don't mean like—

"Exactly. But you believe in an after life, though, don't you? You do?

"Yes. I thought so.

"Good. I do too."

A pair of soft lips. A fleck of ash.

Back Home

Snow fell heavy; flakes brushed across K[ ]'s car like thick, wet lashes. Several hours ago, when she began her trip back home, the sky was a wall of brushed metal, the sun only a hazy spot, a circular glint like light reflected on a pewter dish. Evening had drawn up quickly—*the days were growing longer,* she reminded herself—if only by degrees. Now, with the snowfall picking up, the only light was that generated by her high beams—and this light was swallowed up; the night's blackness a bog for light to be sucked into.

There were no other cars on the winding stretch of road she had come to—she was now in High Falls, and very near her destination. She was fairly sure she remembered the route, even though several years had passed since she'd last taken it. That was to help her mother move out of the house, just a year after her father's death. Strangely (it seemed to her), the woman who bought the house had wound up renting the upstairs rooms to a cousin of K[ ]'s—a cousin she did not know. And now he was dead like her father, and the only person left and able (her mother lived on the opposite coast) to claim (or dispose of) his belongings ("There isn't much," Mrs. Lawrence had told her) was K[ ].

She steered left at the end of a stone wall, which she remembered as the landmark for the street where her former home was located. The snow was accumulating so fast, her vision so impaired, that she almost drove past the turn. She drove slow, afraid she'd hit a deer.

The road dipped significantly—it seemed the ground had dropped out from beneath her—and suddenly she was on an uneven dirt road. *This isn't right*, she thought. She stopped the car and briefly thought of getting out, to see if she could get her bearings, to brush off the windshield and just to stretch out her aching legs. But right on top of that thought was another, *I'm afraid to step out into this night.* So, instead, she backed up to turn the car around. She would locate her tire tracks before they were snowed over, and get back to the road.

She struck something with her bumper. She adjusted the angle of her car and drove forward until again, she struck something. She assumed she hit a curb, so again adjusted the angle of her car, and backed up. As she did, the narrow beams of light from her headlights, peppered with snowflakes, gradually revealed what it was she had bumped into. She stopped the car dead. "Christ," she said aloud, the first time she'd said a word since she'd stopped for a burger on the road two hours before. What stood before her was a slab of stone as good as a ghost. "Jesus, I've driven into the graveyard."

The stone was totally white, *utterly*, she thought. Snow that passed before it disappeared. She wondered how she could have made this mistake. When she had lived here she would drive the final stretch home without even realizing she had done it. She knew the roads, she had memorized every aspect of the pavement (this type of information, she reminded herself, was transitory, permanence, an illusion. Even as she had lived in this place and watched it, it changed, but those changes were instantly assimilated by her). She shook her head—a gesture for no one, with no real benefit but for her own private melodrama—put the car into reverse, found the tracks her tires had cut in the snow (soft tracks now, fuzzy) and drove back to the road. The mistake had, at least, cleared up in her mind where she was and she was able, without further incident, to get to the house.

The house (*my house*) was a warm spot among cold, black trees. K[ ] drove as close to the house as she could, careful not to stray from the driveway— which, unlike the road that circled through the cemetery, was paved (when K[ ] had lived there, it was a gravel drive. The sound of stone crunched beneath a car's tires was once the sound of arriving home).

As she opened the car door and felt the bitter cold night air, the porch light came on. She grabbed her bag from the back seat and dashed through the snow to the porch. The front door was open, and warmth trickled out into the night. K[ ] let herself into the front room.

"What a night," Mrs. Lawrence said, pushing shut and locking the door.

K[ ] stood for a moment, to get her bearing. "It looks so different," she said.

Mrs. Lawrence looked around and tried to remember what the house was like when she bought it from K[ ]'s parents. "It's been so long, sweetie, that I hardly remember what it was like before."

"Of course."

For a moment they both looked about themselves, thinking about the house, then a mental tumbler clicked into place in Mrs. Lawrence's mind. "For Heaven's sake, put down your bag and let me hang up your coat. I have water on the boil so you can get some hot tea into yourself before bed."

They sat in the kitchen and talked about mundane things: K[ ]'s job, the drive, the weather. The topic shifted briefly to the purpose of K[ ]'s visit when Mrs. Lawrence said, "I assumed you wouldn't want to sleep in J[ ]'s room. Your old bedroom was his."

This bothered K[ ]. That her cousin, a stranger to her, lived and died in her room struck K[ ] as both an invasion and a perversion. She thought herself silly for having such a reaction. "I wouldn't want to sleep in my old room anyhow, Mrs. Lawrence. It hasn't been mine for a long time."

"That's good. I cleared off the sofa in the den." Mrs. Lawrence pointed around the corner.

"Thank you."

"So…" Mrs. Lawrence seemed lost in her head for a moment. "Your former room was the biggest upstairs room. That's probably why he chose it. The whole upstairs was basically his, though I used some of the closets and the attic for storage. He kept mostly to your old room. We shared the kitchen and sometimes he would come down and watch television with me. The news, mostly. I don't think he cared what was on, though. I think he was lonely."

"He," K[ ] hesitated. "He was a little unusual, I'm told."

Mrs. Lawrence answered by sucking her lower lip into her mouth and shaking her head. Her hair, K[ ] noticed, was terribly flat.

"Anyhow," K[ ] said, "the den will be fine. It's only for tonight. I don't imagine it'll take me long to sort through one room's worth of belongings if I get an early start. Then I can be on my way."

"You might be able to leave," said Mrs. Lawrence. "But you know how it is around here when it snows."

K[ ] carried her bag into the den. She spread out the sheets Mrs. Lawrence gave her, changed into pajamas and laid down. She focused on the blankness of the ceiling, and thought about what it meant to be back home. The house certainly wasn't like home anymore; she had conflicting feelings of comfort and unease. On the drive up, she had tried to prepare herself for the ways her childhood home might be different. When she thought of the house she was in now, and the version of the house that lived in her memory, they were split, as if she were picturing two different homes. She did not fully believe that one could replace the other. Yet—and this realization was the source of her unease—the changes, some quite dramatic, all seemed to her familiar.

During the first hours of the morning, K[ ] woke from a dream of herself. She stood in a field, its border defined by forest. Her awake self knew this field to be about two miles behind the house (as a young girl, especially during her high school years, she had taken to exploring the woods and had gotten to know them quite well. She got to be so comfortable there, she often sang while she walked, not paying attention to anything but her own voice). In her dream she watched herself doing nothing—she stood still in the center of the field, hands palm-forward. The sky behind her was lightening-blue, as it can only be on the coldest of days.

There was nothing overtly unusual or remarkable about her dream except… she couldn't pin-point why it unnerved her. Maybe because the self standing in the field was her now, at her present age, in a field she'd not stood in for years, or maybe it was the slightly jerky quality of the image: the still picture that was her in the field trembled as if someone off-frame held it and had held it for a long time.

As K[ ] sat on the couch, her heart beat fast, as if she'd made a hard run. *When was the last time I had a dream?* She tried to relax. *I can't remember—in high school? That's impossible. It can't have been that long.* She sat still until the sun rose. Its light was cold like moonlight. Light crept across the snow in the backyard and the snow became blindingly bright—it seemed more than white, seemed more like empty space, like a crisp sheet of paper just fed through the roller of a typewriter.

Judging by the trees in the yard, she guessed the snow was at least four feet deep. Mrs. Lawrence had been right last night; it would be a day at least before the plows reached the roads near the house.

After K[ ] showered, she washed her underclothes and socks in the sink, then slung them over the shower curtain rod. *Just like when I lived here*, she thought, amused.

Over breakfast, Mrs. Lawrence talked a little about K[ ]'s cousin. "When he came to the door, answering my ad for a tenant, and told me he was related to your mother, I thought, 'terrific,' since your mother was so nice. After I showed him the place, I called your mother—just to be sure he was who he said. She was stunned. She told me that he was in fact your cousin, and not a terribly distant one at that. You know, only once removed or something like that. I can never keep track of all the removeds and seconds and halves in my own family, so how can I be expected to remember yours?" She laughed at her own joke. "Anyway, your mother told me that the two of you, when you were both very young—two or three—before you really begin to remember things—you used to be playmates. Your family and his lived near enough, so when baby-sitting was needed, a child could be dropped off at one house or the other." She stood to clear her plate. "Would you like anything more? I've got more eggs in the pan."

"No thanks. Maybe some more of that coffee—it's good."

"I buy the fancy stuff. I figure one should never cut corners when it comes to coffee and tea."

"So, we played together when we were young?" She wished she could remember. Of course, there were small memories—lone moments, mostly—and K[ ] could never be sure which of those were stories she'd been told about herself and which were real memories.

"Then his family left. Your mother wasn't really sure why. Which struck me as funny, since it sounded as if both families were close. I suppose that's no stranger than his coming back twenty-three years later and rooming in the room that once was your bedroom! Your mother said she never heard from them again. She worried for a while, of course, tried to track them down, but after a few years passed, she figured they had reasons for not wanting to be found, and pretty much let it go. She told me she hadn't thought about them until I called."

K[ ] sipped her coffee—which was very good—and thought about a stranger—who wasn't really a stranger—living in her room. Of course, she was picturing her room as it was when she was living in it. Big mirror to practice her ballet, small brass bed, murals she'd painted on the wall and taped-up magazine cutouts of her once-idols. She tried to imagine the room without her things in it, then realized she didn't have to. "I suppose I ought to get to the task at hand."

The door to her former bedroom—*J[ ]'s room*—was closed. Mrs. Lawrence had said that after his body had been taken care of, the room had been closed and no one had gone in since. "I found the idea of going in there a little spooky," Mrs. Lawrence had said. "That's why I was so pleased you were coming to take care of things." K[ ] opened the door, making a point not to hesitate.

The room was painted white and, though neatly stacked and pushed against the wall, was dominated by newspapers and magazines. Against one wall, there was a bed, of course, and beside it, a dresser. In a corner, on top of a pile of newspapers, was an old typewriter. The air smelled metallic—newsprint's acid.

Her first reaction was of disappointment. *My mural has been painted over!* She tried to recall the mural in some detail, but couldn't even recall its subject.

She could remember standing in this room, paints all around her, feeling proud of her work. *Nostalgia is bad. Nostalgia is for unhappy times and unhappy people.* Her own apartment wasn't much different from this room—it too was impersonal. K[ ] resolved to stop being cheap and buy some new drapes and a little more furniture as soon as she returned.

She leaned over a stack of newspapers and opened the window a crack. The sharp, cold air from outside calmed K[ ]. She found a spot on the floor, sat down, and began to look through the first pile of newspapers.

After she'd gone through two stacks, she felt she'd confirmed two things: most of the newspapers were either rinky-dink town publications or tabloids, and that her cousin had an article in every single one. If she could say he had a focus, it would be a focus on the minor and the bizarre. In one small town paper, *The High Falls Chronicler*, he'd written obituaries and birth announcements for several months. In the tabloids, his stories were inevitably about people's encounters with the supernatural. Specifically ghost sightings.

One article stood out. It was in a tabloid K[ ] had never seen on any supermarket checkout lane. Next to the byline was a photograph of the author, a grainy picture of a grave looking young man wearing a tie. The story caught K[ ]'s attention because it was set in High Falls; indeed, the events took place in the forest behind the house. The story detailed a ghost sighting by a stream K[ ] had often walked alongside. The ghost had been seen by a local (whose name was obviously an anagram of her cousin's own) who had been out on a hike. The woods were familiar to the local, so he had no compunction walking through them late in the evening or after dark. He followed a stream that flowed into a small pool, located just outside a clearing. The night was clear, with a nearly full moon in the sky.

As he approached the clearing he heard a woman singing. Her voice was lovely, and he hoped to find the source. He moved toward the edge of the clearing. There he saw the woman. She was young, he had guessed her to be in her twenties. She wore a white dress and sang.

Not paying attention to where he was going, he walked out of the clearing and into the pool of water. This startled him—the way the ground dropped out—and he yelped. The woman stopped singing, and looked at him. At that moment he realized she was standing not just beyond the pool, as he had originally thought, *but on the water.*

He floundered for a moment in the pool, then tore away through the forest. The rest of the article was J[ ]'s bizarre speculations as to why the singing woman was in the woods, who she might have been, and then the article went on to detail some research into the history of local hauntings, which bore little fruit.

The bedroom door opened and K[ ] jumped.

"I didn't mean to startle you," said Mrs. Lawrence.

"I didn't hear you come up the stairs. I was engrossed in a story of my cousin's."

"Really?" Mrs. Lawrence didn't sound interested. "I've made sandwiches for lunch. Are you hungry?"

K[ ] found that she was, noted that the time was already two o'clock, and thought it a good idea to take a break. At the kitchen table, K[ ] asked about her cousin.

"Do you know much about J[ ]'s professional life?"

"Not at all. I am, I'll be the first to admit, a little nosey, but in his case," she paused, to carefully chose her words. "He unnerved me at times. Intimidated me. Not that he was rude or mean in any way, he just seemed so very serious."

"He looked serious. I saw a photograph of him in a newspaper he'd written an article for."

"He was a reporter? I knew he was a writer of some sort. I assumed it was a novel. How could he have been a reporter? He hardly ever left the house."

"Well he wasn't reporting for any prestigious journal, that's for sure. The stories I read were mostly outlandish stories about ghostly encounters. He wrote for tabloids. There wasn't any real journalism. I didn't read anything he couldn't have written with a telephone and a vivid imagination."

After lunch, K[ ] returned to her late cousin's room. The room was cold—with the window open a crack, and with the door closed, the room had probably cooled down quickly. She closed the window and paused to look out over the backyard.

Sans a swing-set, the yard was as she remembered. The end of the yard was marked by a curve of trees. A stream wriggled among their trunks. She tried to remember where the stream flowed (*to a pool?*), but could not.

She turned back to the room and its contents. She didn't think she would go through all the newspapers—J[ ]'s stories were interesting, but not especially worthwhile. She would skim the rest, and what caught her eye, she would keep (*for whom?*). First she thought she would have a look at his typewriter, which looked pretty old. She clacked out an invisible line or two on the black roller, then thought to try it out on paper. Next to the typewriter was a Strathmore box; she put the box on her lap and removed the lid—it sucked at the box, oozed off. When the bottom dropped free, K[ ] saw that, on top of the paper, were photographs. She glanced over at the bookshelf, and saw a case for an old manual camera. She brought her attention back to the opened box, and picked up the first photograph. She recoiled and dropped the photo back into the box. *It's a photograph of me. It's a photograph of me now.* In the back of her mind, she imagined asking Mrs. Lawrence how J[ ] would have gotten such a picture. Did my mother send Mrs. Lawrence a picture of me? Did my mother keep up a correspondence with her? With J[ ]?

K[ ] stared at the picture and knew no one had sent J[ ] the photo. Knew because the photograph was quite obviously taken in the forest behind the house. "This is impossible," she said, and her hand trembled, and the image before her blurred, blurred enough for her to put the photograph face down in the box, and put back the lid. Blurred enough so she could say to herself, *she looked so much like me,* and for a moment believe that the photo was of another woman.

K[ ] did not stay in J[ ]'s room long after the discovery of the photograph. When she went downstairs she told Mrs. Lawrence that she had grown tired; the work a little dull, and that since she was going to be stuck here for at least another day anyhow, she thought she would take a break and maybe call it quits for the night.

"That's sensible. I'll enjoy some company. It gets lonely out here, especially when you're snowed in. I'll make us a nice dinner and we can eat in front of the television."

"That sounds very nice."

"Good." Mrs. Lawrence looked down to her needlework, then looked up again; K[ ] had not decided what she was going to do yet, and still stood at the bottom of the stairs. Mrs. Lawrence said, "feel free to use the phone if you need to let someone know you're stranded here." K[ ] would need to call the office if she wasn't going be in on Monday, but that could wait until Monday morning. Otherwise, there was no one to call.

K[ ] was grateful for Mrs. Lawrence's company. The photograph really disturbed her, though she was unable to address what it meant in any direct way. She did ask Mrs. Lawrence if J[ ] had, during his stay in the house, ever had a girlfriend. The answer was, of course, no. "He did often go out at night," Mrs. Lawrence said. "I thought maybe it was to see a woman." K[ ] helped set up the fireplace for a fire, they made dinner, and they chatted about the shows they watched on TV. A little after midnight, Mrs. Lawrence stood up, brushed the wrinkles out of her skirt, and told K[ ] that she had to be going to bed.

"Goodnight," K[ ] said, and turned to face the dying embers in the fireplace. She recalled sitting near the fireplace as a girl, sometimes laying on the floor in front of it for hours, her parents seated behind her, her father in the big armchair, always, her mother on the couch. She stared at the flame intently; its tongues waved like snakes' bodies crawling in the sand; she marveled at the array of colors in the flame and the shadows the flame cast against the brick (*odd that light can cast a shadow*). The fire died. The only source of light was from the dim lamp behind her. The ash in the fireplace was cold, where only a moment ago was warmth.

Something fell from the chimney into the pile of ash. K[ ] jumped, sat up, no longer sleepy but tensely alert. A plume of ash obscured whatever had fallen. The ash slowly settled, K[ ] was afraid of what might be revealed, and then something else fell from the chimney. She lifted her feet up off the floor and tucked them under herself.

When the ash at last settled K[ ] saw what had fallen into the fireplace. Human feet. She recoiled and made a sharp noise and then fell a leg, it fell perfectly onto a foot and foot and leg were solidly united. The other leg fell. K[ ] pushed herself back against the couch, stupid in her fear. Something else fell, something very heavy, and she knew what it was, though she could not see it, the torso, because the person that was assembling himself was tall enough that, standing upright, only their feet and legs were visible. *I have to scream*, she thought, *to wake Mrs. Lawrence*. She screamed. The sound of her scream—high, piercing—almost wiped out the hideous shuffling of the person assembling.

The assembled person in the fireplace bent into a crouch, revealed itself to be a man, then revealed more as his shoulders appeared like white balls from the dark and finally, leering out from the shadowy hearth, his white face.

K[ ] screamed when he looked at her. His glassy eyes shifted till they met her eyes, and when they did she shut up. He stepped out of the fireplace, dragging soot with each step. His face shone in the lamp light, his features obscured until his mouth emerged from the glare into shadow. His lips framed a word, once, slowly, then again and again. His dry lips parted and his teeth came together over the last consonant. The word was her name.

When K[ ] snapped awake she shook violently and cried out. She stood. A dagger of moonlight fell across the carpet. She walked along that strip of light to the window, unable to release the image of the assembled man's mouth making her name. *Since when do I have nightmares?* She was accustomed to sleep without dreams. To the absence of visions in her life.

The strip of moonlight led from the house to the darkness of the forest. She imagined what it would be like to be out in the snow, pictured herself standing in the snow, facing herself. Saw herself framed by the window, then again standing in the snow, and this idea of two selves spun, stretched out across the white yard.

When she broke free of her rumination she realized she was falling asleep standing up. She walked quietly up the stairs to J[ ]'s/her room, lay down on the floor, and drifted into the dreamless sleep she knew best.

K[ ] woke, disoriented, it took her a few minutes to reconstruct where she was. J[ ]'s/her room. Her strange, dead cousin's room. And her room, the room in which she had lain awake at night as a teenager and wondered about her future *would anyone ever love me?* The room she was now meant to empty out once and for all, and, since yesterday, the room that contained the photograph that couldn't be. She had the urge to look at the photo again, though she was afraid. She looked over at the camera on the bookcase, and wondered if J[ ] had taken the picture himself. As she lifted the lid from the paper box, she tried to establish an explanation, so when she saw the photograph again, it would not be too much of a shock. Perhaps the girl was a relative she had not met, it was a photograph of her mother, it was an older picture of herself taken while she still lived in the house. These were rational explanations, but, as she held the picture in her hand, she found she was not convinced by any of them (her hand trembled as the hand in her dream had trembled). Rather than hide the photograph away again, as if it were something dangerous and alive, she placed the photo on the typewriter, propped up between two rows of keys.

Looking down at the keys, K[ ] saw there were sheets of paper, typewritten and annotated in longhand, beneath the typewriter. *Another tabloid story, never submitted*, she thought, and she thought, *because he died*. She slid the pages out from under the typewriter. What she read was another version of the ghost story she'd read before. A man walked through the forest. He followed the stream and a woman's voice. When he found her, he saw that she stood not beside a small pool of water, but on the pool of water.

At this point the article deviated from its published counterpart. Instead of a speculative meditation on the local ghosts the woman might have been, J[ ] wrote about astral projection, "the ability to release one's consciousness from their body in order to let their consciousness travel." J[ ] wrote, "I believe it is possible not all astral projection is consciously permitted, but that sometimes the consciousness leaves the body to go where it feels right. Anyone who encountered such a consciousness would likely mistake it for a ghost. I suppose they would not be entirely wrong."

At the bottom of the first page was a date written in heavy black ink that bled through the page. J[ ] wrote this version of his story a year after the ghost version was published. And just a month before he died.

A spell was broken by the noise of pans in the kitchen. K[ ] went downstairs. Mrs. Lawrence was at the counter, pouring cream into a cup of coffee. K[ ] thought Mrs. Lawrence looked perturbed, and she wondered if she shouldn't have slept in J[ ]'s room.

"I didn't intend to sleep in J[ ]'s room," K[ ] explained. "I'm not sure why I went up there last night. I suppose I thought I'd get some work done."

"That's what I assumed when I saw you in there."

"Mrs. Lawrence?"

"What happened in the living room last night? Did a log roll out of the fireplace? Did you try to clean it up?" Before K[ ] could answer, Mrs. Lawrence added, "I came down this morning and there was a trail of ash across my carpet. The ash looked as if it had been walked in—I could see footprints in it. Bare feet. Can you tell me what that's all about?"

K[ ] left the kitchen without answering. She went to the living room.

Mrs. Lawrence followed her, "I cleaned up."

With the evidence gone, K[ ] could doubt Mrs. Lawrence. But she didn't doubt her. K[ ] considered making up a story and she considered telling Mrs. Lawrence the truth, but neither option struck K[ ] as… useful. She did know what would be useful, though. "I need some air. I'm going for a walk."

Mrs. Lawrence looked uncertain. "Dear, I didn't mean to yell."

"You didn't yell."

"I was just hoping for an explanation."

"I just really need to get out." K[ ] put on her shoes.

"Cabin fever?" Mrs. Lawrence forced a laugh. "Well, wear my boots, honey. And let me get you a hat. You didn't bring a hat, did you?"

K[ ] took the hat, swapped her shoes for the boots; K[ ] put on her coat and opened the back door. The light outside made her eyes ache.

"Do you know when you'll be back?"

A dim thought emerged at the back of K[ ]'s mind: *she should be used to strange behavior.* Other thoughts, *did a man assemble himself and step out of the fireplace? Did J[ ] take a picture of me in the backyard when I wasn't there?* crowded her head for attention. She said to Mrs. Lawrence, "I'll be fine."

Covered with a layer of ice, the snow held K[ ] for an instant before her weight pushed her boot down, packing the foot of powder beneath her rubber tread. Keenly aware of each step she took, K[ ] made for the black line the little stream had cut into the snow, a black line that led deep into the forest. She stepped onto the frozen stream, saw clear water running beneath; the ice creaked, but bore her weight.

The air was sharp; the cold, clean. She felt how filthy the air in the city was, how terrible. Here, the air smelled of water: a stony, mineral smell; and on the air were hints of pine and the sweeter smell of chimney smoke. K[ ] bent to pass under pine boughs, heavy with snow. When she bumped branches, snow fell across her jacket, froze her bare neck, melted into her shirt collar.

The trees thinned, and the stream flowed into a clearing. At the heart of the clearing was the pool. She stepped off the ice, onto the field. The field was white, the sky, blank; trees wrote their way along the horizon. K[ ]'s foot slipped out from under her, but she kept her balance. *The pool,* she thought. She stepped cautiously forward, stopped, and thought, *I'm standing on the pool.*

She turned around and faced the path she had made. Where she had walked on the stream, there were no boot-prints, no mark of her passage, as though she was placed in the field by an invisible hand and urged to the pool. When K[ ] saw herself walk out of the forest, she was not particularly surprised.

She—K[ ] from the forest—stopped at the edge of the wood, and looked at herself—at K[ ], who stood on the frozen pool. K[ ] heard her breath leave her mouth, saw the cloud. She thought of J[ ], of his trips to this pool, his late-night outings. The reason for his outings—he went out to look for her.

She thought of the plows, how they would come soon enough, and the roads would be clear. K[ ] could return to the city. She knew that the snow would melt, that the earth would turn muddy, and that from the mud would spring grass and flowers. The pool would once again become liquid and it would not hold her, not the K[ ] that worked a job that bored her in a city she'd become inured to, but never liked. The forest would be dense with green, the air would be warm, though at night—K[ ] knew—the air would still carry a chill. She knew, finally, that she would be here, exactly where she stood, to see all these changes. K[ ] knew this as she looked at the rest of herself, who stood still in the shadow of the trees.

A String of Lights

No afterlife, a phrase, indignant, someone, a man, his voice, not to my left where the tall tables and the open windows were, to my right, but I couldn't locate the speaker, but then, "You really don't think so, do you?" A guy, at a table with two other guys and a woman, all pretty young, maybe graduate students. The woman said, "No. There is no afterlife," and the man said—he looked like anybody—the man said, "Then what's all the universe for?"

I finished my drink, tipped the bartender, wished her luck with the GMAT, and crossed the street. I'd lucked out with a parking spot right across from the bar, which I'd thought when I'd parked would be great for when I walked out with Cheryl, but she hadn't shown.

A long enough drive back to my apartment to think about what I'd overheard: "No afterlife?" and "Then what's all the universe for?" All the universe. Did afterlife equal universe? No. Earth was in the universe. No. With a universe so big, there was room enough for just about anything. No. Scratch that. In an infinite universe, there was room for *everything*. Including THE AFTERLIFE. So. In death we travel to another part of the universe. Okay. So the afterlife's like a solar system? Is a solar system? A planet? My musing kept me company all the way up to my driveway. Above the car, trees—some animal rustled in the dark branches—that owl, the one that'd scared Cheryl so much. Where was Cheryl? Her phone was off, as per usual, and I didn't feel like leaving another message. Up through the tree branches, the night sky was murky, too much light by the front steps to see anything. Another noise, a squeak, a sponge on glass: Leslie's apartment was dark; the sound didn't come from Leslie's apartment. The second floor apartment was dark, of course, though for a moment, at the lower right corner of the left-most window, a pinpoint of light, brilliant and clean white. But Leslie had yet to rent the middle apartment. It'd remained empty for months, now. There were days when I was home alone and the emptiness of the rooms below me became oppressive. But! the quiet was good for sleeping.

My desk light, blue in the attic window. The squeak forgotten. I unlocked the front door.

Another drink, tumbler beside my computer, email, and there it was, Cheryl hadn't stood me up, she'd only been late letting me know she had to cancel (why did it never occur to her to call?). She wrote: "I'm stuck here, late, because Neal (her boss) FAILED to show up and the client DEMANDED that someone finish the brochure by *very* early AM because it was quite due and *their* client…" I'd been to Cheryl's office, late at night: I knew what she must look like, now. Lights out except for the lamp in her cubical, the light from her screen, her thick hair disheveled by her own hand, eyes shiny. I wanted to be with her and was tempted to go, but it was 10 PM and maybe she was gone, and if she wasn't, she probably *didn't* want to be interrupted. So a quick email of encouragement, carefully *not* mentioning our cancelled date.

The other email in my box was from a co-worker, I think, but now I honestly don't remember who the email came from, and I deleted the email, so I can't check. The email was nothing personal, just, "Check this out," or something, and a link. I sipped my drink and sleepily clicked the link.

The page that came up was crowded with photos, stills from short films. At the center of the page was a square—at first black, then not, this:

A girl—as young as 15, as old as 19 (though a scrawny 19 she'd be)—in a bedroom. A spare bedroom, a bed behind her and on the wall a framed picture of two houses, white, simple houses. She was modestly but not prudishly dressed, a T-shirt, jeans. She sat at the edge of her desk chair, held her knees to her chest and said, "Hi, I'm Denise" and that she was starting a video diary and didn't have much to say but that she liked books and photography and old movies. Then, a little inspired goofiness, she pushed her wheeled chair (it looked like an office chair from the 1950s) and rolled back on a parquet floor, past her bed, until she bumped the wall behind her.

There the image froze, Denise, eyes wide (startled by the bump—or *acting* startled), mouth shut tight, her whole figure in frame, small, skinny.

I watched the three other video diary entries Denise had posted, and then returned to the first.

There—along the wall—I paused the little video—a candelabra with three white candles and above a framed photo of an elderly woman, dressed in black. And then my phone rang: Cheryl.

A half hour later, she and I were undressing each other, me a little drunk, her exhausted and wired. We had fun, sleepy sex which concluded satisfactorily with dozy sleep, a joint trip to the bathroom and then real sleep, until my alarm woke us and we split, Cheryl to her place for a quick change of clothes, me to my office.

Before Cheryl's phone call, I'd gone back to the first entry of Denise's video journal because of something she'd said in her third:

"I'm not going to tell you about my religion because I know you would make fun of it."

And so Denise offered a mystery. Suddenly what had been only a cute and well-made video journal was colored new; ceased to be just the mild complaints of an ordinary, bright and lonely girl—"this town is *so* boring" and "my parents suck"—and became a little more interesting/complex.

While at work but not working, I tried to guess at what her religion might be. Of course, I started with conservative Christian religions: what Christian religion would a teenager expect to be made fun of for believing?—

but a teenager fears persecution for *anything* that singles them out, and so Denise's fear of being teased wasn't much help. Still, I thought, Southern Baptist? Mennonite? Mormon? But she complicated those guesses, too—she talked often about science, her love for it, its centrality in her reading—and she was homeschooled, so presumably her parents, who presumably shared her religion, who likely *gave* religion to her, were encouraging her to study science, which included Darwin (I know because she admired him especially). Most of my day passed in such thought—did Denise deliberately mention her love of Darwin as a clue? Still, I figured Christian, but nothing too orthodox. She was creating an online video journal, after all, and her clothes were not so conservative. And then I thought, as I drove to meet Cheryl for dinner near her office ("Rescue me! My ass-boss just gave me another past-due assignment!"), teenagers are often very proud of their religion, are more confident about religion than adults. Cheryl kissed me in front of her office building, then waved up to where I presumed her boss was, and said, "I'm sorry, I'm gonna have to go back after dinner." She slumped, did a little exhausted-prisoner-walk to my car, and said, "And I really wanted to have sex tonight, too."

That changed the focus of my thoughts. I suggested a million scenarios that put us in bed together, but ultimately all Cheryl needed was a good meal, some non-work conversation, a glass of wine ("Just one! Okay. Two."), and a ride back to her office. When I got back to my house, I stopped on the second floor landing and put my ear to the door of the empty middle apartment. A creak... nothing... a pipe—the radiators kicking in for the first time since April... nothing... a phone, the faint ring of a phone—was someone in there? My cell phone was buried in my bag, muffled by papers, I fumbled around (the phone's blue light the brightest light on that second floor landing), "Hello?" Cheryl was coming by after all. And she was going into work late the next day, so I needed to brace myself for a late night.

During the next few days, I didn't think much about Denise's video journal, or think to check for new entries. Mystery aside, other distractions kept me occupied. What brought my mind back to Denise was Cheryl, who one night ranted about mega-churches, because of an article she'd read in a back issue of *The New York Times Magazine*, that'd turned up in her office. "I've done perfectly well without religion," she said, leaning back in her chair, plate near-full (mine, half-eaten). "Why would anyone want to believe in God, especially one who promotes bad music and bad TV?" This was the most she'd ever said about religion.

"A most compelling argument," I said.

I remained non-committal. My occasionally Protestant parents left me with a sort-of faith in something. I'd been to a dozen services in the last year because my previous girlfriend sung in a choir and the masses they sang were undeniably beautiful. She left me for someone who wasn't non-committal—no doubt a good decision for her. I did believe in some kind of supernatural thing, that thing that occasionally made lonely moments profound.

Cheryl was pretty much in the same boat as me, at least I thought so, and she backpedaled, which was a quality of hers I perversely adored. She said, "Oh, I do believe in God. And I totally believe in Bach."

I didn't know Cheryl all that well, but that was easy to forget when I was with her.

"You just reminded me of something," I said, and I told her about Denise's video journal.

"You're just watching it 'cause she's a cute teenaged girl, sicko." Then she leaned close to me, deliberately allowing me a grand view of her cleavage. "Are you already tired of this old flesh, darling?"

We went to a show after our dinner, a band Cheryl liked, and I didn't think about Denise again until early in the morning (Sunday). While Cheryl slept in my bed, I was inexplicably awake, a terrible sick nervousness all over me—too much to drink, perhaps. Wearing boxer shorts only, I went online, checked my email, then remembered Denise. I watched four new journal entries.

The second of the new videos introduced a friend, a boy, her age,

Alan. His role was to appear disinterested in Denise's doings, to pretend to read (sprawled across her bed—as I watched I remembered being in the bedroom of a high school crush—how sacred and confusing) while she made her video.

Denise: Today I ran into Janet. She was in my biology class before I stopped going to school. She used to call me alien-girl. I don't know why she was mean to me except that I asked the teacher lots of questions…

Alan: (without looking up from his book) She was just teasing you.

Denise: I asked a lot of questions and then Janet told everybody that something was going on between me and the teacher so I had to leave…

Alan: You didn't have to.

Denise: (Rolls eyes) …school.

During the last of the new videos, someone opened the door to Denise's bedroom—apparently unexpectedly. Denise's reaction was to stand, her back to the camera (putting me at eye-level with her rear-end). Though a little muffled, I heard,

Denise: Mom?

Alan: No…

Denise: It's you.

Alan: Who?

Denise: Come back later.

and

Denise: Don't worry, it's good.

When Denise turned back to the camera, her expression was grave—for only a second, but a freezable second, and I did freeze it, her face, deadly serious.

And then I let it go, and Denise shushed Alan, who asked, "Who was that?" and Denise said, "Alan loves just about every girl he sees." Alan protested, but was shushed again: Denise winked and puckered her lips, "He's so sensitive," and then turned on Alan, and pounced on the bed, her long self stretched out at Alan's knees.

Denise became real to me three days later. I left the office in the afternoon for a client meeting and saw Denise, seated in the backseat of an Outback. She looked bored as she stared out at the street. My first instinct was to duck out of sight, then I remembered that I didn't know Denise, nor she me. As the car passed, she looked through me, I wasn't even there.

That night, as I waited for Cheryl to stop by ("I can't stay but a drink would be nice") I checked to see if Denise had posted another entry and she had. Initially a teenage lament about a party she wanted to go to but couldn't. She had, she said, "An honor bestowed upon me, an honor bestowed by my church."
Denise: I have to learn a long speech. I read it last night. It is very beautiful.
[Inter-cut with footage of Denise hanging a string of white lights along the wall, close to the ceiling, above that picture of the two white houses.]
Denise: We quote one of The Great Sermons, the lovely part about the strand of white lights that stretches out, deep into space.
[Denise twists the string of lights once around a nail.]
Denise: And when a single bulb is faulty, the whole string of lights will fail; we fail until we pluck the dead lights.
[She is on her toes, on her bed, tapping a little black nail into the wall, the strand of lights draped over her shoulder; I think she must be tall; her legs are so slender.]
Denise: We stretch out.
[Denise plugs the lights into an outlet. The lights fail. She mugs for the camera, a comic frown.]
Denise: Finding those dead lights can be a trick.
[She puckers her lips and leans into the camera and mouths something, a word like "solder."]

Cheryl decided to stay after I poured out the last of our first bottle of wine. She slouched back on the futon that served as my couch. She looked up at me with her down-turned mouth. She was very slim; every time I undressed her I was amazed how small she was. She was highly energetic in bed. I tried to mask how out-of-breath I was and I admit she did most of the work.

We slept hard after we came: but I woke with a shout in the middle of the night. And there Cheryl was, small and pale, sitting naked in a wooden chair she'd taken from the dining room, seated at the foot of my bed. I thought, at first, that she was staring at me.

Across my dark red comforter were diamonds of white light, cast by the street light near the window. I sat up, slid back, away from Cheryl, disturbed by her lack of expression. Her eyes, open. And seated so straight. I waited for her to speak, I imagined I heard her say, "You terrible crumpled leaf; you dried thing."

She did not speak, had not spoken. She was asleep and her eyes were closed.

I carefully got out of bed and walked past Cheryl, into the dining room. I poured myself a drink. Again I thought how I didn't know Cheryl well at all. We'd been together for a month. I felt a lot of lust and maybe more, I *said* more. Cheryl came into my home, was invited. I took off my clothes, I got drunk; how vulnerable I allowed myself to be with her. I finished my drink. In the kitchen. I filled two glasses with water. I wasn't sure how to wake her. I stood in the kitchen, cool glasses in hand, and felt as if the floor was being lowered, had the strong sensation I was being sucked into the empty apartment below.

When I went back into the bedroom, Cheryl was in bed, asleep.

The next morning: "I did *not*," and she laughed at herself, put her hand to her mouth—an utterly disarming gesture—and we laughed together, and she went so far as to imitate herself, what she thought she must have looked like, and sat rigidly in the chair at the foot of my bed, eyes open and blank, mouth as unsmiling as was possible. Even this imitation was a little unnerving—it put me back into the frame of mind I'd been in. But not for long. I kissed Cheryl and she melted for me, her back relaxing, her body taking on the languid slouch that was her normal pose.

"I must go," she said. "Even though Neal said I could come in late, he means, like, five past nine and not," she looked at the clock beside my bed, "well I'm going to be getting in at 11. I'm going to shower here, you lucky devil. I brought some clothes." From the bathroom she tossed the borrowed boxer shorts she'd worn to bed into the bedroom. "No," she said, "you may not join me, I must be clean!"

On my way out I stopped on the second floor landing and paused to listen at the door to the middle apartment. I tested the doorknob. What compelled me to try it, I'll never know, I'd stood by that door so many times before, but I tried the doorknob, it turned and clicked; the door was unlocked, had been maybe ever since the previous tenants had moved out, or maybe Leslie was cleaning the place out for new tenants, whatever, I stepped inside.

All the blinds were drawn; I crossed the room to raise one; something—I looked down—glass crunched beneath my shoe. I opened the blind and the floor glittered in the sun. Where I'd stepped were shoe-sized patches of crushed glass and around my prints were larger pieces of filmy glass. I stared dumb at the circle the glass made, then looked up and saw that all the light bulbs in the ceiling were broken. In each socket—there were six in a circle—were the bases of each bulb and their black filament. The same damage appeared in every room—I opened blinds as I went, walked along the edge of each room. In the bedroom, a window had been left open.

The breeze was chilly but the air was a relief. I left, eager to be out of that place, unnerved and without an explanation, glad for the office, for the jocular client I had a meeting with, glad for the receptionist, who wanted the latest on my love life.

And so I didn't think about the glass in the empty apartment until after work, when I bumped into my landlady, busy sweeping leaves from the front walk.

"Leslie," I said.

She stopped sweeping and removed the cigarette from her mouth. "Hi David."

As soon as I thought to mention the broken glass to Leslie, I thought better of it—I didn't want to explain why I'd been in the empty apartment. I asked, "Any more news about the empty apartment?"

Instead of a quick answer, yes or no, my question elicited a funny look and a, "Why do you ask?" promptly cut off with, "No. Can't seem to rent the place. Not that I mind the quiet." She pulled on her smoke, and raked.

The next day was Saturday. Unexpectedly, Cheryl had cancelled our Friday night plans, a girlfriend "in trouble" she had to see. So I woke alone, an unusual occurrence as of late. The sunlight in my room was clear and called for wakefulness. I rose, dressed, and went out with more gusto than I'd felt in some days. After a croissant (steaming, oily with butter and butter-sweet) and a coffee, I decided to walk. I set a gas station as my destination, where I could buy a newspaper. The morning was cold, though the sun bright. Only September, I caught whiffs of snow in the air—impossible—the earliest snow might come late October. Still, nice to think about snow. Cheryl had told me that winter was her favorite season. I wished she was with me but was also glad enough she wasn't.

I was really enjoying myself, feeling carefree, until I reached my destination and saw that car I'd seen before, with Denise in the backseat. I froze—a few feet behind the car—and saw that her friend Alan was in the car with her. I approached the gas station and got a clearer view of Denise's friend. He sat rigid, and his face was stricken—utterly pale, tense.

My first instinct was to approach the car, to ask if anything was wrong, even, to introduce myself (the feeling I knew these people was strong even though I did not know them, not at all). I stopped myself, and stood and took in the scene: an Outback, Denise the teenaged girl of the mysterious religion and her friend, a boy who no doubt was in love with her but would never get anywhere romantically with her, and a driver, an adult—a woman—the way the shadow was I couldn't see more. And there they were, a tableau, the car by a pump but neither being gassed nor with the engine on. No one inside the car moved except Denise—she leaned against the window, then sat back in her seat, then touched Alan's face, etc. Not frantic, impatient.

Alan's look disturbed me and so I stared at him. I gradually began to believe that he was not alive at all. Not dead, but a facsimile, a wax dummy made for the car. This notion was dispelled when Denise flicked Alan's cheek and he flinched. So odd, that flick—playful but cruel. Denise saw me, and returned my stare until I broke off eye contact and went into the store for my paper. When I came out, the car was gone.

I could not walk back to my apartment fast enough, I walked foolishly, on the cusp of a run, newspaper pinched under my arm. When at last at home, I watched the latest entry of Denise's video journal:

[Denise's bedroom is dark, lit only by the three candles beneath the photo of the old woman. On the bed is a shape—Alan. Above his head, the picture of the white houses. The camera floats toward him, halts at medium close-up. The camera operator turns the camera around. Close-up of Denise, who smiles. She turns the camera back toward Alan. He appears to be sleeping.]

Denise: Listen—

[The microphone picks up Alan's voice. His speech is sluggish; he talks in his sleep.]

Alan: A string of lights… their candles trail endlessly though infinity… in the black sky of the universe… and each bulb… a glass blank… those bulbs that are no good… unmade…

[Denise turns the camera on herself.]

Denise: He's such a sensible doll, isn't he?

[Denise turns the camera back to Alan. He still appears to be asleep, but he is violently trembling. A hand—Denise's—reaches toward Alan. A dark figure, who presumably had stood behind Denise, steps into the frame toward Alan. End.]

I watched through all the films again, and every one, even the first, the most charming entry, revealed a dark color, but offered no explanation, and

I really could not say what it was exactly that had me so troubled. The phone rang—Cheryl wondered if I was free and if she could come over. As I said yes, I heard yells from outside. Phone in hand, Cheryl talking, I walked to the window—the yells were kids playing, I thought, then—the yells sounded as if they were closer than outside, as if they came from the empty apartment below. I said, "Yes, come over," and I shut off the phone.

I opened the door to my apartment and leaned out into the hall—the stairs down to the second floor apartment were dusty-sunny. The yells could very well have come from outside—the yells were gone—a creak from below set me in motion. Down the stairs to the second floor, to the door of the unoccupied apartment.

The living room was empty—the glass had been swept into a corner—but what absolutely stunned me was the picture of the two houses. The picture was hung, crooked, on the wall between the two windows that faced the street.

One window was open, and a very cold wind blew snow onto the sill. Though the snow was totally improbable, it was the picture that disturbed me most.

A creak on the floor behind me—

"David."

"Cheryl," I said. Her presence gave me courage. "Cheryl, follow me."

We walked from the living room into the dining room into a hall. From a room at the end of the hall Denise came: she held a white, digital camera. She held the camera high, so it partially blocked her face; its lens aimed at me.

Cheryl put her hand on my shoulder.

I heard footsteps, followed them, in my mind, from the second floor landing, to the living room, to the dining room, to the hall, to somewhere just behind Cheryl.

Cheryl said, "Hello, Leslie."

I could not turn away from Denise or from the camera's eye. Cheryl's hand burned my shoulder.

Adam Golaski

"Snow in September," she said. "How perfectly unusual."

Denise lowered the camera from her face. She went back into the room from where she'd come.

Cheryl said—and she pushed me a little, toward the end of the hall: "You know about the string of lights. Let's go see what's left of Alan."

Montana

What Water Reveals

Where water recedes, land is revealed. Beneath the oceans of the Earth lie a vast, unexplored landscape, as foreign to humans as is the surface of Pluto.

Water reclaims what it reveals, too: eventually, all the world will be ocean and frozen like Jupiter's Europa. Humans may have left by then; charging like a white bull through space. Or they'll be here, as fossils, or here, waiting. In Time, there is room for great patience.

Nicolas rides his newly acquired mountain bike alongside the Clark Fork river, follows a narrow trail cut by other bikes. Today, there are no other bicyclists; none ahead of Nicolas and none behind. The weather is right. No gray cloud cover. Only lone, white clouds that keep the vivid blue sky from appearing too unreal. And along the trail everything's gone green or muddy brown. Nicolas sweats. He wears a light coat, nylon pants, t-shirt. No one knows where he is—there's really no one to tell (though he has numbers in his cell phone). He's gone off on this ride as part of a major personal effort to feel better, to reclaim his life. He's already lost weight. Subtract eight to twenty beers and a bottle or two of liquor a day from your diet and see that you don't lose weight. He dodges branches, catches brambles and hops over tree-roots. It's April (at last); plants creeping and bursting. He wonders why there's no one else on the trail: it is Tuesday, he thinks, but such a beautiful day—and after a long nasty winter that buried everything with snow—he thinks, surely people would be playing hooky. He isn't truant. He's unemployed. He doesn't dwell on his situation. He was fired a little over two months ago and that set off a whole chain of events leading to this morning. The ride occupies his mind. Navigating muddy ruts without taking a spill and dodging branches frees his mind from worry and fear.

The trail is high above the river. To his right is brush and trees—just thick enough to block his view from the wide walkers' trail that follows the base of Mount Sentinel. If he were to jerk his hand to the left, his bike would fly through a thin tangle of young trees and bushes, fifteen feet into snow-cold water. When he starts to think that way, his arms tremble.

Nicolas squeezes the breaks before a hump of dirt. The trail slopes down and away from the river. Beneath arched pines the ground is covered with a mat of gold pine needles. Nicolas relaxes his grip on the breaks and his bike rolls forward. Sun penetrates the thicket over his head in smoke-shape patterns on the ground. He's slightly nervous he'll encounter a bear fresh from hibernation. There is no bear ahead, and the stretch of dark is brief. When Nicolas emerges, he passes an abandoned grill and another. He stops and gets off his bike to get a sense of where he is. The drop to the river's edge is just five feet; he jumps to a sandy patch of land level with the river. "A beach," he says.

The water is amber-clear. He can't sense how cold it is with only a quick dip of his finger; the water's quite cold. On the other side of the river is I-90. A truck passes, a car. Though he feels alone, he's far from the middle of nowhere. Directly opposite where Nicolas stands, the river splits around a narrow island. Tall, dry grass covers most of the island. The grass vanishes into a coppice of pine trees. He can't see past the pine trees to the end of the island. Nicolas can't tell how old the trees are from looking at them, but they're fifty-footers and dense—the heart of the coppice is night-dark, darker than the sunken stretch of trail Nicolas rode through.

His left knee hurts a little from the ride. He's mildly worried by this; he's too young to have problems with his knee. He's certainly given his body a hard time, though. Who knows what he's done to his knee, crashing into his apartment night after night of drinking, blacked-out. He doesn't want to think about this, so he considers ways to get across the river to the island. Too deep to ride across and too rocky. He walks along the river—in the direction he'd ridden from but below the trail, hidden from the trail. A few yards from his beach, the rocks rise up, almost make a stone path to the island. Not quite—on his weak knee he isn't sure he could hop across without falling and perhaps, he thinks, "breaking my knee or cracking my skull." Further down the river bank is a sheet of plywood, river-detritus caught among exposed tree roots. Nicolas gets the board and lays it over the rocks that jut above the water's surface.

The make-shift bridge holds. Nicolas walks a slight slope toward the center of the island. The grass is knee high. He's sure he hears an animal moving through the grass—he's no longer sure—"the wind blowing through the grass?" A tree, felled but still with leaf, shivers in the breeze and Nicolas gives the sound to that. Caught in the branches of the tree are logs, branches, twigs. He picks up a suitable walking stick and pokes his way to the opposite side of the island. The flotsam held by the felled tree has made a cradle of water, and eddy where scum has collected and, "shoes. How many pairs of shoes?" He starts to count but loses interest. He imagines himself falling into the garbage covered pool and manages to revolt himself; the oily water, the tangle of wreck below nagging at his legs, "stealing my shoes," he kids himself from his dim fantasy.

On the spine of the island—a grassy hump that runs into the little forest—is a log. Beneath the log is a nest of garter snakes—Nicolas is startled as one slips from beneath. Against the log is a man-made structure. Two heavy branches lean against the log, set a few feet apart. Across the branches are sticks and boards. Like a lean-to, but too low for anyone to find shelter. Maybe a pack was kept dry and maybe there's still a pack beneath. He looks down the island, toward the little forest. He calls out, a feeble, "Hello," then another, "Hello!" He steps back from the low lean-to and with his walking stick knocks the sticks and boards from their branch supports. Nothing is revealed but a damp patch of earth about half a man long; a patch that runs under the log, where the snakes nest; a few millipedes writhe in the sunlight—they scurry toward the snakes to be devoured.

Nicolas looks back at his bike. He's not worried someone will steal it, but he's a little uncomfortable with how far away he is from where he was: his bike seems small. The cars on I-90 seem small. Though he can see houses, and knows that beyond the narrow bike trail is the oft-used foot trail, and even though it's broad daylight, and still morning, he feels lonely and nervous, nervous as he'd feel in a dead-end alley in New York City.

And for this he feels foolish. He'll see the far end of the island, go back to his bike, ride into town and treat himself to a good lunch. He shouldn't spend the money, but he needs to spoil himself these days.

He follows the spine toward the trees. Just ahead of the little forest is a dead tree, thick—thicker than any of the trees in the coppice. The dead tree's branches are long gone. The tree's top is a splintered spike, a point like the tail of a dinosaur. Among the stegosaur spines is a crow which calls as Nicolas passes beneath. The crow's caw is guttural, as if the bird had phlegm caught in its throat. Nicolas turns, looks up, catches a glimpse of something moving near the log that had supported the low lean-to.

There are no trails on the island and no trail amongst the trees. The ground is covered with pine needles—black, not golden. Nicolas can see lines of light—the far end of the island, he presumes.

After a few steps into the coppice, he turns again and sees a man standing where the low lean-to had been. Nicolas thinks, "He must've come over on my plywood bridge." Nicolas gets the distinct impression that the man sees him and so Nicolas waves. The man doesn't wave back. Nicolas walks into the coppice, away from the man. "He can catch up with me if he wants." Nicolas reaches the other side of the island. There is a little sandy strip and the river, tumbling toward him. For a moment, without looking up or around, he imagines the rippling water as the ocean's edge, imagines he is standing by the Atlantic, on a sunny spring day, gulls calling—

The crow caws its unhealthy caw. Nicolas turns and sees the man's shape among the trees.

"Hello," Nicolas says.

The man doesn't reply, just shambles forward. "That's the word for it," Nicolas thinks, "shambles. He looks drunk. I don't want to deal with that." So Nicolas walks to the end of the beach and begins to walk around the little forest. As soon as he does, the man changes direction. Nicolas doesn't want to be ridiculous, so he says hello again, still walking away from the man. The man remains silent; the man's shape is a wavering line of sunlight. Nicolas continues along the forest, then dashes through—he doesn't care anymore about looking ridiculous. And when he glances back, he sees that the man isn't far behind—though his movements have the wobble of drunkenness, those movements are quick.

Nicolas finds himself disoriented and runs a little toward the felled tree. Looking up, seeing I-90, he realizes his mistake and makes a diagonal dash toward his plywood bridge. Though he took a good hour poking around the island, it's not large—his bridge is just beyond the log where he disassembled the low lean-to. Nicolas jumps to clear the log—

he falls further than he expects to, comes down hard, feels all the impact in his knee. He has landed in a hole. Where the low lean-to was is now a deep hole, the bottom sodden with river water. Nicolas isn't sure his left leg will work at all until he hears a branch snap. The sound is electric; Nicolas is out of the hole.

He is seated at the edge of the hole, a hole that runs deep beneath the log. Struggling in the water are dozens of slithering snakes. He thinks of the shoes swarming in the eddy beneath the felled tree. Nicolas hears a truck on I-90, its iron rumble as small a sound as a pebble bounced into a puddle. Nicolas doubts the man is even a man, thinks, insanely, that he's a bear or a rotten tree stump. Nicolas mumbles, "Dear blessed Jesus Christ on Earth," and shouts, "I admit I am powerless…" and he's on his feet, and he sees that there's no man on the island at all. He's alone on the island and all that is unusual, all that is frightening, is that where an hour before was an organized pile of sticks is a big hole. Nicolas limps across his bridge. He takes the time to tug the plywood board off the rocks. He tosses it as far as he can—not very—but the river takes it, spinning it along past the island.

Nicolas pushes his bike as fast as he's able along the narrow trail. Once he's on the main trail again, past the university, past the field where a softball game is on, he stops muttering, "I admit I'm powerless over alcohol and that my life has become unmanageable." He stops by a bench and cries. His mouth tastes as if full of gin.

The shorthand version of A.A.: become humble enough to believe that you will not always be able to take care of yourself without seeking help and become confident enough to know that you are capable of making good decisions. The serenity prayer: God grant me the serenity to accept the things I cannot change, the courage to change the things I can, and the wisdom to know the difference. Tom hopes Nicolas isn't hung over, though Nicolas sure looks it. For Nicolas to give up two months of sobriety would be a shame. Nicolas pours himself a cup of the coffee Tom brewed for the group and sits down a few rows in front of Tom. Nicolas has looked hung over the past several days, Tom notes. Nicolas worries the edge of his Styrofoam cup. Andrew speaks: "I don't have much to say except that I'm grateful not to be drunk today. I woke up from a bad drinking dream—" some in the room nod their heads— "and I was just so relieved that I hadn't picked up for real I decided to come down to a meeting." Andrew is thanked; Tom smiles. Tom wishes Nicolas would speak—he hasn't yet, even though Tom's been urging him to do so. Still, Nicolas is at the meeting, he's been at a meeting every day for two months, that's something. Tom approached Nicolas after Nicolas's first meeting. You can tell who wants to talk by who lingers. Tom gave Nicolas a list of numbers and names and a list of meetings and times. After some of the meetings, Tom, Andrew and Nicolas would go for coffee or breakfast. A woman wants to speak. She says, "I dropped the kids off at school this morning. All I wanted to do after that was go home and go back to bed. I got so angry in the car, so angry that I had to go to a meeting. I was so certain all the other parents were on their way to a job or back home to relax, have an easy breakfast, all worry-free. I really dug my nails into the palms of my hands, you know what I mean?" A few nods from the group. "I feel better now," she continues. "I feel as if I'm cooled down and now I'm glad I'm at a meeting, glad I made it. I know I'll feel better for the rest of the day."

And other little stories are told. The basement of St. Paul's is dark until the sun, released by a cloud break, shines in through stained glass. The whole room takes on a yellow and rose glow. The air is full of dust. The coffee urn chugs as someone pours a cup. Instead of folding chairs, the group sits in pews that once served the congregation upstairs. Tom wishes they were in a Protestant church instead of a Catholic church—Catholics don't believe in cushioned pews.

After the meeting Nicolas lingers. A good sign. Tom asks him for help cleaning up the coffee.

"You got coffee duty?" Nicolas says.

"You're up soon."

"I can't make a pot to save my life."

Tom says, "Are you okay? You look worse for wear."

Nicolas carefully lifts the hot filter from the top of the urn, drops it into a wastebasket. He says, "You had your breakfast yet?"

Tom shakes his head.

"I'll buy you a bagel."

Andrew is in the church parking lot, smoking. The three walk to a nearby bakery and sit outside at a little metal table. The sun is out and on them; the mornings are still chilly. Andrew sits and smokes while Tom and Nicolas get breakfast. Their coffees steam. Nicolas watches Andrew's cigarette for a moment, says, "Something really strange happened a few days ago." Andrew didn't want food; just coffee. Tom begins to unwrap his bagel; he does this methodically, tugging at the paper until he finds the final fold. He works as if unfolding a fragile road map. Nicolas tells Tom and Andrew about his experience on the island.

"Someone chased you?" Tom asks.

"I don't know anymore. The more I think about it, the less sure I am that I saw anyone. All I know is there was a big hole in the ground where there wasn't one before."

"Have you been back?"

"No."

"You really got scared."

"My mouth tasted like gin."

Tom nods, takes a bite of his bagel. "Are you thinking of going back?"

"Not really."

"Good. I don't think you should."

"You think I was in danger?"

"In danger of going to a bar, yeah."

"That's not what I mean."

"I know."

Nicolas drinks some coffee. He has a little more and takes a too-big bite from his bagel. He speaks with his mouth full: "I didn't go back but I sort of checked on the island yesterday."

"What does that mean?" Tom wipes the corners of his mouth with his napkin. Andrew listens, sips his coffee, starts another cigarette.

"I rode alongside I-90 east and took a look. I guess the snow-pack has really been melting fast because from the highway it looked as if most of the island was underwater. I could still see that little forest, though, so I knew I was looking at the right spot."

Andrew speaks: "Those trees are probably twenty years older than you. Maybe more. Maybe fifty years. They didn't sprout up when the drought started. I bet there've been times when the island was much bigger, too, when it wasn't an island. The rivers used to flood parts of downtown Missoula. Hard to imagine that happening now."

"Yeah."

Tom asks, "You been looking for work?"

"Not since Tuesday."

Andrew says, "I got a little yard work I could use a hand on. I'd be happy to put a little cash in your pocket."

"You don't have to pay me to help you with a little yard work."

Tom cuts in, "When Andrew says 'a little yard work' he means major landscaping."

"Still." Nicolas finishes off his bagel. "Okay." Nicolas asks, "What do you think about what happened?"

Tom says, "I would have been scared shitless too. Maybe you had some kind of hallucination. Maybe you over-exercised."

"Not likely." Nicolas pats his gut. "Look, I can write off the man, too, but what do you make of the hole?"

Tom pushes his bagel aside. Andrew has a sip of coffee, coughs and says, "You probably dislodged something when you knocked apart that pile of sticks. While you were away, the river water did the rest." Andrew exhales a silver smoke-cloud. "Montana's funny. There's a lot underground out here. That's why men came out here—to dig. They left all kinds of holes all over. Ever see the Berkeley Pit? Some of the towns out here are riddled with underground passageways. To keep people warm, to keep the Chinese out of sight, for men to sneak to bars and brothels without their wives seeing. And then… where there's mountains there's caves, I guess. With all the tectonic crashing and what-not, ice ages, glaciers. There are worlds underground out here."

Behind the refrigerator in Nicolas's kitchen, a small hole in the cement floor opens up, no larger than a tea-saucer. Nicolas is shaving. He turns on the faucet at the moment the cement in his kitchen collapses, so he does not hear the little wet noise it makes.

Nicolas's former girlfriend Rachel helped Nicolas get sober. Once he'd gone a day without drinking she thought their lives would become normal, that they would go to parties with their old friends and go out on the weekends and all that would be different would be the sparkling water in Nicolas's wine glass. This, of course, couldn't be true: for Nicolas, a walk to the post office was a difficult prospect without a little alcohol to make him who he was. Nicolas broke up with Rachel on his third day of sobriety. He did so as abruptly as possible. He didn't care to have back the clothes and books he had at her place. When those items appeared in an anonymous box in front of his apartment, he resealed the box and dropped it off at Goodwill. Good riddance. The dollars left in pants pockets, the receipts from liquor stores, the angry-sad note from Rachel asking Nicolas to at least explain why he was breaking up with her. She'd dealt with his "problem" for so long, she thought she, "at least deserved an explanation." Nicolas himself didn't know. During those first days, he wasn't convinced he was an alcoholic. He wasn't sure he'd ever go back to another A.A. meeting or that he wouldn't go out and get blind with gin later that night, in the evening, ten minutes from where he stood. He'd risen from a beautiful dream: Rachel's freckled face, red hair. Eyelashes tumbled-down on her cheeks, five lashes, six black lashes. Nicolas put a finger to her cheeks and brushed each lash away, I love you lash, I love you, I love you lash, I love you and Rachel embraced him. He didn't dream of Rachel as often as he dreamed of drinking. The drinking dreams were more real. He woke up with a hangover. He woke up afraid that he'd had a drink. He woke up and cried.

Nicolas works in the morning scraping paint with Andrew. Nicolas likes to work with Andrew because Andrew doesn't talk much. Andrew is older by a decade than Tom and Nicolas. He's been sober for twelve years. He likes to say, "I smoke to stay healthy." Rain spits and sputters for a little while; Nicolas and Andrew keep working. Andrew hopes to put a coat of primer on his shed before evening. Clouds open up and Nicolas and Andrew run into Andrew's house for cover. The rain hasn't let up by the time they've put away a six-pack of cola, so Andrew gives Nicolas a ride home. "You want your cash?" Andrew asks. Nicolas wishes he could say no but he knows he can't so he nods.

When he gets back to his apartment he discovers an inch of water on the kitchen floor. He calls the landlord and passes half an hour picking up his apartment—finding higher ground for his books, emptying the floor of his closet, taking boxes out from under his bed. He finds, a moment before his landlord knocks on the door, three small bottles of vodka stashed in a shoebox. The landlord knocks; Nicolas stuffs the vodka into his pockets.

The landlord tosses a yellow slicker on the floor of Nicolas's living room and plants two muddy boot prints beside it. "I'll have someone come in and clean up later," the landlord says, a wave of his hand in the general area where he intends to walk with his muddy boots. Nicolas mutters a "sure" and glances at the permanent black streaks his landlord left on the living room wall the last time he came in to do some emergency repair. The landlord sloshes around Nicolas's kitchen: swirls of mud from his boots. Nicolas fingers the vodka bottles in his pockets. He's sure the landlord notices his misshapen pockets and he's just as sure the landlord knows what's in his pockets, even, what kind of liquor. Nicolas almost says something like, "I didn't know I had them," when the landlord says, "This isn't coming from a bad seal in the window or the wall—" the landlord peeps out the ground level window— "This is coming from under the apartment."

"I don't understand."

"I don't understand either since *this* is supposed to be the basement." The landlord grips the refrigerator plug. "Anything perishable?" Before Nicolas can say yes the landlord yanks the plug from the wall. "Don't want to get 'lectrocuted. Give me a hand." Nicolas steps into the pond in the kitchen and the two men pull the refrigerator away from the wall. The landlord says, "Shit."

"What?"

"I don't know how this can be."

"What?" Nicolas touches the vodka bottles and starts to sweat, wonders if he'd stashed other bottles behind the refrigerator during the same blackout he'd stocked his old shoeboxes.

"There's a hole in the floor. Did you notice that before?"

"No." The landlord's eyes drift over Nicolas's pockets. "No. I cleaned back there last week." And Nicolas remembers that that's true, he did clean behind the refrigerator, he would've already found any stashed bottles.

"Hold on," the landlord says. Nicolas stands still, water soaking into his shoes.

The landlord dips a cheap, wooden yard stick down into the hole. "Deeper... shit," the landlord mutters. He opens his toolbox and takes out a lead bob. He ties it to a coil of fishing wire and drops it into the hole. "Jesus," the landlord says. "I don't know exactly how much coil was left but that's, that's at least twenty feet. There's gotta be a sub-basement in this building I never knew about." For a moment the landlord is excited, thinks he's got a whole extra floor he can make into apartments or at least to rent out as storage. "Damn," he says. "I'm gonna have to pump." The landlord grabs his toolbox and yard stick and heads out of the apartment.

Nicolas imagines dumping the vodka into the hole, but he isn't sure the little bottles will sink. He imagines drinking the three little bottles in rapid succession. The landlord reappears in the hall outside Nicolas's apartment. He says, "Forgot my slicker!" Nicolas nods, grins, rolls the little bottles in his pockets.

Ten minutes, more, pass before Nicolas realizes he should have insisted the landlord put him up in a hotel until the problem is solved. Nicolas considers using the cash he earned today for a room, decides instead to go out for a bite—he remembers, "hungry, angry, lonely, tired"—and decides to take care of hungry with the money he earned. On his way, he tosses the three bottles of vodka into a dumpster behind an ice cream shop.

Rain makes rapids of the street gutters, whirlpools of drains; rain blasts from breaks in the gutter around the roof of the all-night diner. Nicolas orders a lumberjack special; comfort food. An arm of the Clark Fork runs beneath the diner, runs under Broadway and Front, connects with the Clark Fork near a footbridge that once carried freight cars. Up the river, the island (as Nicolas calls it) is completely under water, its coppice of trees now growing from a river bed. The sticks Nicolas broke apart have washed away, his plywood bridge is lodged half a mile down river, underneath the Orange Street bridge. The rivers haven't been this high in ten years, and with winter snow-pack still breaking up, the river will only rise higher. In the mountains, it's snowing.

Since the rain doesn't let up during Nicolas's dinner, he assumes the water on the floor of his apartment will have risen. When he steps into his apartment he sees that the opposite is true. The kitchen floor is dry. The hole in the floor has grown slightly bigger—the size of a dessert plate. Nicolas plugs in his refrigerator. The refrigerator rattles and concrete pebbles break free from the edge of the hole. Nicolas aurally follows the pebbles as they fall. They hit a shallow pool of water far below. He knows the landlord couldn't have pumped out the sub-basement in the time Nicolas was out. A small deep hum comes from the hole—air from beneath. The hum lets up, starts up again. Nicolas lays on the floor and with a flashlight peers into the hole. The space below is more like a cave than a sub-basement; Nicolas remembers, *There are worlds underground out here*, and thinks of the island, re-experiences a little slice of the fear he felt that afternoon. He doesn't want to push the refrigerator over the hole, because he doesn't want the damn thing to fall through. He clears off a near-bare cupboard shelf, takes out the shelf and lays it across the hole. "That's better," he thinks, because at least he can't see the problem. "And it can't *moan* anymore," he says.

Nicolas can't think of anything else to do but go to bed. He takes two Tylenol PM and begins to brush his teeth.

He steps out of the bathroom. A shape at the corner of his eye.

From the threshold of the bathroom, Nicolas can see into his kitchen.

A shape steps from behind the refrigerator. A man except—

Rather than a face a ragged mouth opened so wide the lower lip is the chin the upper lip is the top of the head and where there would be teeth is rot, where a tongue would protrude is rot, black rot, swarming rot. From this mouth a low hum, a rattling throat. The man takes a step forward—his foot falls on the plank that covers the hole in the floor. Nicolas bolts for the front door and the man takes another step forward. Nicolas, in the hall outside his apartment, his hand still on the doorknob, turns for a glance at the man's progress and the man is almost at the door, stride huge— "Blessed virgin mother!" Nicolas shouts; he slams the door shut, and says, over and over, "…could restore us to sanity, could restore us to sanity." He notices he's still holding the doorknob when he feels it turn under his hand and he's free, out the back of his building, into the pouring rain. He runs for a few blocks, can hardly breathe in the rain, seeks cover under the eaves of the closed ice cream shop.

Nicolas thinks, "Where do I go?" and thinks, "There are three unopened bottles of vodka in a dumpster behind this building." He steps into the rain, walks around to the back of the building, and stands in front of the dumpster. He puts his hands in his pockets—*cellphone*.

"Tom," he says, "I just ran out of my apartment because there's a man in my kitchen—" he pictures the non-face a moment, pushes the image from his mind— "and I'm standing in front of a dumpster where I threw three mini-bottles of vodka earlier this evening and I'm very, very close to just climbing in and getting them just to help calm my nerves."

"So why don't you?" Tom says.

"What?"

"What's stopping you?"

"Well Jesus I thought you were going to stop me but—" Nicolas relaxes; slightly. "I don't want to get drunk," he says.

"Hold on a second." Nicolas hears Tom shuffle through some papers. "It's nine, isn't it? You've missed the last meeting. You say there's a man in your apartment?"

"Yeah."

"Are you safe?"

"From the man?"

Tom laughs. "You want to meet me at the police station?"

"Jesus, really? No. No, I don't. You think I should? No, I can't. That's too much. But—"

"I can get a cup of coffee with you. I can be downtown in fifteen minutes."

Tension pours from Nicolas's body like water. In the coffee shop, with Tom, Nicolas tells Tom he's sure the man was just a hallucination. Tom isn't convinced; before Tom and Nicolas are finished with a cup of coffee, Tom convinces Nicolas to go to the police station—"I hate the police," Nicolas says. An officer drives over to Nicolas's apartment building, where Tom and Nicolas are waiting to let him in. The three go into the building, and into Nicolas's apartment.

The kitchen floor is covered with an inch of water. The board Nicolas put over the hole is floating near the kitchen threshold. "What's this?" the officer asks.

Nicolas can't make sense of the water, but only says, "Part of my kitchen floor collapsed. I guess there's a sub-basement underneath that's filled up with water."

"You probably don't want to stay here tonight," the officer says.

"I hadn't thought—"

"Good. Did you call your landlord?"

"I did."

"And what did he say he was going to do?"

"Pump out the water."

"Unless he has his own pump that's not going to happen anytime soon. There's flooding all over the area. He won't be able to rent a pump until the rain stops." The police officer steps into the kitchen and idly peers into the hole, now shoulder-wide. "What the?" The officer shines his light onto the hole; the water reflects the light back. The officer angles the light a little, crouches and leans close to the hole.

Nicolas backs away from the kitchen, walks backward toward the apartment door.

Tom asks, "What's there?"

The officer stands and steps away from the hole. "Nothing. For a moment I thought I saw something. I might've." The officer chuckles and says to Nicolas, whose eyes are wide and frantic: "Sir, you might want to drop a line down there and see if you can't catch a trout!" Tom says, "Really?" The officer says, "I might've seen a fish down there. Not impossible." The officer shuts off his flashlight. "You got a big problem here, but it looks as if your intruder's gone, so I'll be on my way."

Tom says to Nicolas, "Did the landlord tell you he'd pay for a hotel?"

"No. I thought about it after. I had the vodka in my pocket."

Tom nods. "Sleep on my couch tonight. We'll go to a morning meeting together. You've had a bad day. Call your landlord in the morning and tell him he has to pay for a hotel until he's got your place livable."

"Should I mention the man?"

"If you want to. But—" Tom looks around the apartment. "What man?"

Nicolas puts clothes, toiletries and the Big Book into a duffle.

When the officer came into the apartment, the officer pushed the door wide open. The door remained open as they stood in Nicolas's apartment. The officer left the door open when he left. Tom and Nicolas closed the door after themselves as they left. No one touched or saw the *inside* doorknob. So no one saw, stuck to the inside doorknob, the flecks of black, putrid skin, cells water-heavy to the point of bursting.

Rachel and I met at the base of Waterworks Hill, Nicolas recalls, awake on Tom's sofa. I hadn't had a drink yet that day; I knew after our walk I'd take her out for lunch, maybe to the Old Post where they have an afternoon lunch special, AKA cheap beer. This was summer, and Rachel was wearing little khaki shorts and a white blouse, like a hiker bought out of L.L. Bean, except better looking, busty, long legs. Her socks, expensive socks designed to wick away sweat (she told me all about the socks), were folded neatly above her hiking shoes. Her red ponytail stuck out the back of her white baseball cap. And the freckles! Lord they were everywhere (I knew, everywhere). We walked a short incline, then followed a path left, that led us along a ridge overlooking downtown Missoula. The air was dusty white, the sky pale.

"What's that dome?" I asked Rachel.

"That's a cistern, that's where the water comes from, that's why this is Waterworks Hill."

She was fast outpacing me; I enjoyed having her in front of me. After lunch, we could pick up a few cans of beer and go see a movie.

She said, "They don't need a water tower because of the hill."

Grasshoppers clicked into the air.

"Come on," she said, and laughed at me for being slow. The grasshoppers looked like orange moths when they jumped. They vanished by camouflage when they landed in the dry grass. I'd seen the valley from Mt. Sentinel and Jumbo. The view from the side of Waterworks wasn't as impressive but better somehow. Not as distant. The downtown looked nice, kept after and brick, but outside the downtown, alongside I-90 and beyond looked desolate, dry. The sun was high and I was sweating hard: the band around my waist soaked, my chest and back soaked, my hair. Drops of sweat fell onto the inside of my sunglasses.

At a broken split-rail fence we made a right turn up the hill—it didn't look too bad but was very steep. I put my hand to Rachel's butt once, and she squeaked, but soon she was out of reach. I kept hoping she'd stop for a moment. I stopped, let her gain more ground.

We passed a little pine, which I thought would make a perfect Christmas tree, and a power shed. The ground leveled and Rachel stopped. On our right was rich green valley. If I looked in just the right direction, all I could see was green and mountains.

"Thank you," I said. "This was worth the climb."

Rachel laughed—a bright bird laugh that put me at ease. "We're going past the peace sign." She pointed uphill. "There used to be a peace sign. Now there are just stones. There used to be a reflector for the phone company up there, and people would spray a big peace sign on it. The phone company kept washing it off and people would spray on another. When the phone company didn't need the reflector anymore, there were a lot of us who didn't want it taken down."

The whole effort sounded stupid to me, but I didn't say so.

On the other side of a valley, horses grazed. Little blue birds flitted low to the ground, keeping ahead of us as we walked toward the former peace sign.

"There's no one up here at all," I said.

"No one hikes here this late in the morning. Too hot."

"So you're just crazy then?"

"Sure," she said, and I loved that answer.

On our way down she pointed to ridges in the side of the hill. She said, "Those were shore lines. Missoula was once a glacial lake—the valley enclosed by great walls of ice." She waved her hand in the direction of the downtown. "That was the bottom of a very deep lake."

A single jet dragged its cloud-line across the sky. I loved Rachel for what she knew and I loved her for how great she looked. I was lucky and I knew it and I was afraid one day she'd know it too and leave me. My brain should have been working overtime to figure out how to get her into bed before lunch, but all the way down to where I'd parked my car all I kept figuring was how soon I'd be able to get myself a beer and how long it'd been since I'd last had one.

A pattern of light, sliced by Venetian blinds, travels along Tom's living room wall. Nicolas follows the light. He's erect, remembering the way sweat had collected among the invisible little hairs between Rachel's breasts, beneath her nose.

The heat from that remembered summer morning nearly drowsed Nicolas to sleep. The white sun-glare, which filled his mind's eye, made it hard to keep his eyes open. From the edges of the glare infringed a tattered black ring, and then the whole of the image was black and cold and Nicolas saw the man's face again, his non-face, the putrid open mouth. Nicolas, wide awake, replayed his first visit to the island. Counted each trip he'd made to the spot on I-90 where he could see the island at a presumably safe distance. He would go to I-90 right after meetings and sometimes later in the day. Each time he went, the river had risen a little higher.

Just after five in the morning the rain stops.

Tom and Nicolas go to an eight o'clock meeting. Toward the tail end of the meeting, Nicolas speaks to the group. "…I just want to say that what makes staying sober hard for me is fear. I guess I was afraid before and that's why I drank, so I didn't have to be afraid. Everything I do sober is new. A couple days ago I froze up in the supermarket [he doesn't mention that he thought he saw a man like a shadow run from one end of the market to the other], I didn't even buy what I'd come to get—all I needed were eggs. I had to work up the nerve and go back later. I worry that people can tell I'm an alcoholic, that I'm not walking like everyone else or I'm saying something wrong. All this fear. It doesn't help they took my license. I feel like an asshole riding everywhere on a bicycle. It doesn't help that I can't remember what I did for large parts of the last nine years—people might know me and I wouldn't know them, and they'd know me as a drinker. Sometimes people wave [a shadow-figure beckoned, the shadow-figure stood next to a tree with a great hole in its trunk and the shadow-figure waved]. I just pretend I didn't see them. On top of being afraid that people think I'm a jerk, I'm afraid I'll pick up again…"

After the meeting, Andrew, Tom and Nicolas go for breakfast. Tom says he's buying, because Nicolas finally spoke. Andrew asks, "You free to come over and help with the shed? Shingles might be dry enough to finish removing the paint." Nicolas agrees and Nicolas is glad neither Tom or Andrew question what he said at the meeting. For a time, Nicolas feels relaxed.

Andrew tells Nicolas that the supplies are in the shed. Andrew heads into his house for a fresh pack of cigarettes: "I'll be right out," he says. Nicolas crosses the sodden backyard and opens the shed. He pulls the light-string hanging from the uncovered bulb. In the back corner of the shed are carefully stacked paint cans, primer, paint-stripper, folded tarps and the putty knives Nicolas and Andrew had been using. On the floor, in front of the paint supplies, are six planks of wood, all varying widths and lengths—scraps from past projects. Instead of a stack, the planks are laid on the ground side-by-side, which Nicolas thinks is a little odd until he gets closer and realizes the planks are covering a hole in the cement floor.

"Christ," he mutters. He backs away.

"What's the matter?" Andrew asks. Nicolas looks over his shoulder, sees Andrew in the doorway.

"What're the planks for?"

"A rotted patch of cement caved in. I guess all the rain soaked the ground beneath. You wouldn't believe it, though, how deep it is. My guess is there was a septic tank here, or a well."

"There's a hole like that in my kitchen."

"Shit, that's terrible."

Nicolas stops a moment, sure one of the planks is vibrating a bit. "Those're like, those're like the sticks I found on the island," he says.

Andrew slaps Nicolas on the back, pulls on his cigarette. "There's nothing to be afraid of here."

Nicolas looks at Andrew, at the glowing coal of Andrew's cigarette. Andrew's hair is thin and unwashed. He's missing one of his front teeth and his other front tooth is bright yellow. Nicolas sees Andrew's face as a kind face. Andrew's eyes are sunken, surrounded by soft wrinkles. He isn't old, just about forty, but he looks older. Nicolas can see clearly the shape of Andrew's skull. He sees the flesh rot from Andrew's face, Andrew's eyes sink and shrivel, Andrew's lips pull back high over blackening gums. "I can't work today," Nicolas says. The planks tremble: a wind underground. "I need to go."

Andrew nods, says, "There'll be work here for you should you change your mind."

Nicolas is grateful and leaves. The sun is high. Nicolas can't think where to go. He spends the day in the Southgate plaza, watching teenagers shop and talk in groups. Young girls and boys, petulant, ignorant, thrillingly unhappy. He eats pizza for lunch and for dinner. He checks into a motel near his apartment and falls asleep with the lights on, the television on. He falls asleep with the taste of gin vivid in his memory.

Late April in Missoula: chance of hail and snow; mountain snow-pack breaks up and fills the river; black flies cloud the air. The sky remains bright late. By July, it'll be light till ten at night. By July, the drought will've shown itself again. Shining just below the surface of the Clark Fork, visible from the Higgins Street bridge, a shopping cart. Fly fishermen will stand between the Madison Street Bridge and the footbridge, casting line. Boys and girls will spend all day floating down the river on oversized inner-tubes.

Lumber trucks rumble past Nicolas's hotel. Nicolas wakes and feels the cotton-dry of a hangover. For the third morning in a row. He wakes fully and knows he didn't touch a drop of alcohol, except for the little bit of mouth wash he absent-mindedly rinsed with the previous morning. The patterns in the textured ceiling are familiar. The carpet is red. He turns off the television. At the edges of the window, where the curtains don't quite reach, are pale blue bands of light. Check-out time is eleven. The clock: 9:32. "This morning," he thinks, "I'll go home." He thought the same the first morning he woke here and again the same the second morning. A mass of take-out boxes and empty soda cups line the dresser. He hasn't been to a meeting since he went with Tom. Three days ago. Three days ago.

Before he got sober, he cured hangovers with a bloody Mary, or something made with V-8, or with Red Bull. "It's not a real hangover," he says. As if this matters.

The little taste of alcohol he'd had when he'd rinsed with the mouthwash had nearly set him off. "I can't just have a little alcohol." He thinks about the vodka he threw away, "what a waste." He's thought about the vodka often: hundreds of times, thousands. How often does he blink? His cellphone is on the dresser, dead. He doesn't have a charger. There's a phone by the bed, of course, but he doesn't want to call anyone. He stares at the ceiling. The beat of the blood in his temples is a hard, dull beat, a knock on a tree stump. The clock: 10:47. Since spitting the mouth wash into the sink three days ago his mind has been going crazy, a rush of words and black holes, bottles and black hole faces.

He's slept in his clothes for three nights. He doesn't know where he left his duffel. It could be in the room, for all he knows. "All right, all right, I'm going," he says and swings himself off the bed. Before leaving the motel room he slips into the bathroom and drinks the rest of the mouthwash.

Nicolas crosses the street and buys a bottle of gin. As he leaves the casino, he spots his girlfriend's car in the parking lot. He doesn't want her to see him with the brown bag under his arm. In the bright sun there's really no way to hide, but he runs around to the back of the casino, climbs over a chain-link fence and up a grassy slope, crosses train tracks, then follows I-90 east. There's no logic.

He decides to kill the bottle on I-90, overlooking the spot of the river where the island was submerged, but when he finally gets to his lookout, he sees that the river has receded quite a bit, that the island is nearly completely exposed. This drains even the will to drink from Nicolas—for an instant. He considers calling Tom after all. A pat down of his pockets reveals no cellphone. He remembers that the charge had gone out of it anyway. He walks down the highway ramp, brown paper bag tucked under his arm. With every step the rolling weight of the bottle cries its soothing siren call and with every step Nicolas attempts to ignore the call, one more step, another. He crosses Broadway and the footbridge, walks the Kim Williams trail until he spies the little path that runs alongside the river.

The path is slick. Nicolas soaks himself as he brushes against bushes and tree branches.

"I can't think this through, I can't take this slow," Nicolas thinks. "I can't take a drink, I'm powerless against alcohol," he thinks and he says, "My life has become unmanageable," and, "restore me to sanity." A branch whips his face.

He doesn't hesitate at the dip in the trail, plunges down and nearly falls on his ass. He drops the bottle and panics until he determines that the bottle didn't break. He leaves the brown bag on the ground. Nicolas mutters, "This clear liquid in this clear glass bottle is more refreshing than water more cleansing more clear and cool." Nicolas knows this is a lie and resists for as long as another step, and another.

Where he'd made his plywood bridge is now too wide for that, and the plywood is gone besides. Nicolas steps into the water. First he doesn't feel the cold, then the water shocks his ankles—deeper, his calves. "A little drink would warm you up," he thinks.

Across from where Nicolas stands is the eddy, where the sneakers are caught. To his left, the grassy spine, the rotten tree the raven had called from and the coppice of pine trees. All this is sodden and slimy. The log lies a few feet from Nicolas. And built against the log is a low lean-to, "The same low lean-to," Nicolas thinks. "Impossible," Nicolas thinks.

"Not impossible," he says aloud. "Anyone could have put that together. From the same sticks."

Nicolas dares himself not to open the bottle of gin.

Nicolas dares himself to take apart the low lean-to as he'd done before. He approaches the structure, "a pile of twigs," hesitates a moment and kicks down, hard. The sticks snap apart, scatter. There is no great hole beneath. A patch of wet, bald earth.

"Nothing!" Nicolas shouts.

He walks—staggers a bit, as if drunk—toward the little forest. He thinks about what to do with the bottle. "Give it to the sneaker-god," he says. "Toss it up onto the dead tree," he thinks. Behind him, he hears the sound of earth moving, wet dirt being pushed aside. Nicolas turns around. His face expresses a sense of inevitability. "Here comes," he says. The sun is afternoon high. Hardly a cloud crosses the sky. I-90 is busy. People are jogging and walking the Kim Williams trail. From Mt. Sentinel, a person could easily see Nicolas and the shadow-figure.

Nicolas faces the man with the wide-open mouth. A mouth like a rotten hole in a tree-stump, like a sink-hole. It is not a man at all, but something that has been buried a long time. Its body is man-shaped but a shimmering shadow figure lost sometimes in the bright sun reflected off the river. Its mouth is huge and working, twitching at the edges and rotten tongue squirming like an ebon baby snake. Behind the shadow-figure, from the hole it made as it climbed from earth, are gurgling sounds. Birthing sounds. The sealed bottle of gin in Nicolas's hand feels heavier than it possibly could.

They Look Like Little Girls

The Greyhound bus slowed to 50 mph somewhere between Spokane and Missoula. There wasn't much traffic on I-90, just trucks; their headlights emerged from the black curve of the horizon and then blew past, rocking the bus, spraying the bus with gravel. And so, each time a truck passed, the thirteen year-old girl (Kallista) woke. She was glad, though; when she dozed, she picked up the thread of the same bad dream. She'd been traveling for ten hours and it was much later than her accustomed bedtime (9 PM on school nights). She tried to read to stay awake, but she was so tired the book'd become all a jumble, one line twisting round the next.

The bus chug-chugged, jerked everyone forward and back.

The grad student (Genevieve) was undisturbed by the bus's turbulence because she'd gulped down two Lortabs with a slosh of scotch just before she'd got on the bus. She'd be washed-out when she woke up, she knew, but she couldn't face the ride and she hated chit-chat. Each time she drifted out of her blackout, into actual sleep, she ventured a little further along the course of her own bad dream.

The factory worker (Hammond), tired, longing for a smoke, was upright in his seat, rigid, stretched taut as if sprung, not eager to get off the bus but damned if the bus was going to make him late for his first day at the next factory, another lumber job; nicks on his face from wood chips shot through the air, sawdust in his lungs, sap and grease on his hands—one factory job to another, the next. He'd fallen asleep almost as soon as he'd boarded the bus just outside of Spokane, but had slept no more than an hour. He'd jolted awake and *wouldn't* go back to sleep.

The recently retired history professor (Walter) was also wide awake. He sat with his back to the window, a thick knit cap between his head and the plastic window pane, and looked at Genevieve asleep in the seat across from him. For the past hour, he'd had two seats to himself, as did Genevieve, as did, he guessed, anyone still on the bus—in Spokane, most everyone got off. Only a few of us, he thought, are going on to the great cities of Montana. He'd attempted to make a sketch of Genevieve, but his eyesight wasn't very good and the light on the bus was dreadful—hard, flat white, grainy as if sand had been tossed into the air. He didn't presume to have intentions on the sleeping student, though imagined various conversations they might have.

The over-weight and over-friendly driver that had picked them all up, had been replaced in Spokane by another, a tall man whose cap cast his face in shadow. He spoke, for the first time, in a flat voice, low like the hum of the bus itself, but each word that tone carried was clear: "The bus is experiencing mechanical trouble. We will stop in Mullen, where another bus has been sent to take you to your final destination." After a pause of a minute or more the driver added, "We at Greyhound are sorry for any inconvenience this may cause. Thank you for choosing to travel Greyhound."

"As if we had a choice," Walter muttered. He looked back at Genevieve, and jumped a little—seated next to her was a figure, sitting upright in the aisle seat, and though the figure should have obscured Genevieve at least partially, it didn't, quite—and then there was no figure—a trick of the poor light, a hallucination brought on by simple exhaustion. In spite of Walter's reasonable dismissals, he was much disturbed anyhow: the figure was like the figure that had occupied the nightmare he'd had when he'd first boarded the bus.

The Mullen station was hardly a station at all—more of an enclosed shed with benches and a ticket window. The driver held the station door open for Genevieve, Walter and Kallista; Hammond remained outside for a cigarette.

Kallista stood by Genevieve in the middle of the station. The station was cold—Kallista wished there was someone she could lean up against. She'd gravitated toward Genevieve because she was another girl, but Genevieve was asleep on her feet. The front door opened, and Hammond stepped inside, hands crammed into his jacket pockets.

The driver unlocked the ticket booth, went inside and was immediately on the phone. Genevieve, in a thick voice that startled Kallista, said, "I'm freezing." Hammond pointed to three unplugged electric heaters, huddled together in a corner. Hammond plugged in the heaters and they shook to life. Kallista let her body relax, though the station was no warmer. Walter said, "Why don't we bring those closer to the benches"—of which there were two. Without any help, Hammond moved the awkward and obviously heavy heaters, one at a time, so they made a triangle around the benches—two behind the girls, one behind Walter. Kallista sat next to Genevieve and introduced herself. Genevieve grimaced—meant as a smile?—then tilted her head back and shut her eyes.

The driver stepped out of the ticket booth. He stood under a blinking fluorescent bulb; this light obscured rather than made clear: "Another bus will be along in an hour. We at Greyhound are sorry for any inconvenience this may cause. Thank you for choosing to travel Greyhound."

Walter said, "This is outrageous."

Genevieve said, "It happens."

Walter quieted.

Hammond said, "I agree with him," but only Kallista heard him speak.

Kallista watched the driver walk across the station and step out into the night. As the glass door closed, his back shimmered; light on the glass, Kallista figured. When the bus started up, everyone looked at each other. Walter leapt up when they heard the bus roll away from the station.

Walter said, "Son of a bitch." Kallista giggled. Walter said, "He's just going to leave us here?"

Hammond said, "He's just going to limp it to a garage." Walter looked at Genevieve—she stared blankly ahead. Kallista felt suddenly very nervous. She said, "I'm Kallista. I'm going to live with my grandmother in Bonner."

"Bonner," Hammond said. He smiled in a way that put Kallista at ease. "I'm going to a new job in Bonner. A pleasure to meet you." He put out his hand and Kallista took it. She turned her head down and away. Hammond said, "I'm Hammond. Are you warm enough?" Kallista nodded. Genevieve said, "I'm fucking freezing." Hammond gave her a stern look and glanced at Kallista. Genevieve shrugged. Walter grinned and said, "These heaters aren't doing much good. But they are warm. The way they're circled around us, we should be fine for the hour."

They sat facing each other, Hammond and Walter on one bench, Kallista and Genevieve on the other. The three heaters, as tall as men, stood around them, coils glowing orange, casting little heat. When the wind picked up outside, a draft cut through the station. After a few minutes of silence, Kallista said:

"I had a bad dream on the bus."

Everyone looked at Kallista.

Hammond bit his lower lip.

Walter said, "The bus was uncomfortable and noisy. It's no surprise you had a nightmare." He thought he was being kind; he looked to Genevieve for approval. Genevieve offered Walter no approval, nor any sign of interest in what Kallista had said.

Kallista's Bad Dream
began in the girl's locker room at the city pool. She had been dropped off by her mother for her weekly swimming lesson. She changed swiftly. She could hear other girls' voices, but couldn't see the girls. The showers were running. The locker room floor was carpeted with hard, gray industrial carpeting, which Kallista believed was teeming with fungus and bacteria. She wore bath sandals, but with open toes and no back, they seemed feeble protection.

The air in the locker room was gray like the carpet. And miserably damp. Light twisted and turned through steam from the showers (they must all have been on, they must all have been at their hottest). Kallista closed her locker door and jumped: a girl—an older girl—had been concealed from Kallista by the locker door. The older girl was naked. The older girl stared at Kallista. Around the older girl's eyes were dark circles of runny mascara. Kallista wasn't allowed to wear make-up, and why would she want to, she thought, if it would make her look so awful. The older girl seemed in no hurry to dress. No clothes were set out, no wet suit across the bench. Kallista turned away—not too quickly, she hoped—and took a step toward the dim exit sign. Another girl, another older girl, strode past Kallista. She was also naked—no towel, no slippers. This older girl's hair was stringy, clumped together by damp. The showers stopped. The voices grew louder. Kallista walked quickly to the locker room door.

The pool room was empty. Kallista went right into the water, where she felt comfortable. She was a strong swimmer and the water was cool. She knew she should wait for the instructors to come before going into the pool—the buddy system had been drilled into her since the first swim lessons she'd ever taken—but she was calm now, the spell the locker room had cast, broken.

Kallista began laps, swimming a steady crawl from one end of the Olympic pool to the other.

In the middle of a lap, she looked down to the bottom of the pool, and saw a boy on the floor.

Light rippled like white tiger stripes around the boy. Kallista tread water, gazed down and for an awful moment she thought he was dead. He grinned then, and began to float up toward her. This wasn't one of the boys from her class—she kicked hard, to get out of his way, to get to the edge of the pool.

The boy's hand clasped Kallista's ankle for a hot second.

She kicked free, swam, the boy behind her—how had she not seen him before, why hadn't she worn her goggles, where were her instructors, she couldn't breathe—she reached the ladder and pulled herself up. The boy stopped a few feet from the edge of the pool, treading water. He looked as if he had a wet paper towel over his face, his skin rippled and translucent.

Kallista asked, "Why did you chase me?"

Kallista felt a hand on her shoulder and a warm breath at her ear. Older girls, some in bathing caps, some with goggles, otherwise naked, all of them naked, emerged from the shadows of the pool room. Dozens of girls, not all older than Kallista, some much younger, practically babies with water wings on their arms.

Kallista looked frantically for the instructors—she shouted their names—"Julie!" and "Mark!"

The girls pressed forward—Kallista felt their bodies press against her own. She tried—ridiculously—to reason with them—"There's a boy, he chased me"—but she was pushed to the lip of the pool and over, into the water, where the boy took hold of her suit and pulled at it, pulled her under.

Kallista was free for a moment. She'd squirmed out of her suit, and she surged forward, but the girls fell into the water, their bodies crashing down around and on top of her—

Kallista opened her mouth, and took in a great gulp of water.

Something bumped against one of the glass doors of the bus shelter. Hammond couldn't tell which. He got up and went to the front door. A single floodlight, set above the door, illuminated a small stretch of dirt surrounded by woods. Wind whipped the trees in tight circles. He crossed the room to the front door. He could see a short stretch of the road that led back to I-90 and more trees. The station was deep in the forest. Why would anyone ever come here, he thought.

He turned to the group and said, "It's really cold outside our little circle." He meant to make the group feel cozy, to make some part of the station seem appealing. The door behind him banged and he jumped a little—not enough so the others would notice, he hoped. When Hammond turned he caught a glimpse of what looked to him like a large dog before it vanished into the dark.

The door couldn't be pushed open, it opened out, but still, Hammond clicked the silver dead bolt in place and pushed at the door to be sure it was locked.

"What was that?" Walter asked.

"A dog," Hammond said. Hammond crossed the room to the other door and locked it, too.

"Why are you doing that?" Walter asked.

Hammond didn't answer, just began to walk along the perimeter of the room, poking at vents and testing windows.

Walter said, "I said, why—" but there was another bang, this time at the back door, and Walter's question fizzled.

The windows in the station were high—Hammond could just peer out if he stood on his toes—and the only other door was the door to the ticket booth, which was locked—he checked. He returned to the circle. The weak heat hardly took the chill off. He wanted a cigarette, but he wasn't going to go outside.

Kallista asked, "Is there just one dog out there?" The front door banged.

Hammond said, "I think so—" The back door banged— "Or two. But they can't get in."

Genevieve said, "The doors are glass."

Hammond said, "Shatterproof, I guess. They're strong. I'm sure."

"And why would we be afraid of dogs, anyhow?" Genevieve said.

Kallista said, "I'm afraid of dogs."

Genevieve said, "Don't be stupid."

Hammond said, "Come here, Kallista." She came over and sat next to Hammond. Walter shifted to the end of the bench, stood. Hammond said, "I don't like those dogs either. They walk funny." Genevieve showed interest for the first time all night. "But," he added, "we're inside and they're outside. And the bus will be along soon." He looked at his watch. "In a little over a half hour." In the wind, the station's joints moaned. Genevieve said, "I'm freezing, are any of you freezing?" Walter nodded, crossed his arms over his chest. Hammond said, "Everyone is cold."

Hammond's Bad Dream
was set inside a factory. Hammond worked at a conveyor unlike any he'd ever worked at before—the whole factory was like the idea of a factory—a grim factory that had as its purpose nothing but providing men with dangerous

work. He was surrounded by gray machines, all casting heat and generating asynchronous noises, like clinkers in a furnace, like gears whose teeth no longer truly meshed. He could see no other men from where he stood, but heard them: curses, shouts (of instruction, of pain). On a gangplank, which ran from one end of the factory to the other, splitting the building in half, paced Hammond's supervisor. Hammond racked his brain for the name of his supervisor—he knew it, he knew he knew it, but all he could conjure were letters. Hard letters.

His job was to guide logs into the open mouth of the machine he stood next to. The machine had no buttons—no starter, no emergency stop. Hammond had yet to look into the machine. The logs were massive, from some primeval wood; in all Hammond's years working for lumber companies, he'd never seen logs like these. They glistened. And the noise they made, huge, dropped from an unseen hand onto the belt, kicking wood bits and red spray high into the air, shaking the belt. The smell in the factory was not of fresh cut wood, but burnt oil.

The logs tended to come at Hammond askew, or to roll toward Hammond. If he was not quick, he would be crushed, either pinned against the machine he worked or beneath a log. And Hammond's arms were stiff. All that kept him going was going, a momentum of anger and fright.

He glanced up at his supervisor who'd stopped pacing. Though the supervisor wasn't moving, he wasn't still, either. The supervisor's body shook, a constant blur.

Hammond knocked a log back on track. In the moment before the next log dropped, he glanced at his hands: they were covered in blood. He let slip a yelp—heard his yelp mimicked by someone else in the factory. The blood was not his own, he realized, after he wiped his hands on his jeans. Another log came. He adjusted it, and again there was blood on his hands. When the log hit the blade inside the machine—Hammond heard but did not see this—the log returned a spray of red that left Hammond sticky. He didn't have time to look into the machine before the next log came, so slick with blood Hammond could barely guide it. An upward glance: his supervisor was gone. A feeling in his hand, a dull throb—Hammond sucked in air, whimpered—he'd lost a finger. A log charged down the belt—Hammond corrected its passage with his shoulder and was nearly knocked over. His shirt was soaked with blood—maybe his own, too. The sound inside the machine changed. Not cutting, but masticating.

A log knocked Hammond to the ground, as it passed. From the floor, Hammond saw the inside of the machine.

Snapping animal jaws, the face of a great, skinned wolf.

The wind died down. The dogs had stopped banging on the doors of the station. Walter sat next to Genevieve. She knew she didn't like Walter. Her pills had worn off. She wanted more; she wanted more scotch, too. "Aw, fuck," she said. They all looked at her. "I left a bag on the bus."

They all looked down at their own bags.

Kallista said, "There's your bag." She pointed to the backpack set on the ground beside Genevieve.

"Yeah. That's my other bag."

Hammond said to Genevieve, "Ease up." He put a hand on Kallista's back. "This is a little girl. A bus'll be here in twenty minutes. Your bag will be fine."

Instead of irritation, Genevieve felt bad. "I'm sorry. I don't mean to be such a—" she looked at Kallista and curbed her language. "I'm tired. I hate busses and I hate sitting in freezing cold bus stations even more. But I am sorry."

Walter put his hand on Genevieve's shoulder. She gave Walter a look and he took his hand away.

Hammond looked at Kallista. "Okay?" Kallista nodded.

Walter said, "So," he looked at Hammond, "What was your name?"

"Hammond."

"So, Hammond, what's that new job you're starting?"

"At a lumber yard. I'll be cutting lumber."

Genevieve asked, "You're a carpenter?"

Walter laughed.

Kallista said, "He's more like a lumberjack."

Hammond smiled. "That's closer. I do dumb work. What about you?"

Genevieve said, "I'm a grad student." She was embarrassed by this.

Hammond nodded. Walter asked, "What are you studying? I'm a professor, or, rather, I was a professor. History."

"Folklore." Genevieve looked at Kallista and Hammond, who both looked confused. Most people did when she talked about her work, so she'd come up with an explanation she thought was interesting and easy to understand. "I study stories about monsters and things like that."

Hammond grinned. Kallista said, "Cool." Hammond said, "Where you headed?"

"Dillon."

Walter asked, "For research?"

"I wish. No. I feel stupid now. An old boyfriend invited me, and I just broke up with a jerk, and, you know. I don't why I'm telling you all of this. I guess because I'll never see any of you again. How about you?" She asked Walter. "And you?" She looked at Kallista.

Walter said to Kallista, "You're going to live with your grandmother, right?" Kallista nodded. "I'm visiting an old friend—a little bit like your old friend—what's your name?"

"Genevieve."

"Genevieve. Lovely." He tapped his knee. "A bit like you, but many more years have passed. I just retired. And, because of some bad—we'll say investments—I'm broke."

Genevieve disappointed Walter when, instead of asking him to explain further, she asked Kallista, "Why are you going to live with your grandmother?"

Kallista looked down at her shoes.

Hammond said, "You don't have to say."

Hammond stood up. Kallista asked, "Where—"

"I'm just going to the door, to take a look."

Hammond walked to the front door. Kallista followed—Genevieve thought Kallista might grab onto Hammond's leg, then thought, with a smirk, that she'd certainly like to. Kallista and Hammond stood at the door. Genevieve decided to join them. As she stood—her head rushed a bit—she heard Kallista ask, "What time is it?" Hammond said, "One-fifty."

Hammond sighed when he looked outside. Kallista said, "Look, it's snowing."

Genevieve stood next to Hammond, behind Kallista. The snow made her nervous. Hammond took out his cigarettes, glanced around, spied the No Smoking sign, and lit up. He said to Kallista, "You won't ever do this, will you?" Kallista nodded gravely. Genevieve smiled. The snow had accumulated quite a bit. In what, Genevieve wondered—ten minutes? Kallista said, "There are tracks," and Genevieve could see them too. Dog prints, she assumed, but Kallista asked, "What kind of prints are they?" Genevieve and Hammond looked closer and saw that they looked like human prints—small, and only the front half of the foot. Genevieve noticed splotches of red around one of the prints. Hammond said, "Kallista, why don't you go back to the heaters. It's freezing."

"I'm not cold."

"Come on. You're cold. I'll be right over." Reluctantly, Kallista obeyed. The more Genevieve looked, the more blood she saw. Never large stains, just splotches.

Genevieve was about to say something about the blood and the prints, to air out the situation, when one of the animals emerged from the shadows and charged the door.

That's not a dog, Genevieve thought. The animal hit the door hard—on the glass a smear of greasy blood. Kallista screamed, drowning out the sounds Genevieve, Walter, and Hammond all made. Genevieve grabbed Hammond's arm—Kallista and Walter hung back—Walter held Kallista's shoulder so she couldn't run. The animal stood, stunned, then staggered back into the shadow. Genevieve asked the question aloud, "What was that?" When Hammond didn't reply she added, in a low voice, "It looked like a little girl."

Genevieve's Bad Dream
was a recurring dream, a dream she'd first started to have during the month before her breakup.

And had ceased having shortly after the breakup.

Until she'd fallen asleep on the bus.

The university library windows were opaque. Genevieve put her face to a window. Not night, the glass was black, she knew because at night from the library windows she usually saw the lamps that followed along the walkways, and stars, and the moon. When had the glass been changed? And to what purpose?

Her books were unopened. On her desk was a thermos cup of coffee and a foil chocolate wrapper. Evidently she'd smoothed the foil and folded it into a triangle, though she could not remember doing so. She was compelled to unfold the foil, smooth it out again, and fold it again.

When finally she was able to put the foil aside and open a book, she discovered she couldn't read it because of the flickering of the fluorescent bulb above her; this light obscured rather than made clear.

Genevieve moaned; a sort of surge of anxiety came over her; out of the corner of her eye, a reflection in the window, a wispy figure moved. She knew she had to read the material set in front of her. That she would fail an exam or be unable to write a paper or something worse would happen if she wasn't able to read and understand the material. She spotted the figure again. A small figure, an undergrad, she thought, moved from one stack to another. As she looked after the undergrad, she saw a man, dressed in dark colors, appear from where the small figure had come. The man looked at Genevieve and said, "Hello."

How had she not she recognized her own boyfriend?

She said his name, then, "I'm so glad you came. I can't work at all. What are you doing here?"

"Just going through the stacks," he said. Somehow Genevieve thought this was meant to be funny and so she laughed. He didn't. He walked in the direction where the undergrad had gone.

"Where are you going?"

She found herself unfolding the chocolate foil to smooth it out once more. She wasn't sure how long she'd been at it. The thin square of foil threatened to flake apart. She forced the folded foil down, and followed her boyfriend. She knew he could calm her, would make simple suggestions that would make it possible for her to study, or maybe even take her back to his apartment. She would've gone willingly, and gladly ignored her work for pleasure.

He was on his knee, looking at a mark on the floor.

"What's going on?" she asked. He looked over his shoulder at her, jumped up, and ran off. She called his name. His footfalls were muffled and beneath that noise was another: a quick, wet sound. The mark on the floor looked to her like a footprint made by a small, bare foot. She touched the mark. It was wet. Her fingertip came back red. She was not surprised. She rubbed the blood off onto her jeans. She knew the mark was left by the undergraduate who was not an undergraduate.

But the lone print confused Genevieve. The story it told, as if the undergraduate had jumped from the stacks, landed on one, bloody foot, only to leap up again. Genevieve looked up. Were there prints across the top of the stacks?

She found herself back at her desk, folding the foil into another neat triangle. The glare from her book hurt her eyes. She was never going to get anything done, she thought. She called her boyfriend's name.

He was right in front of her. The bulb above still flickered and made it impossible for Genevieve to get any sense of her boyfriend's details—what he was wearing, his expression. There was, she was sure, a black luminosity about him. She was sure he was looking directly at her, then just as sure that he'd looked away. He walked away, gave no indication he even heard her when she pleaded with him to just stay, to please just stay.

She went quiet when she saw the undergraduate, who must have been hiding behind her boyfriend. It was small, with the physique of a child. Though it wore no clothes, its sex was impossible to tell; it had no skin. For a moment it did nothing. Genevieve frantically unfolded the piece of foil on her desk. When the undergraduate dropped down onto all fours, its blond hair brushed the floor.

Walter called to Hammond and Genevieve from the circle of heaters: "Why don't you two come back here away from the door."

Hammond didn't reply.

Genevieve turned to Walter and said, in a low, serious voice, "Can we barricade the doors?"

"With what?" Then Walter asked: "Why?"

Hammond said, "The bus will be here any moment and when it comes it'll scare away the—" Hammond seemed to think for a moment before completing his sentence—"dogs."

Genevieve said, "Maybe." She let go of Hammond and walked to the ticket booth. She rattled the locked door.

Walter said, "What are you doing?"

Genevieve didn't answer, just rattled the ticket booth door. Walter left the circle of heaters and Kallista and stood behind Genevieve. He said, "Maybe we could use the benches to block the door." Genevieve nodded vigorously. Walter said to Hammond, "Give me a hand."

Hammond shrugged. He picked up an end of a bench. Kallista paced back and forth between the front door and the ticket booth. The back door banged. Genevieve screamed and started to kick at the ticket booth door. Hammond dropped his end of the bench. Walter took a timid step toward the back door, to try to see what had left a smear on the glass. He asked, "Genevieve, why did you want to barricade the doors?"

Kallista ran over to Hammond and—

A bang against the front door, and another—

The front and back doors shook in their aluminum frames. The animals threw themselves against the glass. Walter was positive there were more than just two animals out there, that they were taking turns, systematically weakening the hinges, the glass. He could see that the animals—whatever they were—they didn't look like dogs—were circling the station, and now he saw dozens, moving in and out of sight. They moved on all fours like dogs and they were covered in blood and yellow globs of fat—except for the tops of their heads: there dangled long, matted hair—

Kallista stared out the front door. Shock, Walter thought. Struck dumb. And why not?

Genevieve put her back to the ticket booth door, stood wide-eyed. Walter said, under his breath, "I can't believe this. This is my nightmare—" And the animals stopped circling the station.

They stopped circling, and they howled. Such a high pitched howl, the glass doors trembled. Walter was sure the glass would shatter. Genevieve and Hammond covered their ears, but Kallista—

The bus rumbled toward the station. Hammond looked at his watch and shouted, "Right on time! Right on time!"

Genevieve and Walter went up to the front door, stood just behind Hammond.

The bus stopped. The door opened and the driver stepped down off the bus. The same driver that had brought them there. And all of a sudden Walter was sure it was the same bus, that the driver hadn't gone anywhere. Hammond banged against the glass door and shouted at the driver, shouted at him to look out, made frantic gestures that from the other side of the glass was a ludicrous pantomime. The driver took no notice. The driver unlatched the storage under the bus and took out a duffel bag.

Genevieve said, "That's my bag." Walter almost said, Of course, but kept his mouth shut. The driver turned—his back to the bus—and looked at the four passengers in the station. Very slowly, the driver unzipped the duffel bag. Genevieve said, "What is he—" The driver began to remove, one by one, the items in the bag. Sweatpants. A bra. T-shirts. And so on. He tossed each item onto the snow. One of the animals emerged from a shadow and sniffed at the pile of clothes. The driver dropped the empty bag on the ground. He reached to his belt, and unhooked a set of keys.

Hammond, Walter, and Genevieve stepped away from the door. Genevieve said, "We're okay, now, right? We're going to be okay." The driver unlocked the door and opened it wide. There was a black luminosity about the driver. The driver vibrated; a haze of blur, a halo.

The driver stepped into the station. He looked at Kallista and touched her head. She relaxed, closed her eyes and saw a soft sun behind her eyelids. As if pushing a finger into jelly, the driver pushed his hand through the white skin of Kallista's forehead, pushed down until his arm was half way inside her. Kallista's skin became raw all over, and she clawed at her clothes. The driver twisted his arm as he pulled it out of Kallista—her jaw dropped open, and she moaned a low moan of ecstasy. Her lips withered around her mouth.

The animals filed in and formed a circle around the driver and Kallista. Perhaps twenty or more. Their bodies wept blood and lymph. They had no lips. Their human teeth shone. One of the animals reared up on its hind legs and stood. Like Kallista's own, its hair was long and blond.

The Man from the Peak

The sun left tatters in shades of red across the sky; tatters that shriveled through purple, indigo—to black. The stars didn't come out. Instead, oil-gray clouds. I kept the car going, up, steering around the worst ruts and rocks in the road. I drove under the no trespassing sign, kept driving up. The forest around me was thick—the leaves had come in, hearty and wet: spring. I wondered if this would be the last time I'd make the drive up to Richard's. I thought so. Richard was leaving. Moving east. So, a farewell bash. Sarah would be there, too. With a sound like marbles clicking, or teeth, the wine bottle and the whiskey bottle on the passenger seat bumped against each other.

Richard's house stood in the shadow of the mountain's peak. I turned off the car and sat, let my eyes adjust to the darkness, listened to cooling engine skitter. The walk to Richard's was lined with paper lanterns—no doubt Sarah's touch. I grabbed the bottles, set them on the roof of the car, lit a cigarette and looked up the peak. I heard people talking—some of the voices outside, from the hot tub, no doubt, and muted voices from the house. There were a dozen cars parked in front of my own. I opened the back door of the car and took out a small package—a book for Sarah, a collection of short stories she and I had talked about the last time the three of us—Richard, Sarah and I—had been together. I tucked the book under my arm, took the bottles and walked up to the house. I rang the bell and a woman wearing a bikini opened the door. She looked at me—looked me up and down as if I were wearing a bikini—laughed a little and brushed past me outside. As she passed, she asked, "Did you bring your suit?"

The house was long and narrow. To my left was the guest room, to my right a kitchen and a television room/bar. Michael, an old friend of Richard's who I'd come to like, was busy mixing drinks. He'd explained to me once that he took up the role of bartender at parties so he could get to know all the women. I approached the bar and said, "I'd say the hot tub is where you want to be tonight." Michael nodded, ruefully. I handed Michael the bottles I'd brought. "Good stuff," he said. "Good to see you," he said. I shook his hand and patted his shoulder. "What'll you have?" he asked. "A glass of that whiskey," I said. He said, "Try this instead," and poured from an already open bottle. I put my cigarette out in a red-glass ashtray by the bar and had a sip. I nodded my appreciation. "I should announce myself," I said, and backed away.

The living room: a large, open space dominated by a fat couch and a grand piano (Richard didn't play). Sarah was on the couch drinking wine. When she saw me, she stood, crossed the room with a quick, woozy stride and put her arms around me.

"Watch the wine," I said.

She stepped back from me, a wounded expression on her face. I took her glass and rested it on the piano. She put her arms around me again and said, "I get so excited when you come. I always do. It's so silly. I always am so excited to see you."

"It's good to see you too." We kissed, as we did whenever we saw each other; I'm not sure how this greeting got started, but our kisses were long and on the lips; she'd been dating Richard as long as I'd known her.

"Have you seen Richard yet?" she asked.

"I just got here."

"Can I?" She tapped the cigarette box in my breast pocket. She slipped her fingers into the pocket and smiled at me. "You always have the best cigarettes." As she lit up, she eyed the wrapped package under my arm.

"It's for you," I said.

She unwrapped my gift, dropped the brown paper to the floor. "You found a copy," she said. She opened the book, careful with the spine, a delicate touch on the yellow edge of each page she turned over. "You're the only one who ever gets me books." She tapped her necklace: an elegant, expensive silver knot. "Richard always buys me jewelry," she said, with a frown.

We caught up, a little; a little about Richard's preparations for leaving, though we skirted the issue of whether or not she'd be going. We would have that conversation later. I needed to drink a little more, to meet everyone. I looked past Sarah, at the women on the couch. Sarah said, "That one's Carmilla—she's a stunning bore—and that's Kat—fun, fun, fun. They're friends of Richard's. From where, I do not know. Come, I need more wine." We left her glass on the piano, made our way up to the bar. She fell into a conversation with Michael. I walked off—I didn't feel like standing around while Sarah and Michael talked.

Richard was in the yard, beer in hand, talking with someone I didn't know. Just behind him was the hot tub. The woman who'd answered the door was in the tub with a couple of guys. Before Richard spotted me, the woman said, "You should come in, it's perfect, cold outside, warm in here." She giggled. One of the guys leaned over and whispered to her. She pushed him away.

"David, you made it," Richard said.

"I wouldn't miss it."

"Well I'm glad, you know."

He introduced me to his friend, and to the guys in the tub. He didn't know the woman's name and she didn't supply it. "Come on and sit," he said to me.

I sat on a cooler. Richard and his friend were talking about Boston, where Richard was moving. I'd never been to Boston, I told them, though I'd heard it was like San Francisco. We talked about San Francisco, Seattle, Portland.

The woman in the hot tub interrupted us and asked me to get her a beer. I got up to get a beer from the cooler. She stood. She was very thin, no hips, but gifted with significant breasts. She leaned forward—bent at the waist without bending her knees—and brought her bosom to my face. Freckles swirled into the dark line of her cleavage. "Thank you so much," she said, and took the beer. The guys in the tub were happily gazing up at her tiny bottom—those men were nothing to her, made to carry her bags and perform rudimentary tasks while she gazed off in other, more interesting directions. I'd met women like her many times before. "My name's Prudence," she said.

"Of course it is," I said.

"You really ought to join."

"You know I'm not going to."

She did know, too, and smiled a wide, long smile.

"But I'll be here all night," I said.

She settled back into her pool.

I lit a cigarette; for a moment, a flame cupped in my hand; I drew my hand away, and looked up to the peak. A man, briefly illuminated by moonlight before the clouds closed up, appeared at the top, moved toward the house. I said to Richard, "Does someone live up there?" Richard told me he didn't think so. I tried to point out the man—who I could still see, as a dark shape on a dark background—but Richard couldn't find him. "I'm going to go in, get a real drink," I said. Richard said he'd be in shortly. I shrugged and walked around to the front of the house—an eye on the man walking down the mountain.

Most of the people at Richard's party weren't attractive. They might be fit and many were dressed in expensive clothes, but most of his friends looked average and, upon getting to know them, were. The exceptions were notable. Michael, a transplant from the coast, a man of style; Kat and Carmilla—just beautiful; Prudence—a manipulator I appreciated; and Sarah. Kat and Carmilla were seated on a small couch in the guest room, surrounded by four or five guys and one unfortunate looking girl (pasty, a large, flat nose and hair forced into a strange shade of red). They were all watching a movie—Kat spotted me in the doorway, shifted on the couch, shoved at one of the guys, and gestured for me to sit beside her. They were watching *The Man Who Fell To Earth*, that beautiful David Bowie film—

I let myself get drawn into the movie. Kat ran her hand in a circle on my back. When the unfortunate girl sneezed, breaking my mood, I excused myself and walked down the hall to the bar. I passed the front door just as there was a knock; the door was answered and I heard, "What, you need a formal invitation? Sure, come on in, you are welcome to come in." Sarah joined me at the bar and took my arm. We collected drinks and Michael and I went out onto the back patio. Mercifully, the three of us were there alone.

Sarah stole a cigarette and complained about Richard's friends—"Present company excluded."

Michael then brought up the subject Sarah and I had danced around once already: "What's in Boston for you? I mean, I know Richard has a great job, but what are you going to do?"

Sarah looked at the floor for a moment, took a drag and a drink and said, "That's just the thing, Michael."

I was eager to hear her explain to Michael just what that thing was—I thought I knew but I wanted her to say it—but instead she stared past Michael, back into the house. I turned and Michael turned and we all watched a very ugly man walk past the back patio door toward the bar.

"Who the hell was that?" I asked.

Sarah said, "I don't know, but—" then drifted past me into the hall. Michael and I looked at each other, then followed—I dropped my cigarette on the patio floor.

The ugly man wasn't at the bar by the time we stepped into the hall—no one was.

He was in the living room, behind the piano, playing the adagio from the *Moonlight Sonata* on Richard's out-of-tune grand—the result was not lulling or melancholic, as the adagio is, but dissonant and eerie.

No one else seemed to share my evaluation of the music. Everyone—the whole party except Prudence and her men—were gathered around the piano watching the ugly man play, laughing when he made an exaggerated flourish over the keyboard, but rapt, totally caught up—so that they all jumped when he moved into the more upbeat allegretto. I wanted to jump too—each out-of-tune note grated on my nerves.

I stared at the ugly man as he played. He was bald. His head was long and boney, his eyes lost in shadow. His skin was a dark brown—not like Michael's, no, he didn't look African—the ugly man was black all right, but his skin was waxy and all over there was a patina of green—the green of rotten beef. I couldn't help but imagine what it would be like to touch his skin—my finger, I was sure, would sink in, as it would in a pool of congealed fat. His ears were large and pointed. His mouth was small—pursed as he played—and his teeth were too large for his tiny mouth. His two front teeth were the worst: jagged, yellow, buck-teeth.

I was greatly relieved to see that Sarah did not appear to be under his spell. She stood in the corner watching not the ugly man, but the crowd—and Richard, who stood with a stupid open mouthed expression on his face, clapping like a little girl every time the ugly man crossed his hands over the keyboard. I could hear, barely audible, David Bowie's voice in the guest room.

The ugly man stopped playing the piano then, and it dawned on me that he must be the man I'd seen coming down from the peak. He waved his hands in the air, and this seemed to release everyone. There was some applause, and people returned to what they had been doing. I watched Kat and Carmilla walk back toward the guest room, Michael made a bee-line for the bar, and Sarah and Richard walked over to me. I noticed the pasty girl with the bad dye-job standing next to the ugly man, looking down at him as he caressed her hand. The perfect couple, I thought. I led Sarah and Richard to the bar and insisted that Michael open the whiskey I'd brought—a far better whiskey than what he'd served me when I'd arrived.

I asked who the ugly man was.

Sarah said she didn't know. Michael and Richard acted as if I hadn't asked the question. I put my hand on Richard's arm and asked again, and he said, "Which ugly man?"

I took Richard's response to be a joke and gave him a forced, weak chuckle. My whiskey was a relief. I needed a moment alone with Sarah—I wanted her to have a chance to finish what she'd been saying earlier, I wanted her to tell me that there was nothing for her in Boston, that she had no intention of ever joining Richard in Boston and was only pretending so as not to break his heart before his big trip.

I felt a hand on my shoulder. I was certain it was the ugly man's; I was surprised—relieved—that the hand belonged to Prudence. "I'm out of the tub," she whispered.

Sarah and Richard were talking; I asked Prudence what she wanted to drink and she held up a beer. "I'm all set in that department. Did you know they're watching a movie in the guest room?"

"Yes," I said. I followed Prudence down the hall. She'd put on a dress over her wet suit—somehow, with the bands of wet, clingy material around her waist and her chest, she seemed more naked than she had before. I'd catch up with Sarah later, catch her when Richard was off chatting up one of his boring friends.

Prudence and I entered the room—*The Man Who Fell to Earth* was still on—had Bowie yet revealed his alien identity? Kat and Carmilla were on the couch, and to my satisfaction, Kat shot Prudence a nasty look and beckoned me to a spot beside her. Prudence, first in the guest room, took that spot. Small as her hips were, there was no more room left on the couch. When she saw this, she slid off the couch, onto the floor, and offered me the spot Kat had already offered. Regardless of the outcome of my conversation with Sarah, I knew I would not leave the party alone; I considered, even, the possibility that Prudence and Kat's attentions would prove useful in gaining Sarah's attention.

Kat stroked my hair; Prudence my leg. The other men in the room couldn't help but glance away from the television to look first at the women, then at me, wishing themselves in my position.

Just before the movie ended—a sad, pale scene—I'd been lulled by all the petting—the ugly man, the man from the peak, walked past the guest room. I caught a glimpse of him, just as he walked out of sight. Except for Prudence, the people in the guest room left: the guys, Carmilla and Kat. Before I could dwell on this much, Prudence was on the couch beside me, hand on the inside of my thigh, mouth drifting toward my face. I knew that face, drifting sleepily, a drunk woman about to kiss me. I let her kiss me. We kissed. Her tongue darted in and out of my own mouth. Her open hand pressed against my erection. My hand on the damp cloth covering her right breast, my hand on the damp cloth at the small of her back.

I broke off our kissing. I said, "Let's get something more to drink." Though she gave me a petulant look, I knew she would do as I asked and I thought—for a moment—this woman actually knows what I'm doing, understands, would have ended the kiss herself, shortly, if I hadn't. In that moment I preferred Prudence to Sarah. The moment was fleeting.

The ugly man had been speaking—addressing the entire party, it seemed. When Prudence and I stepped into the living room, he waved his hand as he'd done before, and the crowd dispersed as it had before. Everyone left the room except for one person, one of the guys who'd been in the hot tub with Prudence—I watched her watch him talk to the ugly man and Prudence said, "I knew he was gay." I wasn't sure who she was referring to at first—I didn't think the ugly man was gay—and then I realized who she meant.

"Who is that man?" I asked.

"I don't know. I've been outside all night."

"Didn't you see him come down from the peak?"

"From the peak? There's nothing up there. I'm going to get another drink."

She left me. I lit a cigarette and went out onto the patio. Richard and Sarah were out there, though Richard was talking with one of his friends and Sarah was just standing around, looking bored. She brightened when she saw me. I gave her a cigarette.

"Why don't we go outside a while," Sarah said.

We left the enclosed patio. We heard voices, coming from the direction of the hot tub. We walked out into the dark yard, toward the woods.

"What was that guy talking about?" I asked.

"Which guy?"

"The ugly guy. They guy with the buck teeth."

Sarah turned up a confused expression. When she pulled on her cigarette, her face was illuminated. She had, I thought, the most perfect face. Between her eyebrows, just above the bridge of her nose was a circular patch of skin very smooth and brighter white than the rest of her face. I wanted to put my fingertip on that spot. I did. She scrunched her face up and giggled, brushing my finger away.

"So that's what that button does," I said. "So," I said. "You didn't finish what you were saying earlier."

She didn't answer me, but pointed, and I forgot what I'd asked when I saw what she was pointing out. The man from the peak walked across the lawn—on a line parallel with our own course, maybe twenty feet away—with the guy he'd been talking to in the living room. They walked toward the edge of the wood, where a woman—the woman with the bad dye-job—lay on the ground.

"What is going on over there?" Sarah asked.

I said, "I'm sure we don't want to know."

"Do you think she's all right?"

"She looks fine to me," I said, though there was no way I could actually judge, from where we stood. "We should leave them be," I said, but I asked, "Who is that guy anyhow? I saw him come down from the peak."

"Which guy?" Sarah asked.

"The bald guy." Right when I said that, he was out of sight, he'd stepped into a shadow that made him all but invisible. So I said never mind.

On the patio, we finished our drinks. Sarah took another cigarette. She looked around—there were other guests on the patio, but none we knew more than just in passing. Richard had gone inside. Sarah said, "I'm not putting any pressure on you, David, but I'm not going to Boston."

Sarah seemed like herself when she said that, more than she had all night, and I was glad, I'd known it, known she would leave Richard for me if I'd wanted, and I did want that, and I hadn't been wrong.

All the voices on the porch seemed to rise in volume—there was a scream—I decided from inside the house—but no one paid any attention.

Several hours later, I stood in front of Richard's house, trying to figure out why there were twelve cars, not including my own, in the driveway. The party had started to die about an hour before; people had slipped out one-by-one. I realized, as I stood in front of Richard's house smoking, sipping a cheap glass of whiskey, that I hadn't heard a single car go. Even if people had carpooled, had designated a driver, there were still too many cars in the driveway.

My thoughts weren't adding up in any significant way. I was in a haze of drunk and sleepiness—not so far gone that I wouldn't be able to collect Sarah and leave soon, but dull enough that my lines of thought were short.

I stared for a while at the mountaintop. There were no houses, that I could see, higher than Richard's. If the man from the peak lived up there, he must have walked from the other side of the peak, and that looked to me like a hell of a walk.

I coughed, caught a coughing fit, felt a hand on my back.

"Prudence?" I managed, still bent over.

"No, not Prudence."

The voice was a voice I hadn't heard once that night, but I knew whose voice it was.

"Taking in the air?" the man from the peak asked.

I saw a laugh on his face; he was laughing at me.

"Smoke?" I asked. "Whiskey?" I held out my drink and my cigarette.

He held up a hand—his fingers were long, his nails were long.

"You don't drink," I said.

He just grinned his stupid ugly grin, a set of teeth crooked and misshapen. That his speech wasn't impeded by his malformed mouth was a wonder—indeed, his voice was the most soothing voice I'd ever heard. "So who are you?" I asked.

He said, "I'm an invited guest," and I remembered what I'd overheard earlier that night.

I said, "I watched you come down from the peak. Are there houses up there?"

He looked at the peak, followed its upward rise with his head until he'd found the very tip and said, "No, there are no houses."

I thought maybe he lived in a tent or a trailer home and was just having fun with me, making me ask my questions just so. Normally, when I think someone's doing that, some cute girl who thinks she's coy or some clever boy trying to impress, I walk away without so much as a fuck you and that puts them out, and then they beg me for my attention. Normally, that's what I'd do. But I said, "But do you live on the peak? In a tent? In a trailer? In a mobile home?" I gave that ugly man from the peak all the options I could because I was desperate to hear his answer. For some reason: I was desperate to know.

He said, "I live in the peak."

I didn't know what he meant by "in the peak," but I smiled—I felt that dumb smile spread on my face—I smiled and nodded as if "in the peak" made all the sense in the world.

I asked, "So what is it you're doing in the backyard?"

He gave me a straight answer. An awful answer. And for a moment I could see him exactly as he was; all of a sudden I could see him, see that his clothes—from pant cuff to shirt collar—were drenched in blood and gore. Blood dripped off his shirt sleeves, blood was pooled around his feet, there was blood on the top of his bald head and there was blood all around his mouth. The blood around his mouth was the most horrible, smeared around like finger-paint. Before I became hysterical, I couldn't see the blood anymore. He looked ugly, but his clothes were clean. His pant cuffs flapped in the breeze. His bright white shirt sleeves were rolled up just below his elbows.

I wondered, if he could do that, why he didn't make himself look handsome to me. I think he knew my thought, because he said, "Charisma. You know what I mean."

I laughed. He walked back into the house. I stood shaking my head, enjoying for a moment the great joke. Then a wave of nausea passed through me and I vomited—all spit and whiskey—and my head was clear. I rushed into the house—for Sarah, I thought, where is Sarah? The guest room was empty. No one was at the bar. Richard was seated on the piano bench next to the man from the peak, and they were playing "Heart and Soul." The man from the peak playing the chords, Richard plinking out the simple tune with a single finger, laughing like an idiot.

I ran into Prudence out on the patio. She was drunk, but when she looked at me I knew she was still in control: I'd known from the moment she brushed past me at the front door that the big breasts and the flirty girl-voice were all for show, plumage that got Prudence what she wanted. I'd known that she was like me in that way, and admired her for it. So instead of just ignoring her for Sarah I stopped and told her that we were all in a lot of trouble.

"I'd sort of picked up on that," she said, pointing with her thumb toward the backyard. Her calm was wrong, a part of all that was wrong that night. She said, "I was just leaving. My car's blocked though. I was trying to find someone—"

"So go out to my car—it's silver, it's the last one in the driveway. Go out to my car and wait for me. I'm going to get Sarah."

She said, "Sarah? Fuck Sarah. What do you need Sarah for?" I sensed her control was limited, or running low, and so she obeyed me, started toward the driveway. Better to do as I said, then to do what the man from the peak asked her to do. I went through the near-empty rooms, finally went into the backyard, where I knew everyone must be.

I tried not to understand too much of what I saw. Since there was no moonlight, no stars, I couldn't make out the exact details anyhow. But the yard was lined with bodies. Many stripped of their clothes, all flat on their back. The bodies, piled like sandbags, formed a wall along the edge of the woods. They were neatly stacked but for a few strays—I saw Michael's body, not five feet from where I stood.

And then I saw Sarah, on her feet, wandering in a daze. I became aware that "Heart and Soul" had stopped. I could hear Sarah's feet brush through the grass.

I couldn't speak—had no impulse to. I ran to Sarah, put my arm around her and guided her toward the side of the house, away from the patio door which was opening, away from Richard, who staggered out into the yard, singing, "Heart and Soul." He fell in love, he sang, "madly."

Prudence was not in the driveway, and I thought fine, if he has her, that'll buy me and Sarah some time, and I'm going to live, and Sarah, too. I pushed Sarah along the driveway, dragged her. I opened the car and put Sarah into the passenger seat, then started the car and backed up to turn around. In the headlights, the car still facing the wrong way, toward the house—I saw Prudence, on her back. Her body must have been just out if sight, just under the front bumper. She jerked, once. I couldn't help watching her breasts: a spray of freckles that vanished into her cleavage.

The mountain road was so rutted, I couldn't go fast, not without taking the chance of breaking an axle.

We were close. Very close to the bottom of the mountain when I heard the bang from the inside of the trunk. I jumped on the accelerator and I could feel a heavy weight shift. Sarah stared calmly ahead, as if we were on a day-trip. There was another bang, and the trunk burst open. I couldn't see anything out the rear-view mirror—just the silver trunk lid. I drove, swerving around boulders, bouncing in and out of pot holes, cursing each time the front end of the car ground into the dirt, until, incredibly, the man from the peak stared at me through the windshield. He clung to the hood on all fours, his arms and legs wide apart, face inches from the glass. He wasn't hiding himself: his teeth were bared and he was filthy with blood, dribbling blood onto the glass, foaming blood from his nostrils.

I felt, suddenly, quite serene. I brought the car to an easy stop. Sarah and I stepped out.

The man from the peak hid himself again. He hopped off the hood with a single, graceful flex of his legs. I heard stones crunch under his shoes as he walked up to Sarah. He looked at me while he put a hand on her right shoulder. And she relaxed completely—I wasn't sure what kept her from collapsing. He grabbed her hair and yanked, forcing her head to the side. She winked at me as if she were about to get a treat she'd been waiting for all day.

Did I make a move to stop him? No. His eyes locked onto mine. And any desire for survival I'd had, any wish for Sarah to live, just slipped away—was leeched from my thoughts. I reached into my breast pocket, slowly removed my cigarette pack, took a cigarette, tamped it against the box, lit it and smoked. I stood, smoked, watched as he tore a chunk of flesh from Sarah's throat with those stupid buck teeth of his and opened his mouth to the jet of blood that burst from her artery. I watched him and he watched me and was he grinning while he drank? Oh, surely he was and I smiled back at him, smiled and smoked my cigarette, smoked so hard the filter flared up before I finally dropped my cigarette and stamped it dead.

I looked up after watching my own foot twist a cigarette butt out on the dirt road and they were gone. He and Sarah were gone. I stared up at the top of the mountain. Stood for at least an hour. Finally, I was released. Trembling, I slid into the driver's seat and drove down off the mountain into Rattlesnake Valley, as blue light crept across the sky.

I listened to the radio for three days. I had the dial somewhere between stations. Sometimes one came in stronger, sometimes the other. I heard news, I heard a minister Bible-teaching, organ music, chants—when both stations grew weak I heard a murkier broadcast: two voices, disharmonious music, swamp-static. I'd ordered all my meals by delivery for the last few days. Greasy wax paper curled in on itself; half-eaten sandwiches, flat soda, Styrofoam. I spent the day in a leather arm chair. I slept there—I woke often to be sure that all my windows were fastened, that the bolts on the door had been shot—that I hadn't been careless after a delivery boy had come by, though, each time I closed the door on a delivery, I locked up, leaned against the door and double-checked the locks. I worried the skin around my fingers and smoked—I'd found a stale pack in my bedroom; not my brand, someone else's cigarettes, some woman I'd brought here had left her cigarettes. I tried to think of ways that I could have stopped what happened from happening, but there was nothing I could've done. I could've done little things differently—not waited so long to take Sarah away (not sent Prudence on her own). Yet, even these small acts seemed out of the realm of possibility to me—that I couldn't have behaved any way other than the way I behaved. My own personality, my own desires, took on monstrous shapes in my mind.

On the third day I remembered the book that I gave to Sarah—that slim collection of short stories. An image of that book popped into my head, completely unbidden. And once that image was there, I couldn't shake it—try as I might. As if the image of that book were being broadcast directly into my head. The book must still have been at Richard's house. I could picture it in each room: on the bar next to a clear, empty bottle; in the guest room on the couch; etc. The book, then the empty room all around it. My thoughts returned incessantly to the book. The book as object. The book as icon. The book as literature—how did those stories tie in with the events of that night? At times, just as sleep would come over me, the stories in that book would seem clearly prophetic—how could I, having read the book, not have known what was going to happen at Richard's party?

I left my apartment to retrieve the book. A small part of my brain screamed at me not to, pointed out that going anywhere near Richard's house was lunacy. I drove up the mountain, tapped the steering wheel, chewed on the end of an unlit cigarette and drove under the no trespassing sign to Richard's. I would get the book and leave. I would have the book. The sun was high and bright, there was nothing at all to going into Richard's house and getting the book and then leaving with it, set on the passenger seat or, perhaps, on my lap. Once I had the book, I would be able to settle back into my rational life.

Prudence's body wasn't in the driveway. I remembered the wall of corpses the man from the peak had made.

I was glad there was still a mess from the party—bottles, ash trays full of butts, objects displaced, leftover dip, etc. If the man from the peak had taken the time to clean the house—that might have made me crazy—if the house had looked as it did on the occasions I'd come to visit Sarah when Richard was away, I'd've been greatly disturbed. There had been a party. The man from the peak had come.

The moment I touched the book I knew that I hadn't come for it after all, and that I hadn't come of my own will.

The peak was a black spike surrounded by sun. I climbed toward the peak. I sweated heavily in my dark clothes—if someone had stood at Richard's front door, would they have been able to see me at all? Just shy of the boulders that crowned the mountain, I found the crevasse I knew was home to the man from the peak. "I live in the peak," he'd said.

I sat down at the edge of the crevasse. A jagged, open crescent in the side of the mountain, as if a sliver of the moon had burned its impression onto the side of the mountain. When I leaned over, I felt a gust of wet air, like breath; it reeked of ammonia and dirt. I'd smoke until my cigarettes were gone and by then there wouldn't be much light left. I didn't want to be here but I found that it was impossible to leave.

The Dead Gather on the Bridge to Seattle

The raccoon wasn't eating garbage—the can hadn't been knocked over—it was eating another raccoon. From across the yard, Roger could see that the raccoon's little mouth glimmered with gore. Roger unlocked the trunk of his car, unzipped a narrow case and removed a shotgun. He looked for the raccoon with his flashlight—it was no longer standing above its cannibalized mate. He jumped when the light fell on the raccoon—large as a dog and shambling toward him. Roger called out, once, a single profanity eaten up by the surrounding woods. The raccoon wasn't startled, didn't draw back or run as any raccoon would when confronted by a man. Roger cursed again and shot the raccoon. It burst open, as if rotten.

The phone in Roger's mobile home rang.

Roger dashed up the back step into the kitchen where he'd left the portable. He glanced at the wall clock—a little past eleven—then at the caller I.D.—his sister Vivienne. "Viv," he said. "Oh, hello, Martin," he said. "Is everything all right?" he asked. He said, "Fine. Martin, what's this about?" Roger set the shotgun down on the kitchen table. He picked up a pizza crust left from his dinner. He took a bite. "She's sick?" He tossed the crust down. "How long have you been at the hospital?" The light above the table dimmed. "I don't know what I can do." Roger pushed the kitchen door shut. "It's fifteen hours," he said. "She asked?" Roger looked again at the wall clock. "I'll leave in a few hours." "No? OK. I'll be on the road in an hour. Still, I won't be there until tomorrow evening." "Five o'clock. I'll call from the road." "Yes," Roger said, "I'll call."

Roger stared at the shotgun on the table; he let his eyes un-focus over the dull gleam it gave. He thought about the raccoon, and of how sick it must have been, and of how it sickened him. He tried to recall what had woken him. The phone wasn't what'd woken him, neither the raccoon—he was surely accustomed to the noise animals made during the night. The prospect of the drive did not appeal to him, but for Vivienne to ask him to make the trip, all the way from Decker, from Montana to Washington, to Seattle, was extraordinary.

With the cell phone he'd been given by his employer, he called Peter and asked him to cover his route. Peter said he was feeling ill and didn't think he could do it; Roger pressed and Peter agreed. Roger said, "I'll leave the keys to the truck and the freezers on the driver's seat." Roger went out, carrying his shotgun and a ring of keys. He returned the shotgun to the case in the trunk of his car. He checked the freezers—three freestanding units. He unlocked the generator shed and topped off the fuel. He added gas to the truck's tank, too, and placed the keys on the driver's seat. After he'd shut the door to the cab, he reopened the door and took the key for the padlocked generator shed off the ring. The time was just before midnight. He set his alarm clock for one AM, and lay down.

Roger slept, but hardly.

He called his boss: "I won't be able to make the deliveries this morning," he said.

His boss said, "You can't call in sick."

"Peter's covering the route."

"Pete's only been out with you once or twice. You can't have the morning off."

"Don't hand me that, Harry. You can help Peter if he gets lost."

"You can't just call in like this."

"Harry, I haven't taken a day off in the two years I've worked for you. I've covered for everyone, I've even covered for you. Peter will do the route. He'll do it tomorrow too. I'll pay him out of my check so don't worry about payroll."

"Okay, okay. What's this about, anyhow?"

"Personal."

"Are you all right?"

"I'm okay."

"Is there anything I can do?"

"No, but thanks. I have to go."

The sky brimmed with stars. A shooting star, another. A bright, raspberry cloud of light flickered in the sky. Roger squinted at the cloud, perplexed by the sight—not Northern Lights, he didn't think. An animal moved behind the trees that bordered Roger's yard.

Roger filled a thermos with coffee. He hadn't been away since he'd first moved out to Decker. He locked the windows and behind himself the front door. The leaves of the big cottonwood rustled; a sound like a brook. Stars fell, one after another: a shower. Roger had never seen a shower so full, and would've stopped to watch, had he the time. The grass and the trees were black. The car turned over smoothly; the gas tank was full, the oil clean, tire pressure good. Roger kept his car neat. On the passenger seat were a handful of CDs, all gifts from Vivienne. Vivienne was the only family who kept in touch with Roger since his move. He drove off his property, onto the dirt road that began his daily delivery route. In an hour, Roger would be on the highway, headed away from his customers, away from Decker. With enough coffee, he thought, and some No Doze he'd buy at the gas station in Lodge Grass, he might not have to sleep.

Roger's car was all he'd kept from his former life. The car didn't belong in Decker, and he rarely drove it, a black Saab sedan, a forty-thousand dollar car purchased when forty-thousand wasn't a whole lot of money for Roger to spend on a car or on anything else. When he left San Francisco, he decided to keep the car because it was solid. A powerful engine, four-wheel drive, and black.

The roof of his car reflected the stars. Roger picked up 314.

Spread out, sixty miles north, a little south of the Yellowstone River, were the foundations of fur trading posts. Crumbled dust foundations. To the west of Custer is Junction, which was no more a town but a graveyard, left to its own except for dinosaur bones. Buffalo grazed the plains. Roger drove through the Wolf Mountains with his stereo off. What was dead in those mountains lay still; the wolves ate their kill. Long stretches of 314 were unpaved. Roger's high beams bounced and blurred ahead of his car. Rodents scurried to the sides of the road. He drove as fast as the road permitted, steering wheel firmly gripped as the irregular road wrenched the car right and left, toward black trees and boulders. The Rosebud battlefield, the little rivers.

Lodge Grass, *greasy grass*, the first full-service gas station on Roger's route. The needle still at full, Roger topped off the gas. Two truckers stood mesmerized by the meteor shower, ball caps tilted back on their foreheads. Roger bought No Doze and poured water into a little cone. The clerk said, "There's stars falling all over the North. The radio says it's something special." Roger nodded, waited for the clerk to count his change. As Roger broke open the box of No Doze, a news item caught his attention: a man presumed dead, and in that state for some hours, was revived. A good omen, Roger thought. At the gas station, Roger had a brief window of cell phone reception, so he dialed Martin.

"I'm on the road," Roger said. "I'm calling so you'll have my cell number." Roger said, "I should go," but before he ended the call he asked, "How's Vivienne?" Bad, was the answer. "Do the doctors know what it is?" Roger asked. Only that it's an infection.

From Lodge Grass: Rt. 90 all the way to Seattle. The highway was empty. Roger kept his high beams on and an eye out for deer and bighorn sheep, apt to simply *be* in the road. Roger watched for their eyes. He passed Garryowen, Crow Agency, and Hardin. Billings would soon emerge as a cluster of light. South of Billings, opposite Boothill Cemetery, near The Place of Skulls, was Sacrifice Cliff, where two Crow rode on the back of a single white horse, a horse blindfolded so it could be made to ride off a cliff. Two young Crow returned from a hunt to find their tribe dead by smallpox. They mourned, singing, yelling, clutching one another on the back of a blindfolded white horse. *The place where the white horse went down.* A blind horse, snuffing, kicking dust, led by two anguished Crow off the edge of a cliff.

The city of Billings was electric lights and dark industrial shapes, all set in a cup of mountains and rim rocks. The traffic around Roger grew heavier. Trucks, mostly. Roger wanted a real breakfast, but knew he couldn't spare the time. He'd stop in Billings, though, relieve himself and buy an egg and sausage sandwich from a gas station.

All along the highway were parked cars. People had driven out of Billings to get a better look at the star shower, still in full. The sky carried an aura, a hint of color, a haze of red.

When Roger moved to San Francisco, five years before, Vivienne came with. The realtor who sold Roger his home assumed Vivienne was Roger's girlfriend, and was visibly relieved when Roger corrected her: "She's my little sister." Vivienne's room in Roger's house—the guest room—was small but sunny and featured floor-to-ceiling, built-in bookcases. Vivienne bought books with Roger's money and quickly filled those shelves. Roger's room was large and always felt empty, except on the nights when Vivienne, afraid or drunk or sad would sleep in Roger's room, curled into the green leather chair set beside the fireplace.

Roger exited the highway for the first gas station he saw with its lights on and topped off the Saab's tank. He liked the needle at full. He washed the car's windows and lights. He borrowed a key for the restroom in back, where he washed his hands and face as well as he could with the soap-grit provided. The paper towel dispenser was empty, so he dried himself with his un-tucked shirt. Inside the mart he found a sausage sandwich, which he heated in the microwave and ate while he picked up a glass jar of peanuts, several tall bottles of water, and two apple juices. The clock above the microwave read 2:17. He added elk jerky and crackers to his purchases.

Outside, a man stood by the pumps, lit by fluorescent bulbs peppered with moths and flies. He leaned over and removed the cap from a bright red gas can—Roger heard the ping of a spring-release. A star fell, died behind the mountains; the star shower was over. Another man, wearing a John Deere cap, emerged from shadow, from behind the last pump. Something in the way he walked—the angle at which he held his head—struck Roger as off. Roger put his groceries down on the roof of his car and took a step toward the pumps. The man with the gas can, bent over, pumping gas, touched the bill of his hat, acknowledging Roger. Roger nodded, took another step toward the pumps. John Deere moved like a man short on sleep, someone just up from the thick of a dream.

"Evening," Roger said to the man with the gas can, but with an eye on John Deere.

The man with the gas can released the pump trigger, stood and replied, "Morning, more like it." The man with the gas can then heard what Roger heard, a sickly sound, a rale, something unhealthy between breath.

John Deere fell upon the man with the gas can. Roger ran toward the two men; the man with the gas can yelled out in pain; Roger hit John Deere hard with his shoulder. John Deere's head hit hard against a pump, then hit the ground with a sound like a soggy sponge thrown against a tile floor. The man with the gas can started to complain—"son of a bitch bit"—but stopped when he got a look at John Deere.

The side of John Deere's head had collapsed, as if the skull was ceramic, as if there had been nothing inside—but, splattered against the pump was blood and tissue, a shivering jelly.

The man with the gas can vomited. Roger watched: the man wasn't vomiting because of the gross corpse; he was sick, abruptly, violently ill. The man said, gasping and bewildered, "He bit me," and held out his arm. Roger ran to the gas mart, opened the door and shouted to the clerk, "There's a man sick out there." The clerk glanced at one of the monitors behind the counter—two men, and both looked to be in bad shape. The clerk couldn't quite comprehend what he was seeing and began to ask, but Roger was gone. He wouldn't wait anymore. He didn't have time to get involved. He put his groceries on the passenger seat of his car and drove. Without the stars flashing across the sky, the night was very dark indeed.

Roger drove out of Billings. Though the star shower was over, cars were still parked alongside the highway. A pickup with its doors open wide offered a glimpse of a woman awkwardly asleep on the front seat. People wandered on the median: the headlights of stationary cars lit up men and women who appeared lost—at least, uncertain. Strange sights.

A car pulled onto the highway toward Billings. With his rear-view mirror, Roger watched the car drift from lane to lane. Perhaps a few six packs brought along for star gazing. Or sick. Roger let his mind go to worry: his sister had once been quite needy, but since Roger had left, she'd pulled herself together. To ask Roger to come and see her, well, she must really be sick. Roger put this out of his mind.

He considered the possibility that the police would connect Roger with the incident at the Billings gas station—as Roger was indeed connected. Perhaps the clerk would say something suggestive, "He was in an awful hurry to get out of here," or the police would watch video and see Roger kill John Deere. Roger admitted that to himself: he did kill John Deere, though, he added—and this he said aloud, "His head shouldn't've been like that." Roger felt a nervous-sick, took a swig of water, pressed the gas pedal, and brought the speedometer's needle to 90. If the police came, Roger would probably stop. But he didn't want to think about it anymore so he didn't. He didn't allow himself to think about the incident.

Two years ago, during Roger's first month on the job in Decker, at the warehouse where frozen food was loaded onto the truck Roger drove, enormous cuts of meat but also meals in boxes, vegetables and microwavable burritos, there had been a terrible accident. A truck driver named Davis, a fork lift, a crate, and a cracked palette. Roger heard wood split, a shout, a scream. A crate—three-hundred pounds of frozen food—had crushed Davis's gut and abdomen. Davis's legs lay separate from his body, pumping ever-weaker gasps of blood. Roger knelt beside Davis; Davis was alive; he whimpered and gripped Roger's hand. Davis wept, whimpered and begged. Davis cried because he knew he was dead. Roger had never seen anything so horrible and he muttered, "This is the most horrible thing I've ever seen," but he thought: "I can bear it."

As Roger drove past the Laurel exit, he turned on the radio, let it scan through the empty stations, numbers flicking from one end of the dial to the other without a word or a note, FM and AM—not too unusual, but—a little unusual. A tractor-trailer rushed past, rocking the Saab in its wake. Roger slowed his car, down to 85, and shook his head at the truck driver. Too dark to drive like that. He reached for a CD. Without looking to see which of his sister's mixes he'd picked up, he opened the case, popped out the CD, and slipped it into the player. When he and Vivienne lived together in his San Francisco apartment, he often came home from work to find his sister getting ready for a night out, music loud, sometimes with a girlfriend, both checking their make-up, both dancing, both teasing Roger for his suits. Roger hadn't minded. He liked to see his sister happy. He turned off the music.

On the road ahead, two. little. lights.

Roger hit the brakes hard, glanced at his rear-view mirror—he was alone on the highway. The tires held the road, his belt held him: he did not hit the bighorn sheep that lay in the road. He'd seen the animal's eyes, made gold by his headlights. The sheep's hip was crushed, its hind legs bent, hooves in the air. With its forelegs, the sheep dragged itself toward the car.

That the animal had been hit (very likely by the truck that had passed Roger a few miles back) did not trouble Roger much; certainly, he would not have gotten out of his car to stare if that had been the whole story. Roger was troubled because the animal was calm. There was no fear in its expression, no struggle in its movement. He'd seen animals similarly injured, mostly deer, and always they had looked terrified.

He let the sheep get quite close before he snapped out of his uncomfortable reverie *it's as if it's dead* and got back into his car.

A sign for Red Lodge distracted Roger; he recalled the only fact he knew about the area, that in 1943, the Smith Mine exploded, killing 74 miners. He thought of the sheep again, and he wished he'd shot it. Not to free it from its misery, but because it was horrible. In San Francisco, there were bad periods with Vivienne. He thought of the night he'd woken to find her standing in his bedroom doorway. He'd waited for her to say something, but she'd stood without moving, dressed in a pair of his pajamas, for long minutes—he'd glanced at his clock—3:07, 3:08, 3:09, etc.—until 3:20. He'd gotten out of bed, had put his hands on her shoulders and looked into her face. The illusion that she had no eyes was shockingly vivid, even now, as Roger drove I-90 toward western Montana, toward Seattle where Vivienne lived and was now sick in a hospital. She'd had eyes, of course, dull, blank, surrounded by puffy, gray skin. The illusion had disturbed Roger, but he blurted a cry when drool had dribbled from her lower lip, a great elastic strand. "Vivienne," he'd said. She'd closed her eyes, reopened them—eyes alive again—and she'd said, "What is it, Roger?" When Roger hadn't answered, she'd laughed and returned to the guest room. Some weeks, she'd done that every night. A few nights had been worse and once she'd screamed so much a neighbor had called the police (Roger had been glad when they'd shown up, banging on the door, if only so he could show Vivienne—asleep by the time they arrived, of course—to someone else, so that someone else could say, "She looks fine to me").

Roger drove slow for a few miles. A group of bighorn sheep, clustered at the side of the road, appeared to be normal. He brought the Saab back up to 85, drove fast past Greycliff, Springdale, McLeod and Livingston. Just outside of Bozeman, a car merged onto the highway. Its left taillight flickered, a loose wire, a red wink in the dark. The car exited, turned sharply onto an unmarked dirt road. Roger was once more alone on the road. The sky became silver blue. Roger ate elk jerky and peanuts. He tried the radio again.

A few miles from Main Street, Bozeman, in a trailer park, a teenaged boy, sixteen, woke up. His girlfriend, Dorie, was asleep beside him. His mind felt smoke-filled, vague; his skin stung and was slick and gritty. The night before—generic smokes, beer, and finally—finally!—sex, though stupid, frightening sex—Dorie yelped with pain and his orgasm came too quick and all over her thigh, and when she'd looked at the mess she'd said it was, "Absolutely disgusting." But he was not hung-over sick, not embarrassed or guilty sick. "Dorie," he said, just before his eyes rolled up and he felt his brain shift, slip inside his skull, felt things liquefy.

Thought—as he'd known it—was gone from his head. He pawed at Dorie's body, curious, her neck and her face, and skin came loose as he did. He ate a little bit of Dorie, but quickly lost the thread of what he was doing, wandered away from Dorie, into town.

Outside, the grassy mountains were white, their snow-covered peaks gray. The sky was empty. The teenaged boy was not alone in the park. Others walked sluggishly from their trailers. They had no interest in each other.

Roger was nearly to Bozeman. He dialed Martin's number: the news broadcast he'd found had been hysterical. "Martin, it's Roger." Alongside the highway were parked cars. "Martin, calm down." A man stood by a car, his hand up, a weak wave, but there was something so totally wrong in the way he waved. "Shut up, Martin. Shut up. How's my sister?" Roger clenched his teeth. "You stay there with her. You tell her I'm just eight hours away." Roger pulled the wheel to the left, let his cell phone drop to the floor, just missed hitting a car stopped in the middle of the highway. "Damn it!" he shouted. He reached for the phone and said, "Martin, what's going on?" but the call was lost.

Roger kept his radio off, to focus on driving. More people had parked their cars on the highway. A motorcycle lay on its side. A man and a woman were hugging. Roger slowed to 45. He hoped the traffic—if it could be called traffic—would clear once he was past Bozeman. Eight hours away. Roger wanted to be with his sister *now*, not in eight hours. He felt ridiculous and angry for leaving her. He reminded himself that he had his reasons and thus cleared his head. Had Roger turned on his radio, had Roger's antenna picked up a signal, he would have heard the news that a connection was being made to a world-wide star shower and several new diseases, or one disease with a variety of possible outcomes, a disease that affected not just people but mammals of all sorts. There was a warning about dogs and a story about a horse that tore off the leg of a little girl.

But Roger didn't hear the news, he drove in relative silence, cautiously until the traffic did clear up, just past Bozeman. He accelerated, brought the car up to 85, spied the green dinosaur logo of a Sinclair, and decided to stop in Belgrade to fuel up. He was more than a quarter down, and he didn't like that.

The gas station appeared unattended, but the pumps were on, so Roger filled up. As he stood by his car, he watched the window of the gas attendant's shack. A flicker on the glass; not someone in the station, headlights. The car weaved, and for a sick moment Roger was sure it would crash into the tanks, until it jerked away, rumbled down a dirt path, the gated entrance to a ranch, the gate wide. The pump clicked off. "Hello!" Roger shouted. He screwed on the cap, took half a dozen steps toward the shack, stopped and cried out again. He walked back to the car, opened the trunk, contemplated his shotgun for a moment, picked up a tire iron and a flashlight instead.

He did not go into the shack. He shouted once more, saw the glass door rattle against his voice, shone the light into the room. A few racks of maps were tumbled over. A coffee pot was smashed on the floor. He couldn't see over the counter. "This'll be on Sinclair," he thought, until he heard breathing, ragged like he'd heard before, in Billings, from the John Deere man.

"I'd like to pay for my gas," Roger said to the attendant, who'd come around the corner of the shack. Roger kept the beam of his light low on the man. "I said I'd like to pay." He raised the beam up, from crotch to chest, chest to face—

When the light hit the attendant's face the attendant screamed—squealed, really, a wet, porcine cry. The attendant raised his hands up, presumably to block the light but didn't actually cover his eyes, only held his hands up, on either side of his face.

The left side of the attendant's face showed bone, had the look of something chewed and raw.

Roger moved toward his car, tire iron raised and ready, but the attendant did not move, only screamed. Roger wanted to smash the attendant's face, to shut him up, to feel his head turn to mush at the end of the iron, but he saw no practical reason to do so, and so got into his car, and drove onto the road that led back to 90 West. The attendant squealed and squealed, hands up, tongue circling chapped lips, round and round, well after Roger was miles gone, past Churchill and Amsterdam, past Manhattan, fast approaching Three Forks. There, between Manhattan and Three Forks, Roger calmed enough to pull the car to the side of the road, found the presence of mind to get out of the car—tire iron firmly in hand—and retrieve his shotgun and the boxes of shells from the trunk. Once these comforts were on the back seat, Roger checked to see if he was close enough to Butte to get any reception on his phone.

"Martin, it's Roger," he said. He looked around: beyond his headlights there were only black shapes and nothing much in between. "Martin, what the hell is going on?" Behind Martin's voice the clatter of wheeled, metal furniture, the flash of brushed steel. "You're moving her where?" Vivienne was being moved upstairs, Martin said, because, "…more secure." Roger shouted—he didn't realize he was shouting, the noise from Seattle so loud, "Why secure?" Roger remembered Vivienne violent, coming home to find the glass-top coffee table shattered, Vivienne a mess on the floor, that vacant stare. "Is it Viv?" he asked. Martin shouted back, a "No," but wasn't speaking to Roger. Martin's voice lowered said something like "another patience," and the call died. Roger redialed, hung up—the road again, he needed to be *there*.

He thought he'd heard police sirens more than once, checked his mirrors, but all the way to Butte there was no one else on the road, and even for Montana, even so early in the morning, this wasn't normal. Roger scanned through the radio stations—near Butte there'd be something. He picked up a top 40 station, all pre-programmed, even the DJ, but otherwise there was nothing. Roger opted for silence.

Off the highway, down in Butte, men crawled along the jet-black slag walls, moved over the walls on all fours. A woman walked from a bar to the wall. Her walk was straight-backed, rigid. She grabbed a man from the wall, plucked him from the wall by his foot, dropped onto him, her knees snapped a rib, and she took a bite of the man's cheek. He did not struggle. He moved as if he were still crawling on the wall. A young mother, her child strapped into the backseat of her car, an '81 Rabbit Volkswagen, swerved onto Harrison Avenue, toward I-90. She'd never catch up to Roger, but she'd follow, miles behind, all the way to Seattle.

Behind her, Our Lady of the Rockies, a statue of Mary, mother of Jesus, 90 feet tall, usually brilliant white and lit by floods at night, was dark; all the flood lights were shattered. Mary was a dim shade, her face, blank.

The sky, for the first few hours of Roger's drive, had been distracting with stars and with lights falling to Earth. Then the sky went dead, exhausted, and for hours was gray-black, pasty, murky. At 5:13 AM, the sky got purple and clouds stretched low were visible and the mountains, too, vivid. The shadows of pines and rippled rock cast deep black lines. Roger had made good time—by driving between 85 and 95 most of the trip—yet he felt late, felt an anxious grip on his stomach and groin. All around were cars, most pulled over, like the sightseers' cars back in Billings. By 5:45, the sky was a deep pink.

And ahead, a car—for an instant Roger was sure the car was moving—maybe slow—but as he approached—fast—he saw that the car was stopped and that its front end was just off the road and touching the front end of another car. He jammed the brakes. He thought, *I don't have time to see if anyone's okay*, and, *I don't care*. Roger sat behind the wheel, finger on the door-lock, engine clicking, ignition off. 5:49 AM—still seven hours to drive—the clock went dark, came back to light, blinking 6:00 AM. "Close enough," Roger muttered, and without another thought he stepped out the car, shotgun in hand.

"Is anyone here?"

No response. The sky was empty, growing gorgeously pink, hints of a clear blue sky appearing up high, well above the mountains. A bull, a small shape near the tree line to Roger's left, walked toward the road, something about its gait unhealthy—and Roger heard the sound of gristle, chewed. For a moment he thought it was the crackle of a fire, and carefully examined the cars—the cars were fine, a little dent where the bumpers kissed, it looked to Roger as if the cars had slowly rolled into each other. He walked around the cars—glanced at the bull as he did so and saw that it was closer and that its flank was smeared with mud. The chewing sound grew loud and Roger caught a whiff of something foul, feces. Not the sweet smell of manure; more acrid.

On the other side of the stopped cars was a man wearing nothing but black dress socks. His pale skin was covered with excrement and dirt and blood. His face was buried in the stomach of a still living deer. The deer strained to keep its head off the pavement, its legs kicked. The man was holding the deer down—his strength—

"Stop," Roger said.

The man jerked his shoulders, pulled his head up out of the deer's gut, then released the deer—it struggled to move, but its viscera was spread around the naked man's knees, the deer, falling out of itself. Roger shot the deer in the head; it gave a great kick which broke open the naked man's head—

and a woman sat up in one of the cars and thrashed around, maybe an epileptic—

her head hit the dash and broke apart like glass, its contents, thick liquid.

The naked man, flailing, attempting to keep upright, reached for Roger, clawed at Roger's pant leg. That was when Roger began to think of those people—the John Deere man, the gas attendant, the woman in the car, and the naked man—as dead. Clearly they were not without animation, but they were not alive. Roger shot the naked man.

The bull was now at the side of the road. It's flank was not mud covered but an open wound—a great, wet hole—and Roger knew that it too was dead, that the dead were not just people but animals, too—*the raccoon*—and this gave Roger a terrible, lonely feeling—desperate. From now on, he would only stop for gas. The bull bellowed. Roger got into his car and drove away.

In no time at all, Roger drove past Anaconda, where the dead were lost in the Washoe Theater, confused by the golden deer painted on the theater's curtain, by the copper fixtures that dimly shone, by the rams' heads carved into the ceiling. Those still alive in Anaconda—a dog and a brother and sister, hid from their mother, who knew where her children were, but could not remember how to open the door to the basement.

There are stretches on 90 through Montana where the mountains are far from the road—always in view, but distant. Once far enough west, the mountains move in, the road curves up and among them. Snow drifts in May. When Roger saw the opportunity to fuel up, he did. Gas pumps were rarely manned and were often old—no slot to swipe a card. This worked. If a station looked disorderly or dark, Roger fueled up and left, no worries. He would have welcomed the sight of a police cruiser in his rearview. Once, a car passed, headed east, the back piled with household belongings, and two girls huddled together in the backseat. The driver's expression a warning: the dead were everywhere.

Forty miles outside of Missoula, Roger's cell phone received a flicker of reception, and immediately the phone rang. Roger dropped speed, from 90 to 80, and answered, "Martin."

It was not Martin, but Vivienne.

"Where are you?" she asked.

"About six hours, Viv. Less."

"Oh six hours I'm sick I don't know if I can hold on to my thoughts Roger six hours that's a long time and Roger the thought of you your handsome eyes where is my memory?" something metal hit the floor; someone shouted, Vivienne screamed.

Roger didn't shout into his phone, didn't cry out his sister's name. He dumped his phone onto the passenger seat, reception gone.

Two years before, the day after he left San Francisco, he stopped in Missoula, early in the afternoon. He stopped because he still had a day or two before he had to be in Decker, where he'd gotten a job delivering frozen food. He stopped for no other reason than to sightsee, which he did, he wandered aimlessly, amazed by how good it could be in a city that was not cosmopolitan, that was not San Francisco or New York, the two poles his life had him caught between—had once had him caught between. Spokane had been nice, had shown Roger a little city, emptier on a workday than he'd thought possible and Missoula was like that too, though less industrial, more kind. He ate a fish taco in a restaurant where people could still smoke, and he liked the way people were dressed, some for office work, surely, but many more for enjoying the place they were in and nothing else.

That Roger was romanticizing this place was evident even as he was doing so; a stop at a dingy bar cleared his head, kept the idea that maybe he'd settle in Missoula from fully forming. Afternoon light slanted into the dark bar decorated with license plates and empty bottles, some quite old, all beneath a film of dust. A few obvious alcoholics sat at the bar, a grad student who either thought the alcoholics were noble or who was a young alcoholic himself, and a skinny red head who turned out to be the bartender. She served Roger his beer, washed some glasses in a metal sink, then disappeared into a back room, the door marked with a sign that read: "hot dogs $1." A man in a once shiny baseball jacket turned to Roger and began to talk, without an invitation to do. He told Roger that he accepted his people's defeat, "Indians," he said, "didn't have weapons as good as yours and that's how it goes, I accept that, that's okay. But you should know, you might not have known this, but we have Custer's leg."

Roger, amused, asked, "What?"

"Custer's leg. The Blackfoot. We have it in a bag."

"The whole leg?"

"It's dust now."

The Blackfoot opened his mouth—presumably to smile—but without teeth, what his open mouth indicated was unclear.

"We pass it from tribe to tribe. Depending on the season."

"You mean, Custer, like, 'Custer's last stand' Custer? The general?"

"The government wants it back, so we pass it, tribe to tribe, keep it safe in a medicine bag."

Roger drove, he pushed 100. The feel of the car changed; eventually felt right. He checked for reception—as he passed through the Hellgate, reception returned, and Roger redialed.

Roger left San Francisco shortly before Vivienne married Martin. Martin's family thought it rude that Roger left town before the wedding, and one of Martin's aunt's was foolish enough to say so in Vivienne's presence. Vivienne didn't lose it, in the way she'd lost her mind from time to time while living with her brother, but she did explode, at first delivering a rich assemblage of Czech profanities, followed by an eerily calm explanation of Roger's importance in her life and of his right to do just exactly what he felt he had to do, and concluded with an un-invite of Martin's aunt, which was not reversed, as everyone on Martin's side of the family—even Martin though he never admitted as much—assumed would happen. As Roger was never discussed by his own family, he was never discussed by Martin's.

The phone connected to Martin's phone, and Roger heard noise like people arguing. Roger shouted his brother-in-law's name, shouted, "Vivienne!" A voice, high and hysterical. Roger said, "Vivienne?" But it wasn't Vivienne. "Martin. Shut up. Stop carrying on." A clatter, as if in the phone, the phone must have been dropped. Martin's voice, Martin apologized. "Fine," Roger said. "What's going on with Vivienne?" Martin's explanation made little sense. He said something like:

"The doctors don't know. An epidemic. Hardly any staff here at all. Vivienne is sick, man, sometimes she seems okay and sometimes she loses her mind. And that's what the doctors say, too, that people are losing their minds, like, not crazy, like, their minds are dying. You gotta get us out of here. We can't get out. And Vivienne wants to go."

A scream, Vivienne's, for sure. An animal loped onto the highway. At 100 miles per hour, Roger could not stop for it, dropped his cell phone, gripped the steering wheel so as to keep the car steady, and drove into the animal. Its pliant body burst over the hood of the car, a dog, perhaps, or even a wolf. The car skidded a little, but Roger kept control. The wipers cleared the windshield adequately. When he found the phone, the connection was gone, and no reception.

Roger slowed to navigate the winding roads of Idaho, but was in Washington in less than an hour. Out this way, Route 90 was rarely heavily trafficked, but there was simply no traffic. A couple times Roger swerved to avoid an abandoned vehicle, but he no longer worried about oncoming traffic, and straddled both lanes, preferring to stay clear of the shoulder, where many cars were either abandoned or was the site of unwholesome activity, peripheral glimpses of writhing and bloodied men and women. He crossed into Washington state. Soon, Spokane was below him. Here, he passed cars and trucks, people driving slowly to survey the damage, people heading east. He passed one car headed west, a little Rabbit that quickly receded in his rearview mirror, a red speck on faded gray highway.

Past Spokane, he stopped again for gas. He didn't look for an attendant. He was grateful the pumps were on. He considered the very good possibility that gas stations would dry up, maybe not in the next few days, maybe not in a week, but soon enough. He thought maybe he'd find a gas can and fill it. Maybe grab some food, too, though for now what he'd bought in Billings was plenty. Roger's freezers, back in Decker, were still humming, drawing power from the generator shed. Peter, who'd volunteered to drive Roger's route, didn't make it out of the driveway, crashed Roger's truck into a tree; Peter's head smashed open against the steering wheel.

A man, "Hey, man."

Roger's shotgun lay across the roof of his car.

"Hey man, can you give me a lift?"

The man was not dead, he was a young guy in torn jeans and a waffle shirt, with a dusty pack and dusty boots. Roger weighed the pros and cons of a passenger.

"This pack is killing me." The man dropped his pack between his feet, which revealed a bleeding wound on his shoulder. "I feel terrible, too. Look at this bullshit." The man pointed to his shoulder. "There's some fucked up shit going on."

Roger remained cool, determined to wait until the pump clicked off, then to fill the neck. No gas can, though. Roger sighed. No time, now.

The man asked, "Where are you headed?"

"Seattle."

"Great!"

"To see my sister."

"Seattle's great."

"She's sick. In the hospital."

"Sorry to hear it, man. But that's good for me. I could get this shit looked at, maybe get something for this damn headache."

The pump clicked. Roger squeezed the pump trigger, once, twice, then locked the cap.

"No," Roger said.

"'No' what?"

"I won't give you a ride."

"Why not, man?"

"You're sick."

"You're going to a hospital!"

"You're sick and you're going to die."

"Why the fuck would you say that?"

"How does it feel?"

"I feel pretty bad, that's how I feel."

"No. How does *it* feel?"

Roger lifted the shotgun from the roof of his car.

"You gonna shoot me? You're fucked up, you know that? Stay the fuck away from me. I'll get a ride from a human being. So just stay the—"

And Roger saw it happen. A moment of confusion, a jerky step back, a tremor that traveled the spine to the eyes.

"—fuck—"

Discharging his shotgun at the gas station would be stupid, and the man was no threat. Roger put the shotgun on the passenger seat, and brought out the tire iron.

"—away—" The man shook his head, as if to clear it.

There was plenty time for Roger to get into his car and drive away. The man saw what Roger held and stepped back, appeared to struggle with himself, took another step back. "Just let me go, man."

With the iron raised, Roger closed the distance between himself and the man, brought the iron down, let its own weight do most of the work, splitting open the left side of the man's head. *Not rotten yet,* Roger thought. The man jumped, something electric lifted him from the ground, and Roger swung again, up from his leg, and knocked the man to the dirt with a blow to the man's shoulder. *He's still alive.* Another blow, to the chest, broke ribs. The man cried out. Roger leaned over the man, beating him with the iron, beating him to death.

Roger tossed the tire iron into the passenger-side foot well, and drove away, his interest in the man gone, his need to reach his sister all the more keen.

When Roger left San Francisco, he quit a lucrative job and sold most of what he owned shortly after he learned of Martin's competent handling of a suicide attempt by Vivienne. Martin had returned from work and found Vivienne on the floor of their bathroom. He called for help, removed what pills were still in her mouth, and kept her awake. Once Vivienne was out of the hospital, Roger fully expected Martin to break up with Vivienne, leaving her once more in Roger's care. Instead, Martin took her on a short vacation and proposed. Roger waited for a little while after, suffered quietly and admired Vivienne's ring when she came home, which wasn't all that often. The night before Roger left, he and Vivienne spent one last evening together. They fell asleep together, in Roger's room, warmed by a fire and with no fuss at all.

Roger drove the rest of Washington in a haze. Deep forests. The falls of Snoqualmie. A white barn painted with the word "Cherries." All the energy it took to make the drive came from Roger's body, a knot of anger and lust and confusion untied from Decker to the bridge to Seattle.

Route 90 terminates as a long bridge that crosses Lake Washington into Seattle. He would not be able to drive into the city. The sun was up, the sky, clear. Not blue, exactly. More—white. The bridge was crowded with people, a great, sluggish crowd, biting and clawing at each other and at nothing, spitting blood, smeared with blood, coated and crusted with blood. Roger thought of his sister. *Maybe.* He needed to get across the bridge. He filled his pockets with shells. He would clear a stretch of the bridge, get back into his car and drive until he needed to clear another stretch. He would drive across a bridge of corpses. When the path became too narrow for the car, he would walk. *I am ready to destroy whatever monsters lie between me and my sister and I'm ready to keep her alive forever.* He unlocked the door, stepped onto the bridge, and took aim.

Weird Furka

KADE, a commercial radio station in Furka, Montana, was moving in a few months from its current location, the "Furkabick Hotel," as the DJs had dubbed it, to a new location with a greater broadcast range. The Furkabick Hotel was a three story house, built during the copper rush. The house ceased to be a residence in the mid-thirties, and became KADE shortly after. The station has broadcast nearly continuously, with only short interludes of dead air. KADE broadcast country and bluegrass music and syndicated radio shows until the late 1950s/early 60s, when the last episodes of "The Lone Ranger," "Have Gun, Will Travel," and "Gunsmoke" were aired. The station switched over to an all-country format, which it has remained, adding several politically conservative drive time talk shows, in the early 1990s.

The only exception to this format was an ambient/electronic/experimental music show broadcast Monday mornings, from 1 AM to 4, a time-slot that failed to draw any advertising dollars. The show was created and hosted by Craig Watson, a friend of the owner's girlfriend. Craig lived in one of the few houses left in Furka. He worked as a bartender and occasionally manned the pumps at Manny's. Once KADE moved, and its range increased, and advertisers became interested, his show would be cancelled. He called his show "Songs of Degrees." Virtually no one listened. Craig liked the idea that a sleepless radio listener might roll the dial low and come upon his broadcast, drawn in by unfamiliar sounds.

Craig was usually the only person at the station when his show was broadcast. He loved the Furkabick Hotel, and thought it a shame that the station was abandoning the old house. One more step toward turning Furka into another Montana ghost town. The nature of what he broadcast left him with long stretches when he didn't have to man the boards—twenty minute compositions of water dripping, of string instruments recorded inside vast underground caverns, of people's voices phased into a fold of noise, and phased back into a conversation. Besides, he didn't like to talk too much during the show's broadcast—he didn't want to explain; he wanted listeners to encounter, and take from their encounter what they might. During these long stretches he liked to wander through the empty house. Other than the studio itself, a long unused recording studio, and an office and a front desk on the first floor, the Furkabick was still very much a house, replete with old furniture, paintings and knick knacks. He'd explored the top, second and first floors very thoroughly; the only treasure he'd found was a volume of western themed poetry, which he brought into the studio and read while broadcasting, and occasionally read selections of to his listeners.

Craig decided, that before his show was cancelled, that he needed to explore the basement. He hadn't done so yet because the door to the basement was locked with an old padlock—a skeleton key fit in its face. On the first Sunday of October, with a single swing of a small sledge, he sent the padlock singing across the floor. He located it and hung it back on the latch. With a camping lantern in hand, he carefully picked his way down the wooden steps—nearly falling through a rotted plank. After the nervousness of the moment passed, he thought, "It'd be a long morning laying down there with a broken leg." The air smelled of dust and mildew, and he sneezed more than once as he peered around in the dark space.

The basement was nearly empty. The floor was hard-packed dirt, and wooden support pillars with bark shredded like fur ran in even rows from one end of the basement to the other. Bare wooden bookcases lined one wall. Just beyond the boiler and the oil tank, both red with rust, was a set of bunker doors, which he reasoned must be how the owner and the maintenance people got in and out to check the gauges and the fuse box. On the other end of the basement was a door-less doorway. Craig walked to it and shone the lantern inside. A bare room, with a cement floor, without windows, but with a very intriguing feature: a wooden trap door in the floor. Craig looked at his watch and ran back upstairs—careful to avoid the rotted step—to put on another CD. He sat in the warm studio—the only room with any heat at that hour—listened to the drone piece he'd put on, and contemplated the trap door. The basement had been enough to make him a little uncomfortable—the thought of opening the trap actually scared him a little. "This is silly," he said aloud. The track he was playing had another 30 minutes to it, so he went back down to the basement to finish his exploration.

The trap door was locked with another old padlock that resisted several blows from the sledge, but the latch itself finally gave, cracking out of the wood of the door with such a noise that Craig jumped back, startled, afraid he'd disturbed some animal's nest. He glanced at his watch, calmed down a bit, and lifted the trap.

A strong odor rose up in a gust: a vinegary smell, mingled with the acid smell of old paper. A wooden ladder led into the sub-basement. Craig laid on his belly and hung his lantern down into the darkness. With the light suspended into the small space, the basement around him was pitch dark. The room was furnished with metal bookcases, and the bookcases were filled with records and boxes of reel-to-reel recordings and electrical equipment. Craig was briefly overcome with a nervous, tingling sensation. He started to climb down into the room when he caught a glimpse of his watch. "Damn," he said, and ran back upstairs to the studio. He looked for a CD with a long running time, put it on, and went back downstairs.

He knew that what was in the sub-basement belonged to KADE, but decided to carry as much of his find out to his truck anyhow, figuring that the owner had no idea any of it existed, and that he could return it during the chaos of the move. The job took two hours, and was a lot of hard lifting. The transcription disks and the machine used to make them, were the crown jewel of his find, he knew it, but it cost him a lot of lower back pain and had it fallen on top of him, as he pushed it out of the sub-basement, it could've crushed bones. Again he pictured himself on the floor, unable to move, but this time, so deep in the basement, he might never be found.

At 4, the morning DJ came in, looking exhausted, strung out, thermos of coffee opened and steaming. An hour later, the receptionist came. By then, Craig was in his bedroom, everything hauled in from his truck and set down on the floor around his bed. He looked at the equipment he'd brought home and thought, "What possessed me to do that?" He laughed at himself: he thought of himself as daring when it came to ideas, but not as a man of action. Briefly, souring his amusement with himself, a panic came over him, a clammy mist which filled his head. Just for an instant. He slept soundly.

Craig worked at the bar that same night. After his show and before his shift he usually didn't do too much other than sleep and have a late lunch. On that Monday, when he woke, he had a strong desire to set up the equipment he'd found and go through the boxes of records but decided, after some deliberation, that he'd rather wait until he had a solid block of time. He ate at his kitchen counter and walked to the bar a little early.

Johnson, a regular, was the only patron.

"Craig," he said, when Craig emerged from the kitchen, tying a knot in the back of the apron he wore around his waist.

"Johnson." Craig thought Johnson was okay. Johnson drove a delivery truck, usually at night, and liked to make fun of Craig's show, which Johnson insisted he never listened to.

"I made it through ten minutes of your program last night."

"Yeah?"

"But only because I thought it was the Emergency Broadcast, and the government would come on with important information." Johnson laughed at his own joke. Craig forced a smile.

"How are you doing, Johnson?"

"I'm fine, fine. If I wasn't married I'd be perfect." Johnson laughed again. Wife jokes were also part of his routine with Craig. "You look dreadful, though. Always do on Mondays."

"The show kind of messes with my schedule."

"I bet. When're you going to give that up? You don't get paid, do you?"

"I like doing the show. I like radio." Craig started drying the wet glasses the dishwasher had brought out. He had this same conversation week after week. "But, it looks as if I won't be doing it much longer. Station's moving and they won't be taking me with them."

"That's a damned shame. But if we tune in at the same time as always, and nothin's on, it'll be like hearing your show."

When Craig returned home from the bar he stripped off his clothes, which stank of cigarette smoke, showered and put on clean clothes. He brewed a pot of coffee, brought the pot into his room and set to sifting through his find, which, when Johnson wasn't talking, was all he could think about at work. The first box was filled with 16-inch transcription disks, acetate coated glass. By Craig's reckoning, they were in fine condition—no crystallization of the acetate. The basement room must have been very dry and cool. The next box contained metal disks and a few made on cardboard. He was extremely excited; terrified too that he was now responsible for these fragile recordings. He unlatched a suitcase-size box and was overjoyed to see that it was a transcription machine—possibly the very machine used to make the recordings. There was also a record player, capable of playing the transcription disks—able to switch from 80 to 70 RPMs, and an Ampex tape recorder—the earliest commercially available tape recorder. The third box he opened was filled with tape recordings, the fourth with more, and the fifth with another set of glass transcription disks. "Good Lord," he thought, "If these machines still work, I'll be able to listen to all of this." He bit his fist to control his excitement. He wished there was someone he could tell, someone who wouldn't spread the word all over Furka, resulting in Craig's having to return everything to KADE. He uncoiled the wire, plugged the record player into a socket and clicked the power switch to the on position.

He fell asleep, on the floor of his bedroom, listening to a scratchy recording of a local news broadcast made in 1942.

On Friday, after sitting at Manny's in case a car actually came, Craig went home and put on one of the cardboard transcription disks. In tinny mono, he heard what sounded like some of the ambient music he played on his show. This had him; he wondered if he was about to hear a very old experimental record. Perhaps he had discovered a lost composer. After a few grooves of the disk, though, the music faded, and a man introduced himself.

WEIRD FURKA
TRANSCRIPT NUMBER ONE
Broadcast July, 1947

MUSIC INTRO: Pipes being tapped, individually and faintly at first, then all at once, firmly, louder and faster. Once a cacophony of sound has been created, tapping ceases, and sound fades.

ANNOUNCER: [A deep voice] Greetings, listeners. I wish to welcome you to a new kind of weird radio show. The strange stories you are about to hear are true, and told by the people who lived them. If you scoff at the idea that there is a world outside of our common perception, another world beyond our own, [whispered] *the supernatural world* [no longer whispered], then prepare to have your assumptions challenged; if you already believe such a world exists, then prepare to have your beliefs confirmed. [In a booming, reverberating voice] Welcome to Weird Furka!

HOST: Thank you for tuning in. Tonight, on our first in what I hope to be a long-lasting series of broadcasts documenting the weird happening in our own Furka, I have a peculiar tale told by a housewife, Mrs. Buzzard, who lives in a well-kept house on Broad Street. In an effort to distance this show from *dramatic* shows, and because the modern American housewife is busy all day long, I took KADE's top of the line portable recording device to Mrs. Buzzard's kitchen to capture her weird story.

What you're listening to is a live recording.

[Sounds from the street] Mrs. Buzzard, is it all right if we close the windows? It'll be better for the recording.

MRS. BUZZARD: Certainly. It'll get pretty stuffy in here, though. I'm baking.

HOST: And it smells wonderful. But the noise from outside. [Sound of windows being closed. Sound of an oven door opened and closed] Thank you. You answered a letter I sent out saying that you had a strange story to tell. Is this something that happened to you?

MRS. BUZZARD: [Sounding distant] I wrote it on the card that it happened to my sister.

HOST: I know, but for our listeners. And please speak in the direction of the microphone. So, this weird event happened to your sister?

MRS. BUZZARD: Yes.

HOST: Please tell our listeners what happened, just like you told me on the card you sent. And please speak toward the microphone.

MRS. BUZZARD: Is this better?

HOST: Much.

MRS. BUZZARD: Well, my sister—her name's Clara—is it okay to use her name, or is this like "Dragnet"?

HOST: It's okay to use her name.

MRS. BUZZARD: My sister Clara lost her husband, Sam, to a heart attack. A terrible thing. Of course we were all upset but especially Clara and her son. She was very depressed and cried a lot and had a hard time doing anything. I'd come over and our brother, Francis, would come over too. He fixed up her sink and made sure there was enough coal in the basement, the things Sam would normally do. Sometimes Francis would take Clara's son out to watch a ball game, too.

Now, this may seem a little unusual, but Clara had two

phones, one for the upstairs and one downstairs. You see, they had a very big house, so that way, if Clara was cleaning upstairs and a call came through, she didn't have to run down to the living room.

HOST: Sure.

MRS. BUZZARD: One day the upstairs phone rings. She told me she ran up the stairs without thinking about it and answered it. The person on the other line says that he's her husband, and wanted to let her know he was okay. Though the man on the other end of the line sounded like her husband, she was furious, of course, and in tears, and hung up.

Soon after Francis came by the house and found her at the kitchen table, crying. When he asked what was the matter she told him that she answered the phone upstairs and a prankster said he was her husband. She asked Francis, "Just how cruel can you get?" Well Francis looked at her in a funny way and reminded her that the upstairs phone didn't work. You see, a little before Sam died, he'd started on a project in the upstairs hall and had taken out the phone jack.

HOST: Amazing. A call from the dead.

MRS. BUZZARD: Well that isn't all. The next morning she was in the kitchen washing the dishes and a man walked by the house and she was sure it was her husband. Absolutely certain. She dropped a dish in the sink and chipped it. Before she could go outside to see if he really was her husband—after the call the night before she didn't know what might be true—her son ran into the kitchen. He looked extremely happy and in a rush—you know how children talk when they're excited—he told her that he was just outside playing and his dad walked up to him and smiled and told him that he was okay.

And that's the story.

HOST: Thank you very much Mrs. Buzzard, for sharing with our audience that weird but true ghost story.

[The sound quality changes a bit. The HOST is back in the studio] Thank you very much for tuning in. Tune in next week for another weird but true story.

ANNOUNCER: Weird Furka is a new kind of show, in which listeners hear the bizarre stories of their neighbors. If you've had a weird encounter with the supernatural, please contact KADE, Weird Furka [address]. Tune in next week for another story that will shake you free of the everyday.

MUSIC EXTRO: Same as introductory music, but cut off by the recording.

By Sunday, Craig had found two other episodes of "Weird Furka," all on the cardboard transcription disks. He decided that at some point during his show, he would air all three episodes. He put on a long modern classical piece, one with sounds similar to the intro music for "Weird Furka." Sure that everyone was out of the station, he ran out to his car and carried the disks and the machine he needed to play it up into the studio. Unable to dub the show successfully, he decided he'd just lower the studio microphone and air the show that way; it was short, he would sit silently and listen. He faded out the classical piece as he started the record. The pipe-sounds came up, and then the announcer. There was something about the show that he found utterly compelling. He promised himself he'd do a little library research when he got the time; for now, he listened to the familiar broadcast: the sounds in Mrs. Buzzard's kitchen, the announcer, who Craig was beginning to suspect was the host. He could smell what she was baking, feel the heat in her kitchen. He sat and watched the disk spin. He didn't move at all.

On Monday night, the bar was nearly empty, except for a few regulars. Craig was stacking glasses. He jumped at the large smack of an open hand on the bar, and at the barking of his name.

"What the hell was that?" Johnson demanded.

"What the hell was what?" Craig ran a towel over a dry glass, as if he were polishing a stone.

"I turn on the radio and I hear a voice I thought I'd never hear again. I know the man's dead, so I could only assume my radio'd fell into another dimension or I was tuning in Hell."

"You listened to my show last night?"

"Hell no. I never listen to your show. When I'm driving at that hour I turn the station to something that doesn't sound like a room full of children with busted musical instruments. But last night… were you responsible for bringing Frank Shokler back from the dead?"

"Frank Shokler?"

"The guy who did that show."

"'Weird Furka.'"

"That's the show. 'Weird Furka.' Damn weird all right. Worse 'n weird."

"You know about the show?" Craig put down the glass and the towel and leaned forward.

"Give me a draft and I'll tell you if I know the show."

Craig poured a draft, all the while looking at Johnson, waiting for the story. Johnson waited until he'd had a drink before he spoke.

"I used to listen to that show when it first came on. They used it for filler between Benny and 'Gunsmoke.' I liked those shows so I heard a few episodes of Frank's show." He took another swig of his beer, wiped his mouth on the back of his hand and proceeded. "I didn't like that man at all. I tolerated that show for a while, but when it got really weird—when he got really weird—I tuned out. I'd turn off my radio for twenty minutes rather than listen. And I like a good creepy story from time to time. Hell, back then I probably had a *Vault of Evil* or some nonsense stuffed in my glove compartment. But Frank was a bastard and then he got to be a frightening bastard and I was done with him. Where'd you find that shit?"

"I just dug it out of a library."

"Oh yeah?" Johnson didn't look like he believed Craig, but didn't seem to care. "What possessed you to play it on the air?"

"I thought… it's interesting. It's local. I thought my listeners might like it."

"You ain't got listeners."

Craig knew that was likely. That was one of the reasons why "Songs of Degrees" wasn't going to move with the station. "What do you know about Frank Shokler?"

"Not much. He was in my high school. Didn't play sports. Built a crystal set we'd listen to in shop. I wasn't friends with him. He went away after high school. When he came back, it wasn't long until he was recording interviews with every nutty housewife and derelict in town. Then he was gone again."

When Johnson was finished with his beer, Craig poured another. "On the house," he said.

During the next week Craig set up the Ampex and started listening to the reel-to-reels. Again, local news, a few field recordings of live Jazz shows and an on-the-scene broadcast of a major forest fire. He also found what he had hoped he might: more episodes of "Weird Furka." Since bringing home the recordings, Craig ate all his meals in his bedroom. Dirty plates and bowls had accumulated around the equipment in his room. He brought a hot plate in to heat soup. The rest of his house seemed large and silent, seemed to press down on Craig, so he shut the door of his bedroom when he listened.

He searched unsuccessfully online for any mention of the show or of Frank Shokler. Furka hadn't had a library for over a decade, so after a few hours at Manny's—during which he did nothing more than raise the gas prices on the marquee and sweep out the shack that he sat in—Craig drove to the library in the next town over. He didn't find much there, either. On microfiche were radio listings which provided him a way to date the episodes. He carefully copied out all the dates, then realized no episode titles were given, and there were no titles on the recordings he'd found; some of them were numbered; but he wasn't sure the radio listings started with the first episode. The show was on the air for less than a year. He uncovered a small article from an issue of the *Furka Weekly*, which talked about "Weird Furka" and Frank Shokler's death—

in rather flip terms, Craig thought. The central theme of the piece being that Shokler's death was as strange as an episode of his own show. After making that comment, the article was vague about how he died, stating that, "It may have been a heart condition," and mentioning that he was found at the station. As an extension of the joke the article basically was, the reporter had tracked down two of the women Shokler had interviewed on the show: Mrs. Buzzard and Mrs. Drummond. Mrs. Buzzard talked about how he was still around, "in the air." Mrs. Drummond said about Shokler, "He was a polite fellow. He was skinny. And when we talked—which was really only the once but I remember it like yesterday—he was very intense, as if he were trying to see around me. Or around what I was saying."

WEIRD FURKA
Transcript Number Four
Broadcast August, 1947

MUSIC INTRO

ANNOUNCER: Greetings once again, dear listeners. The strange stories you are about to hear are true, and told by the people who lived them. If you scoff at the idea that there is a world outside of our common perception, another world beyond our own, *the supernatural world*, then prepare to have your assumptions challenged; if you already believe such a world exists, then prepare to have your beliefs confirmed. Welcome to Weird Furka!

HOST: Thank you for tuning in. I'm your host, Frank Shokler. Tonight's mysterious story is told to us by Mrs. Drummond, who kindly invited me into her homey living room. As I've said before, in an effort to distance this show from *dramatic* shows, I took KADE's top of the line portable recording device out of the studio and into the supernatural fire, so to speak. Nothing is scripted. What you're listening to, as always, is a live recording.

Mrs. Drummond, you wrote to me and shared with me a most fascinating story. Will you be kind enough to enlighten our listening audience?

MRS. DRUMMOND: [Nervously] Yes. Should I start?

HOST: Yes, Mrs. Drummond, please begin.

MRS. DRUMMOND: For a time, I lived in a house that was haunted. This was the first house my husband and I bought. We bought it for a song and I suppose that was in part due to the rumors. We liked the idea that there were ghosts and hoped to see one.

At least until we invited my brother to the house for a night. My brother was a serviceman in the first war and on leave, and was driving to see a girl—he married her, in '19. Anyway, at the time, my husband was on a strict medical diet and to support him I went on it too. We served my brother a meal we couldn't eat—I don't think my brother ever saw a meal without a potato! [laughs] We told him about our diet and then moved to the living room and spent a quiet evening chatting. Around eleven, we all retired. We put my brother in the downstairs guest room.

In the morning, over breakfast, my brother grinned at us and asked which one of us was it, breaking our diet and sneaking down to the kitchen? We both denied having gone down. He accused us again and my husband asked him why he was so sure. He told us that he heard footsteps in the kitchen. He said that, with all the activity in the kitchen, he figured one of us was preparing quite a feast. He also added that he was sure he was going to be invited to join, because his door opened, though no one came in.

Well I looked at my husband, and he nodded, and I said to my brother, "You're so lucky. One of the reasons we bought this house was because it is rumored to be haunted by the first homeowner's butler. The guest room, in fact, was the butler's room. We haven't heard or seen anything ourselves, you're the first." Unfortunately, this story really bothered my brother. I didn't see him again until my husband and I moved out here.

HOST: That's quite a story, Mrs. Drummond. Did you or your husband ever see or hear the ghost?

MRS. DRUMMOND: No, we never did. We were very disappointed. I guess we're heavy sleepers.

HOST: Thank you very much Mrs. Drummond.

[Sound changes, back in studio] I find it really quite amazing just how many people have had supernatural experiences in Furka. Until I sent out my letters asking for such stories—and if you didn't get a letter, feel free to write me directly at the station—I never would have guessed. There are enough interesting stories for this show to go on quite a while.

I've been wondering, these past weeks, if Furka is for some reason a place where the supernatural and the natural cross, an intersection to other dimensions, perhaps, and that people—sensitive people—are occasionally granted glimpses. Alternatively, I've wondered if Furka isn't exceptional at all. That if I were to go into any town in Montana, or anywhere in the country for that matter, and ask people to share with me their supernatural tales, that just as many would have stories to tell. Perhaps if we recorded enough of these stories, we would gain an understanding of the mysterious, and perhaps a way to make contact with the other side. This is Frank Shokler, signing off.

ANNOUNCER: And that takes care of another episode of Weird Furka, a new kind of show, in which listeners hear the bizarre stories of their neighbors. If you've had a weird encounter with the supernatural, please contact KADE, Weird Furka [address].

Tune in next week for another story that will shake you free of the everyday.

MUSIC EXTRO

With a little inventive wiring, Craig found that he could digitize the reel to reels, and burn them onto a CD. This made it a lot easier to bring the shows to the station.

Johnson caught Craig's eye from the barroom door. For a moment, Craig thought Johnson was going to charge the bar. Craig backed up a little, wringing has washcloth through his hands.

"Why do you insist on playing that nonsense?" Johnson demanded.

"I thought you didn't listen."

"Shut it, Craig. I keep my radio on KADE for country. But I hear what's on. And I know when Shokler's on the air. I can sense it. And I don't like it."

"Look, Johnson, what're you drinking?"

"What do you think?"

Craig poured out a glass of the local brew Johnson drank. Craig said, "It's a harmless little show, Johnson. It's quaint."

"Frank Shokler wasn't harmless. The show reminds me of bad times."

"He wasn't harmless?"

"I thought his show was gone. That he was gone. You'll stop airing it, right? Go back to that trash-compactor stuff you used to play, right?"

Craig grinned. "I still play that trash-compactor stuff."

"Well play it all the time."

"I don't understand why you care."

"You'll take it off, won't you?"

Craig felt courage swell up inside of him, the same feeling of courage that had him crawling around the station's dark basement two weeks before. "No, Johnson. I don't think that I will."

"Then damn you, Craig." Johnson left, his glass more than half full.

Craig found, among the reel-to-reels, thirty recordings of "Weird Furka," in addition to the three cardboard transcription disks. He didn't want to hear them all at once, he decided. He wanted to make them last as long as he could. So, he listened to a few episodes over and over, laying on his bed or on the floor of his room. Sometimes he listened to one of the other recordings. He started to reuse plates rather than take the time to wash them. Sometimes he urinated into a cup instead of leaving his room to go to the bathroom.

He did a little more research into the media the shows were recorded on, and learned that it was extraordinary for the recordings to have survived the way they did. The acetate coating on the cardboard disk typically became brittle, the petroleum separated out of it, or crystals formed on the surface. The reel-to-reels also should have become brittle, or, if conditions were different, turned into a sort of glue. Recordings made as recently as the 1980s in professional recording studios were unstable. The media "Weird Furka" were recorded on, and the shows stored with it, were all like new. Burning what he could onto CD comforted him, guaranteeing, he believed, the longevity of the show; in the back of his mind, though, he was fairly sure that he didn't have to worry.

In the middle of the night he woke up. He sat up in bed and shouted, "Who?" and he looked around quickly, trying to figure out where he was and—once that was established—why his room was in the state it was in. He recognized, barely, the recording equipment, but he didn't recall bringing in the dishes or the mugs or the hot plate. He was a neat person. He was disturbed by the smell—an unfamiliar, stale smell. And then, a metal corner of the transcription machine glinted, and caught Craig's eye, and he was lost, and then asleep again.

The next Sunday, when he pulled up to the station, he stopped before getting out of his truck, because there was a large black dog standing near the station door. He watched it, illuminated in his headlights. The dog didn't move. He got out of the truck slowly, gathered his CDs from the passenger seat, and walked toward the front door. The dog followed Craig with a slow turn of its head. At the front door, Craig and the dog were side by side. He tried to suppress the terror he felt, sure the dog would pick up on his fear and jump at him; he didn't think he could bear it if the dog barked. Once inside, the door shut behind him, he looked out at the dog. In turn, it watched him.

Up in the studio, Craig warned the DJ about the dog.

"Thanks for the heads up, Craig."

"It was the strangest thing."

"Dogs are like that, sometimes. Nothing to worry about, I'd imagine. He'll probably be gone by the time I leave." The DJ sniffed at the air. "Maybe he smelled food on you."

"Oh, sorry." Craig hadn't done any laundry in the past week. His clothes either smelled like cigarettes from the bar, or like the peanut butter sandwiches he'd been eating almost nightly.

"Don't sweat it. You got your first song ready?"

Craig handed him a CD. "It's track seven."

"OK." The DJ cued it up. "What is it?"

Craig described the piece; the DJ clearly wasn't interested.

"I've been listening to your show on my drive home. You gonna play any of those shows?"

Craig brightened. "Yes, yes I am."

"Where the hell'd they come from?"

"Oh, ah, a friend of mine."

"He found 'em? They sound really old."

"No, no, he makes them. He makes them sound old. It's amazing what you can do with a computer."

The DJ nodded, but didn't appear to believe Craig's story at all. The DJ swung the microphone in front of his face, faded out his song, and said, "That wraps it up for me, folks. Next up, "Songs of Degrees," with your host, Craig Watson. I don't know about you, but I find those little shows he plays to be more peculiar than the music he likes. Hope none of it gives y'all nightmares." The DJ started up Craig's CD, and wished Craig a goodnight.

Craig could hardly stand listening to the music; he desperately wanted to get to "Weird Furka," to hear Frank's voice. He knew he needed to space the shows out, though; they were very short, he'd only brought three, and he was on the air until 4 AM.

When Craig left the studio, the dog was still outside. As Craig climbed into the cab of his truck he said to the dog, "Goodnight, Harold." The dog nodded, and walked off. What he had done didn't strike Craig as peculiar until he was in bed. When he remembered what he'd done, what he'd said, though, he opened his eyes wide in his dark room, and covered his open mouth. Before questions could emerge, such as why his room was in the state it was in, or why he felt so driven to play "Weird Furka" during his own show, a wet feeling came into his body.

Craig found that his desire to hear the "Weird Furka" shows he hadn't listened to yet was greater than his wish to extend his pleasure. On Tuesday night he listened to every episode he had. The shows being as short as they were—ranging from five minutes to ten, he was able to listen to them all in a couple of hours. He left his house when he had to work at the bar, arriving a little late. When he got back home, he listened to them all once more. Three of the episodes, not including the first, featured stories told by Mrs. Buzzard, who became less and less nervous with each show. At first Craig dismissed Mrs. Buzzard as a crackpot and a ditz, but gradually he grew to love her voice, and the way she told a story, and the smells of her home, which he imagined he smelled while he listened. These smells covered the rotten, sweaty smell of his bedroom. One episode struck Craig as a sort of turning point, a moment when "Weird Furka" changed and became something more than just a collection of local legends and personal anecdotes.

WEIRD FURKA
TRANSCRIPT NUMBER SEVENTEEN
Broadcast October, 1947

    MUSIC INTRO
        HOST: Greetings once again. I'm your host, Frank Shokler. If you scoff at the idea that there is a world outside of our common perception,

another world beyond our own, *the supernatural world*, then I hope to challenge your assumptions; if you already believe such a world exists, then I hope to confirm your beliefs; I hope to be welcomed into your brotherhood. This is Weird Furka!

Until now, I have presented the stories of your neighbors. I have recorded the stories in their homes, at their invitation. I think these stories have all been compelling. I considered myself to be among the unfortunate who had not directly experienced anything supernatural.

Perhaps being in the presence of those who have, perhaps because of my recent steady contemplation of unusual phenomena, or a combination of the both, I have recalled a story from my youth, an episode I had quite forgotten until earlier this week. The story came to my memory so vividly, and so suddenly, I doubted it was anything more than a dream. I thought about it, and thought about it, and realized that no, it wasn't a dream at all, but a memory that had been lost to me for some reason. Perhaps suppressed because of what it hinted at, suppressed by my own self in a misguided attempt to keep me grounded in the reality of the day-to-day. Hopefully you will extend to me the same faith you extend to those I've interviewed these past few months. Hopefully you will not chalk this up as a radio stunt or as filler. I assure you, I have many other stories from your neighbors that I will broadcast for you in the upcoming weeks. Please indulge me: upon rediscovering this episode of my youth, I felt an urgency to share it with you.

When I was a boy I used to take long walks in the woods. My parents didn't like that I did it, because they were afraid I'd be mauled by a bear or shot by a hunter. Still, I went. There were trails I knew and loved, because of particular trees or rocks or tiny pools of water in the stream that frogs and fish lived in.

One late afternoon I was climbing on a rock and I saw what I thought must be a firefly. It was a light which flashed for a moment a few feet off the ground. I looked for the light and in a moment I saw it again. I realized then that it wasn't a flashing light, like the light of a firefly, but only appeared to be, as my view of it was obscured intermittently by trees. The sky grew dimmer, the light seemed to grow brighter, and I was sure that it was moving closer to me.

Once I got close to the light—it was a fireball, hanging in the sky, like a Biblical sign—I felt no heat from it, but it was a flame just the same—once I got close, it started moving away from me. I followed it. At times it was difficult, and had I been an adult I don't think I could have gotten through the brambles and dense shrubbery it led me through.

The fireball and I came out of the woods to a field. Along the field ran a dirt road. A mile down was a tall house. The fireball rose and rose and then vanished. I stared at the spot in the sky where I'd last seen it for a while before I looked back at the house. I thought maybe the fireball had wanted me to go to the house, but seeing that tall house out there, having been lead there by a fireball—it terrified me. When I thought about what might be inside that house—

I didn't think I'd ever see that house again. But I realize now, now that that memory has come back to me, that that house was KADE, a good fifteen years before there *were* radio stations in Montana.

It probably sounds as if I'm just making this up, taking up radio time because I don't have a real show, but I ask that you believe me, and I assume some of you good listeners will. This memory came to me like that fireball did when I was a boy, it emerged from behind a thicket of trees in my mind and made itself known as a bright, burning point. I am really unsure what this all means. Is it Furka? Could it be this converted house that I'm broadcasting from? What draws the supernatural world out of its invisible place and into our sphere, where our perceptions are so dominated by five drab senses? I leave you to think on that.

Next week Weird Furka will return in its customary format—I will be interviewing a Furka resident who has had a supernatural experience. What will make next week's episode unusual, is that that Furka resident is a twelve-year-old boy! Goodnight.

MUSIC EXTRO

Craig didn't do anything for a while after listening to episode seventeen for the third time in a row. He let the tape's leader flap as the reels spun around. He was on his back, surrounded by bowls and plates. Upon hearing episode seventeen the second time something had grown in his memory—just a little bit, enough for Craig to detect it. When he played the show again, the memory moved forward, just as the fireball had in Frank's story. That memory of Craig's—that moved forward in his mind—was of the same fireball, and how it had led Craig to the Furkabick Hotel. Sure, the owner's girlfriend, one night at the bar, had listened to Craig talk about his love of radio and had said she would speak with the owner about finding time for Craig to do his own show; sure she had given him directions to the station and told him when to go. But overlapping those truths, was the truth that Craig had followed a cold fireball to KADE that had left him standing in front of that tall house wondering how he'd gotten there.

When Craig couldn't stand the enormous roar of his own circulatory system, he carefully put on the next reel, to listen to episode eighteen again.

He was not excited to hear it, because it struck him as a step back from episode seventeen; he knew later episodes were more like episode seventeen, so his inclination was to skip ahead. Yet—he felt as if that would be disrespectful.

WEIRD FURKA
Transcript Number Eighteen
Broadcast October, 1947

    MUSIC INTRO
    ANNOUNCER: Greetings dedicated listeners. The strange stories you are about to hear are true, and told by the people who lived them. If you scoff at the idea that there is a world outside of our common perception, another world beyond our own, *the supernatural world*, then prepare to have your assumptions challenged; if you already believe such a world exists, then prepare to have your beliefs confirmed. Welcome to Weird Furka!
    HOST: Thank you for tuning in. I hope last week's episode was not too off-putting. Tonight, we have a peculiar tale for you told—with permission from his parents—by a twelve-year-old boy named Jimmy.

        [transitional sounds] How are you today, Jimmy?
    JIMMY: I'm fine, Mr. Shokler.
    HOST: Well, now, Jimmy, you and your parents sent me a very interesting letter about a mysterious experience you had. Would you care to tell our audience your story? And please speak into the microphone, son.
    JIMMY: [Too close to the microphone] My parents and I just moved out here.
    JIMMY'S MOTHER: [In the background] We moved to Cedar Grove less than a year ago.
    JIMMY: [facing away from the microphone] Mom!

JIMMY'S MOTHER: Sorry.

HOST: No, it's okay. Jimmy, if your mother can add details to the story, our listeners will certainly appreciate it. That gives weight to the story.

JIMMY: Okay.

HOST: Please continue.

JIMMY: The neighborhood is still being built, and it goes for blocks and blocks, and in some places, on the outermost points of the neighborhood, the houses haven't been finished or aren't even built, they're just grassy lots. I like to play down there, even though my mom doesn't like me to go so far.

JIMMY'S MOTHER: I worry about animals coming out of the woods.

JIMMY: There are no animals. Except skunks and raccoons and deer.

JIMMY'S MOTHER: Well, I don't need my son getting sprayed by a skunk.

JIMMY: [laughs at this suggestion. His mother giggles] Anyway, I was down there among the unfinished houses—I like to play in them because you can climb on the frames and see out where the roof hasn't been put on yet. One of the houses, that a week earlier was totally unfinished and open, now looked finished. But I could see that the door was wide open, so I kind of thought maybe the house wasn't done yet, and I wanted to see the inside.

    I walked up to the door and hollered into the house if anyone was home. No one answered and besides, the hall was still unfinished wood and the walls were open where they were putting in light switches and plumbing. I walked in and down the hall. On my left were two doors—pocket doors—and I pushed them open. I couldn't believe it. The room behind the doors was completely finished. And I got a weird feeling from it.

HOST: What was that feeling, Jimmy?

JIMMY: That that room had been lived in for a long time. But that's impossible and I knew that. But the floor was polished and clean and there was a carpet—a bear rug, with the head still on it—and a big leather chair and a table and lots of bookcases with books. I went over to the bookcases and looked at the books and a lot of them were in different languages. They all looked old. Some of them were in English and one said that it was ghost stories, so I took it down to look at it and it was really beautiful and there were pictures in it. I figured that no one would miss it if I borrowed it for a while so I took it home with me.

When Mom saw what I had she asked where I'd gotten it from and she told me I had to return it right away.

HOST: Do you remember the name of the book?

JIMMY: No.

JIMMY'S MOTHER: I don't remember either. It might have just been called "Ghosts." It was a beautiful old book, leather bound with gold leaf. We wrapped it in brown paper with a note so Jimmy could just leave it on the front steps and not go into the house again, that we thought, obviously, someone lived in.

JIMMY: Anyway, so the next morning after breakfast I go back down to where that house was. The door is still wide open. I look in thinking I'd just as well put the book back on the shelf if I could. The pocket doors were open, like I guess I left them, but the room was different. I walked down the hall and looked, and the room was as unfinished as the rest of the house.

Before I got spooked I went outside and looked at all the houses around that one to make sure I hadn't just made a mistake. But I'm telling you, I hadn't. Well, now I was pretty spooked and wanted to get out of there. I put the book in the hall near the doorway and took off. I haven't been down there since.

HOST: A vanishing room! Perhaps a room from another dimension, briefly sent to Cedar Grove to deliver a book to young Jimmy here. I want to thank Jimmy for his story, and his mother, Mrs. Johnson, for helping.

[Sound quality changes, back in the studio]

HOST: Just a quick word to wrap up tonight's episode. I have been the subject of some local controversy. Seeing as this is a small town, I'm sure you know of what I speak. You must also know that the rumors aren't true, couldn't be. The people who spread these rumors are stupid, thick-headed people who do not understand—maybe can't understand—the nature of my work. I am building a library of the supernatural, *among other things*. These people who insist I ought to take a step back and learn how to live normally are people who don't understand that my discoveries originate from a solid base. I am a solid person, and only because of this, am I able to attempt to reach into the invisible. There are other dimensions that can be reached, I know it; chances are, I won't discover these places, *but there is a chance that I will*. Please discount those who criticize me.

I hope you enjoyed tonight's broadcast.

ANNOUNCER: And that takes care of another episode of Weird Furka. If you've had a weird encounter with the supernatural, please contact KADE, Weird Furka [address]. Tune in next week for another story that will shake you free of the everyday.

MUSIC EXTRO

Thursday afternoon, exhausted, Craig sat in front of the gas station, staring blankly at nothing. He jerked in his seat when he heard his name. Johnson walked from his truck toward Craig. Craig stood up, tense.

"Leave me alone, Johnson," he said.

Johnson put up his hands. "Give me another chance, Craig. Just hear me out." He stopped walking, and stood about two yards from Craig. "I'm sorry I told you to go to hell. You're a good kid, I'm sure of it. You've been serving me beer a long time. You just need to listen to some sense."

"You've told me everything already."

"No, no, I haven't. I didn't want to. Now, can I come over and sit down?"

Craig sat, and Johnson took this as an invitation. He took a chair off the porch and set it in front of Craig. "Just give me five seconds and maybe I can clear up why I got so angry when I heard those shows on the radio again."

Before Johnson could speak, Craig came alert, and asked, "What's your first name?"

Johnson grimaced.

"Is it James? Jim, Jimmy?"

"Use your head, son, I can't be little Jimmy Johnson. Frank and I were in high school together. But don't look so disappointed. Maybe if you ever got some sleep you would've figured it out: Jimmy's my nephew. Only son of my brother, David, God rest his soul. It's my brother who made me aware of what Frank was up to. Frank was screwing any housewife who'd let 'em. You've heard Mrs. Buzzard on the air, right? She was a frequent guest, wasn't she? She thought Frank was handsome and interesting, unlike Mr. Buzzard—a friend of mine, by the way. Now you see why he made those recordings when their husbands were at work."

Craig fought a grin and asked, "But with Jimmy there?"

"A mother can shoo a child out of the house. My brother was sure something had happened. Bed sheets all thrown about, Mabel—my brother's wife—out of it and exhausted. House in disarray."

"And you're sure?"

"My brother was. Ended his marriage. I haven't seen my nephew or Mabel since. So, I just don't like the idea of Shokler getting memorialized or glorified or anything. That's why I got so angry. I shouldn't have. But I'm calm now."

"That's good."

"I'm just sorry I didn't just lay it all out for you—I can see why you were bull-headed—I'd'a been if someone'd walked into my bar and told me what to do. I'm glad we got that square." Johnson seemed unsure what to do now that he'd explained himself to Craig. He said, "If I were you, I'd get out of this town all together."

"Why's that?"

"Look around you. The town is shriveling up. When was the last time you pumped any gas?"

Craig tried to place in time the small, green pickup that was the last vehicle he'd topped off. He shrugged.

"That's right. When I'm driving through this town I make sure I have plenty of gas 'cause if I ran out here I'd be in the middle of nowhere. Montana has a way of squeezing little towns until they're dead, and this town is pushin' out its last wheeze. Once your station moves, you ought to. Go someplace where you might find a nice divorcée and make a life for yourself."

"I'll give it some serious thought."

Johnson clapped Craig on the shoulder, then took Craig's hand and shook it. "You do that. Now I gotta hit the road." He started toward his truck, stopped and faced Craig. He pointed a finger and said, "You take care of yourself."

As Craig watched Johnson drive away, he grinned. Shokler's rant at the end of episode eighteen had meant little to him, so long out of context, but Johnson had unwittingly provided Craig with the missing history. He knew what Shokler had been accused of, and was certain the accusations were baseless. Sunday night, Craig would broadcast all the episodes of "Weird Furka."

Craig spent Sunday afternoon making CD copies of the last episodes. As he recorded episode twenty-five, his attention was caught by Frank's mention of a dog. Frank told the audience that he had his dog, Harold, with him in the studio, and intended to bring his dog with him to the station from that point on. Craig thought the dog at the station the previous Sunday must have been Frank's—it did not occur to Craig that the dog he'd seen couldn't have been Frank's.

And that night, the dog was there, standing guard at the door. Craig walked up to the dog and said, "Hello, Harold." He knelt beside the dog and patted him, as he would a familiar animal. He stopped petting the dog, pulled his hands back and rubbed his forehead. For a moment he had no idea who the dog was, became terrified of it—and the dog growled. Blood rushed to Craig's head—he could nearly see a cloud-like infusion fill an empty space in his mind—and he resumed petting the dog. When he stood, he held the door open for Harold in case he wanted to join Craig in the studio. The dog didn't move, and Craig knew he was standing guard as he had for Frank.

Craig didn't speak at all to the DJ when he stepped into the studio, though the DJ spoke to him, and set up Craig's show. The DJ said, "Dog out there tonight?" And when Craig didn't answer, he said, "I didn't see any dog there last time." Then he left, and Craig started airing "Weird Furka."

Craig felt happy—giddy. And when, a little past 2 AM, Frank Shokler joined Craig in the studio, he almost took no notice, as if Frank had been there all night. Longer, perhaps. The two of them listened to the radio. The episodes of "Weird Furka" had dissolved from the original interview format into Frank talking for ten to fifteen minutes about supernatural revelations he'd had. Occasionally, a dog barked, and Craig wasn't sure if he was hearing Harold outside or on the radio.

"I was wrong for so long," Frank said. Frank's voice was a clear baritone. Craig admired it as a good radio voice.

"Was there an announcer, or was that you, too?" Craig asked, without looking away from the boards.

Frank smiled, and, lowering his voice, said, "If you scoff at the idea that there is a world outside of our common perception, another world beyond our own, *the supernatural world*, then prepare to have your assumptions challenged; if you already believe such a world exists, then prepare to have your beliefs confirmed."

Craig clapped.

"Nothing else was faked, though, unless some of those housewives I interviewed were making stories up to pass the hours. I imagine that went on a little. Some of the women, though—" Frank grinned, "were very serious and touched, I think, by what took hold of me."

Craig turned in his chair and looked at Frank. Frank, in the other chair, by microphone two, was not a man, but man-like, dressed in a white dress shirt, sleeves held up by cloth bands, a pair of brown, wool trousers, suspenders and two-tone, white and brown shoes. The skin of the thing in the clothes was like moist black cloth. Between the weave, it shone. Craig gasped; just beyond the thing was Craig's book of poetry; he focused on that as he switched on his microphone, drew it close to his lips and whispered, "Someone, please help me."

Frank said, "And what is taking hold of you, too."

Craig turned back to the board, and stared at the counter as it counted down the minutes that remained of the episode of "Weird Furka" he was broadcasting. Gradually, he looked away from the LED light numbers and at Frank again; he couldn't not look at Frank.

"It took me a long time," Frank said, "to realize that Furka wasn't the nexus of the—shall we say *weird*?—but that the nexus was me." Frank shrugged, sort of—at least, that's how Craig interpreted the gesture with which Frank capped his statement. Frank said, "You should put on some of that music you like."

Craig found the way Frank's mouth moved to be horrible; like bubbling molasses. Craig was dimly aware that the last episode of "Weird Furka" had been broadcast. Without thought, he took a CD from the case he'd brought. It was the album he thought sounded like the opening music of Frank's show.

Frank's face rippled. "Johnson has come to rescue you," he said.

Craig knew Johnson's arrival did not mean he should have hope. He knew—almost as if he was outside watching—that Harold had leapt onto Johnson as soon as Johnson stepped out of his truck. Johnson would be found the next morning, dead air broadcasting from his truck's speakers. The papers would declare that he'd been "mauled by a wild animal," though there would be no animal tracks to be found near Johnson's body.

Frank said, "You should gather up all those records." Frank indicated the burned

CDs with a wave of his arm. Craig began to gather them, his will gone; gone since he climbed into the sub-basement of the Furkabick hotel three weeks before.

"Good." Again, Frank's face rippled. "You should've turned that heating plate off when you left your house last. A fire has started already, fueled by your own filth."

And acetate and celluloid, Craig knew. Frank stood up and started out the studio. Craig followed, the episodes of "Weird Furka" cradled in his arm. They walked through the empty house, to the basement door. The lock that Craig had broken still hung like a loose tooth from its latch.

The basement was dry and dark. In it, all that was visible to Craig was the white of Frank's shirt and the band of white on Frank's shoes. Craig followed, and whimpered.

"It's not so bad," Frank said. "It's not so lonely as you've been. Why there's Mrs. Buzzard, who's most pleasant, and Mrs. Johnson." Frank stepped into the small room at the far end of the cellar and bent over to open the sub-basement trap door. "After you."

Craig saw, as he'd seen Johnson mauled and his house in flames, a young boy, up far later than he was supposed to be, recording Craig's final broadcast. Craig got down on his knees, then dropped hard on his butt. He swung his legs over the lip of the sub-basement. Looking down, Craig saw a small point of light. He knew Frank stood over him, but also knew Frank was patient. The point of light grew; his eyes ached as his pupils shrunk to compensate for the ever-growing brightness below. The light, a ball of fire the size of a human head, was cold. The light was there for no more than a handful of seconds—when it vanished, Craig was blinded by the green-yellow circles burned onto his retinas. CD case held tight against his breast, he let his own weight pull him over the edge and dropped into the hole. Frank followed, carefully climbing down the ladder, pulling the trap door shut behind them.

[*for* Conrad and Louise]

About the Author

Adam Golaski is the author of *Color Plates* (Rose Metal Press, 2010). "Green," his translation of *Sir Gawain & the Green Knight*, appears in *Open Letters*. He edits *New Genre* and for Flim Forum Press.

Acknowledgements

Slightly different versions of several of the stories in this collection appeared in the following publications: "The Demon" and "They Look Like Little Girls" in *Supernatural Tales* #9 and #13, respectively; "Back Home" in *All Hallows* #32; "What Water Reveals" in *Strange Tales: Volume II*, edited by Rosalie Parker (Tartarus Press, 2007); and "Weird Furka" in *Acquainted with the Night*, edited by Barbara and Christopher Roden (Ash-Tree Press, 2004).

As I wrote the stories for this book, many people offered their support and many their love. I wish especially to thank the following. Les Poets Bleu: John, Jeff, Matthew, & Jaime. Liz Sanger ("What Water Reveals") & Kaethe Schwehn (KADE). Jeremy Lassen, who recommended I try Raw Dog Screaming Press. Angela. The Kemple family, especially Kate. Jeremy Withers. Mom, Dad, & Marie. And my Zetta, & my Elizabeth.

Other Novels from Raw Dog Screaming Press

Isabel Burning, Donna Lynch
hc 978-1-933293-49-3, $29.95, 236p
tpb 978-1-933293-56-1, $15.95, 236p

Isabel's new job as housekeeper at Grace mansion allows her to observe the habits of the enigmatic Dr. Edward Grace. Captivated by his tales of travel to Africa, she is inexorably drawn into a tumultuous relationship which eventually reveals the Grace family's dark heritage and lays bare every secret, even the ones she keeps from herself.

Health Agent, Jeffrey Thomas
hc 978-1-933293-43-1, $30.00, 290p
tpb 978-1-933293-44-8, $15.95, 290p

Punktown's health agents are charged with keeping the public safe from infectious disease. But for health agent Montgomery Black work is about to consume his life. The problem is a highly contagious and extremely deadly STD, mutstav six-seventy. While trying to prevent the spread of the disease Black could lose everything he cares about but there's no ignoring the suspicion that something far more sinister than the impartial hand of nature is behind the spread of this epidemic.

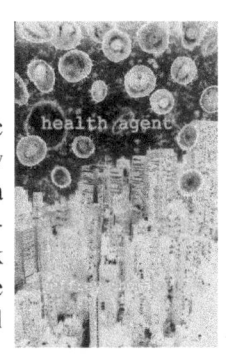

Sin Conductor, John Edward Lawson
tpb 978-1-933293-65-3

Willis Lowery is just your average occupational hazards estimator until one day, while inspecting a factory, he happens across a chemical burn victim. Her name is Dusyanna, and the passion she ignites in him threatens to melt away every fiber of his morals. As he soon learns, there is no escape from her circle of degenerates, so he vows to become the devil to beat the devil.

Blankety Blank, D. Harlan Wilson
hc 978-1-933293-50-9, $14.95, 188p
tpb 978-1-933293-57-8, $29.95, 188p

Rutger Van Trout has problems but the worst is not that his son might be a werewolf. It's not his obsession with transforming his house into a three-ring barnyard or his wife's haunted skeleton. The complication has invaded his community in the form of a new breed of serial killer, who stalks from house to house leaving a bloodbath that would make Jack the Ripper himself blush.

www.rawdogscreaming.com